WRITE ME A LETTER

DAVID M. PIERCE

WRITE ME A LETTER

For my sisters Debbie, Peggy, and Judy

A Greek señor named Persius once suggested that hunger was the "bestower of invention." If this be true, I must have felt moderately peckish when I created the characters, bars, businesses, streets, and a town or two herein, but it took someone a lot hungrier than I've ever been to invent Los Angeles and the San Fernando Valley.

CONTENTS

CHAPTER ONE

The most beautiful woman in the world turned up the wattage in her deep violet eyes, crossed her slim, nylon-clad limbs, leaned slightly forward toward me, and murmured in a smoky half-whisper, "What do you think?"

The tallest detective in the Greater Los Angeles Area—if not the world—one V. (for Victor) Daniel, thought he was dreaming is what he thought.

I have encountered many a lovely mademoiselle in my time and in my wanderings. I say this both truthfully and, I hope, modestly, without in any way trying to give the impression I am, was, or ever will be a professional charmer, a *thé dansant* gigolo, a Burt Reynolds look-alike, a Formula 1 racing car pilot, or a hairdresser. It is merely that in Hollywood and its environs, in one of which I dwell, gorgeous girls are everywhere. I've had my package of baloney, jar of pickled wienies, and six-pack of Mexican beer checked out at Ralph's Supermarket by a girl whose smile alone made my knees tremble uncontrollably starting from the tummy. During the course of an investigation once, I had to regularly visit a health club for women, mainly actresses, strippers, and dancers, out Ventura Boulevard; it pains just to think about it. There was one black goddess on a rowing machine—but that's another story, and one that will not, alas, be told by my humble pen.

And did I not once shake hands with Miss Joan Collins in a bikini? She, not me, in the bikini, thank God. And, once upon an unlikely dream, Miss Tuesday Weld smiled her dangerous smile my way. And was not my own, my beloved Evonne Louise Shirley, one of the world's most fetching of blondes and most lovely of creatures?

True, all true.

But.

I tore my eyes away from the vision who was gazing at me intently from the far side of my desk and indulged in a few more passing thoughts before producing an answer to her query. Some of the thoughts were even printable. Her face was uncannily like that of Vivien Leigh, her eyes resembled those purple wells of Elizabeth Taylor, her anatomy surely was stolen from Janet Leigh, legs courtesy Miss Lauren Bacall, feet by Claire Trevor. . . .

No, no, I thought. That way lay madness, I thought. That way lay direct to the funny farm, nonstop, under severe restraint—but what a way for a guy to go. I thought I'd better wrestle what was left of my bemused brain back to dry land is what I thought.

The time was 11:15 A.M., that was dry land. It was undeniably Monday, April 4, four days to my mom's birthday; dry land again.

And unless I'd done a Rip Van Winkle recently, the century was the twentieth, and the weather in my part of the San Fernando Valley—Studio City, just over the Hollywood Hills from the famed Tinsel Town itself—was thick and muggy, as was a large percentage of the local citizenry.

My office, in which myself and my visitor from another reality were ensconced, was where it always was, on the corner of Victory and Orange, snuggled in between a weed-and-wino-filled vacant lot and a Vietnamese takeout. On the wall to the right as you came in was a last year's calendar I'd forgotten to take down that pictured a bevy of Armenian beauties at play.

My visitor's name was Ruth Braukis, which wouldn't look that good up in lights but what's in a name, anyway, as Percy Bysshe once quipped. She'd shown up at my low-rent place of work a half-hour earlier, and after I had, with some ceremony, seated her in the spare chair opposite mine, she had introduced herself and handed across to me a sealed envelope, which I proceeded to open and peruse, after excusing myself politely for the nonce.

The note was written on flashy cream-colored paper, in red ink, under the heading, "Lew Lewellen Productions," and read: 'Amigo mío—this will introduce Miss Ruth Braukis, a good friend of mine [with the 'good' underlined twice]. Help her with her baby-sitting chore if you can, and if you can't, never darken my door again.'

"Yore pal Lew," it concluded.

"Do you know what this note says?" I asked her.

She nodded; one wing of her raven hair fell across one perfect cheek.

"So who is it you want baby-sitted, or is it sat, Miss Braukis?"

"Or is it whom," she said. "Although I'm not sure either one is the right word. I do need someone collected and then delivered, and Mr. Lewellen said when I called him that if you could look after him when he was on a toot, you could look after anybody."

"Oh, well," I said, scuffling my size twelves bashfully. Then she smiled at me; then my foolish old heart sang.

"He can be a bit of a handful, old Lew, when he's riding the sauce express, that much is true," I said, understating the matter considerably. When the moon was high and full and yellow around the edges and Lew donned his dancing shoes and drinking cap and was ready to howl, even six foot seven and a quarter inches and 241 pounds of V. Daniel had all he could do to drag Lew's carcass home the following dawn, and once it was the dawn after the following dawn, relatively unscarred.

"Who is it you want collected, Miss Braukis?"

"My uncle," she said.

"I had an uncle once," I said. "He had false teeth and his name was Clarence."

"Fascinating," she murmured. "My uncle's name is Theo. He's coming from Estonia."

"Even more fascinating," I said. "Is that the Estonia that's just a few miles east of Kansas City?"

"No," she said, "it is the newly independent country of Estonia, which is next to the newly independent countries of Latvia and Lithuania."

"Oh, that Estonia," I said. "On the Baltic Sea, I believe, not far from Leningrad, or whatever it's called these tempestuons times. From where, I also believe, on the one or two days a year when the blizzard abates, one can see all the way across to brave little Finland." As I've said before, kids, try to stay awake in school, you never know when you might have to impress a walking rhapsody.

"Theo is my mother's younger brother," she said. "I've never met him but I've seen pictures of him and my mother talked about him a lot." Her voice choked slightly; she looked away.

"Talked?"

"That's really why I'm here," she said. "In L.A., I mean, and not back home in Bismark, where we live."

"What a strange coincidence!" I said. "I eat your herring all the time."

4

She gave me a brief glance—of appreciation, no doubt.

"Mother was on a tour out here with some of her girl-friends, and, of course, also to meet her brother. She suffered a stroke two days ago. One of her friends got in touch with me, and I flew right out."

"Bad?" I asked inanely, as if there was any such thing as a good stroke, medically speaking.

"Bad. She's alive, but that's about it, she's still unconscious."

"Ah, hell," I said. "I'm sorry." I thought about telling her about my mom, who had Alzheimer's and who was in a home in the hills out past Glendale, but I figured one mom at a time was enough for her to worry about; it was more than enough for me.

"How can I help?"

She sighed. "It's all such a mess. I don't know what to do. She was supposed to meet Theo at the airport, and then she was going to rent a car and drove him up north to some place near Lafayette, do you know where that is?"

"I do," I said. "It's not far from Walnut Creek, which is not far from Oakland, which used to have a football team, which is not far from the home of a banana-fingered, no-hit baseball team, San Francisco. But why Lafayette?"

"That's where my uncle Teddy lives," she said. "My mother's other brother."

"Why doesn't Uncle Teddy meet Uncle Theo?" I said.

"Because Uncle Teddy is on a home kidney dialysis machine," she said. "He's waiting for a transplant but until then he has to wash his bood or whatever it is every day, which takes hours."

"Gotcha," I said, beginning to think I'd fallen into a particularly melodramatic episode of "General Hospital."

"So Mr. Lewellen suggested you," she said in her husky voice.

"And how do you know him?"

"I don't, really," she said, "but he and mother went to the same college. I think they were sweet on each other because they stayed in touch and still send each other Valentine's cards."

"Ahhhhh," I said. I checked my watch. "Excuse me a sec, I have to make a quick call."

I dialed the number of the courier service I always used. When the girl at the other end answered, I asked her if George was in.

"Just got back," the dispatcher said.

"Tell him Vic says make it four o'clock, not three, would you please, sweetheart?"

"Consider it done, honey," she said.

I rang off. "Sorry about that. Now, Miss Braukis, I take it that as Uncle Teddy can't meet Uncle Theo, and you naturally want to stay near your mother, and there's no other family available, you would like to meet Uncle Theo and escort him north to Uncle Teddy's."

"Well, a hotel right near Uncle Teddy's," she said. "Yes, please. Could you?" She turned on her Lillian-Gish-in-*Orphan-of-the-Storm* look.

"I might be able to," I said. "When does he get in?"

"Saturday morning. I know that's six days away and mother might even be better by then, but I thought I'd try and make arrangements now just in case, so if you were tied up, I'd have time to think of something else."

"Let me just check the little old schedule," I said. I put on my specs reluctantly, got out the little old schedule, which was in fact a *Cosmopolitan* magazine's "Desktop Diary for Today's Woman," a thoughtful present I'd uncovered in my stocking the previous Christmas from my favorite, thoughtful blonde, who was not without a flash of humor from time to time. The year before she had given me a hunter's and fisherman's diary, so if you ever want to know how much the largest pike ever netted in American waters weighed, you know who to call, except I chucked it out when I got the new one.

I opened the diary to the appropriate week, making sure that Miss Braukis didn't get a peek at it. Aside from such domestic trivia as "buy Mom present," "have brakes checked," "thpaste," "mthwash," "1 case ginger ale," and "Jockey shorts," it was as blank as a doctor's expression just after you've asked him how much longer you had to live.

"The time I could find," I said truthfully. "But why me? I mean, why anyone? Why doesn't Uncle Theo just hop a connector flight to Oakland, then take a cab?"

"Because he can't speak English," she said.

"Not at all?"

"Not at all."

"What does he speak?"

"Estonia," she said. "And of course Russian."

"Of course," I said. "What luck my Russian is flawless, Tovaritch."

It was then that the amazing Miss Ruth Braukis leaned forward, gazed at me earnestly from those marvelous orbs, ran the tip of her adorable tongue over her equally if not more adorable upper lip, and oh, dream on, big fella, dream on, asked me in that voice redolent of late nights and saxophones, "What do you think?"

At that point, precisely what would you have done in my position, may I ask? Made some lame excuse, mayhap a pressing appointment with your gum specialist, and turned her out into the swirling smog? Of course I said I'd do it. Of

course I said, in the most reassuring tones, "Leave it to me."
Of course there did occur a brief but satisfactory discussion
of monetary matters, including a hefty chunk up front.

Then I elicited the necessary details from her—the time
Uncle Theo was due in—3:44. Where—LAX. What airline—
TWA. Coming from where—New York. She also gave me Uncle
Teddy's address up north and his phone number; her address
in town, the Fairfax Hotel (on Fairfax, appropriately); another
number where I could leave a message for her; and the name
of the hospital where her mother was—the Hollywood Kaiser,
an establishment of healing I knew all too well and have the
scars, the bills, and a certain redheaded nurse's home phone
number to prove it. . . . Now, now, rumor mongers, simmer
down. I hasten to add at this point that said redheaded's mon-
iker is Duke, he once played tackle for Arkansas State, and as
well as being a nurse, he's also an osteopath who makes house
calls. Mummy's name—June Braukis—a photo of Uncle
Theo, and a letter from Uncle Teddy to Uncle Theo he'd air
expressed down explaining all to Uncle Theo in Russian. One
the envelope was written "Fioder Bièlken," which, on inquiry,
turned out to be Uncle Theo's name writ in a westernized
form of the Ruskie alphabet.

Oh. Speaking (as I just was) of bits and pieces, of bitty
bits and patchwork pieces torn from some greater whole—
oftentimes, especially, in bars late at night—I think that
perhaps all my days (and most of my life) consist of nothing else. And unlike those who search for religion, truth,
love, forgiveness, or oblivion in the bottom of their glasses,
all I was hoping to find was some sort of cosmic superglue.
I thought about asking madam if she happened to know
where I might purchase a large, family-size tube of same,
but I didn't.

I thought about asking her what her favorite color was, or if she liked yellow roses, tangoing, big bands, bigger men, Dolly Parton, autumn leaves, and bygone days, but I didn't. Evonne, I didn't even think of it.

When I had all the legitimate details I thought I might need from her jotted down safely in my memo pad (courtesy M. Martel, Stationers), I escorted her to the door. She said she'd call later in the week if there was any change of plan. I said she could call anyway, just to say hello, merely to hear a friendly voice, if she wanted. She declined my offer to chase up or call a cab for her, saying she had some shopping to do before returning to the hospital. She held out one dainty hand. I took it gingerly in my big mitt. She laid her other hand atop mine as gently as a goosedown feather settling on black velvet, gave me her tremulous smile again, and then she was gone.

I went back inside.

The office looked shabby suddenly. . . but then it always did.

I looked at the six hundred dollars in traveler's checks she'd signed over to me.

I looked at the chair in which she had so briefly reposed. I thought I could detect an elusive, lingering trace of her perfume still in the air. What an enchanting woman, to put it mildly, what a vision of incredible loveliness. And she was tall, too, of course. Great beauty of person requires that one should be tall, shorties can't cut it, Aristotle wrote, although maybe not in those exact words. Would I ever see her again? Who knew what tricks impish Fate had yet in store up his tattered sleeve for V. (for Victor) Daniel.

I had but one slight twinge of unease, or regret—too bad she was so full of shit.

CHAPTER TWO

Don't get me wrong.

I didn't suspect Ruth Braukis of being the biggest liar since the Big Bad Wolf merely because she was stunningly beautiful, although lesser males might be so inclined. That sort of juvenile, chauvinistic prejudice I eradicated from my character eons ago—to be precise, last Tuesday morning just before lunch. Believe me, I had other reasons for my suspicions.

Lew Lewellen was a film producer. Was it likely a film producer would send Valentine's cards to anyone except himself, let alone a college sweetheart from thirty years ago? And I could have been wrong but didn't I vaguely remember Lew's wife telling me once Lew had never even finished high school let alone got into a university. And all that stuff about uncles and Estonia and kidney machines, really. I may be gullible, especially when violet eyes are batting my way, but even I have my limits.

First thing I did of course was to call up the Lewellens. A pretty señorita I'd seen several times at Lew's but whose name I couldn't recall answered, and after I'd said it was me, she said the Lewellens were away for the weekend and could she take a message. I said, "No, gracias," and hung up.

Away for the weekend, eh? A likely story. No doubt Mrs. Lewellen had so instructed her minion to say if I called as she was too nice to lie to me directly. And was Monday, which day it was, a part of the weekend anyway? Not even in Beverly Hills it wasn't. So what was going on? How and why were my old friends the Lew Lewellens involved? Curious, eh, amigos?

I called the Fairfax Hotel; there was no one by the name of Ruth or June Braukis registered. Well, conceivably Ruth was staying in her mom's room and conceivably mom had a girlfriend roommate as double rooms are cheaper than two single rooms and conceivably the room was registered in her mom's girlfriend's name, if you are still conceivably with me, so then I called Kaiser, and guess what, no Mummy there, either.

Then I called up Uncle Teddy in Lafayette or thereabouts. No answer. Then, just to see if there was any truth at all in Ruth's tissue of fibs, I phoned TWA. Lo and behold there was a flight arriving daily from New York at 3:44 P.M., which was some small progress, although toward what, who knew? Then, just for a giggle, I took down my *Reader's Digest World Atlas* from the small shelf of reference books that hung a mite lopsidedly between the Armenian beauties and the fire extinguisher to see if there still was an Estonia. There was, south across the icy floes from Helsinki.

I looked fondly at the loving dedication inside the front cover of the atlas: "God knows where ya came from. Maybe this'll help ya figure out where you're goin'. Luv, Sara. XXX."

Luv, Sara. What a twerp. Sara was a punk poetess I helped out once in a while, God knows why, by giving her some easy chore to do and then giving her big bucks for doing it. Did I say "punk"? I should say "ex-punk." With great cunning, wisdom, and gentle handling, I'd converted her from the rags, shredded panty hose, and safety pins of punkdom, to say nothing of her Day-Glo hair, back to the trouser suits and Hush Puppies of normalcy, and do you know how she repaid me? She got herself Born Again, as did her boyfriend, and they took to showing up at my office looking like those rustics in Grant Wood's painting who are standing outside their barn waiting for rain. All right, they did tire of their antics after a couple of weeks, long after I'd tired of them, and owned up that their whole Born Again routine was done just to tease me, not that I hadn't figured that out all by myself. The atlas, of course, Sara had purloined somehow during her punk period and foisted off on me instead of getting me a real present for my birthday or Mother's Day or whenever it was, something I could really use. Wrinkle cream, maybe, or a twenty-five–dollar gift certificate for my bookie, Two-to-One Tim.

Anyway. I returned the atlas to the shelf, put the checks in the big safe in the bathroom out back, then sat and waited. What I was waiting for was for George, for whom I'd left that phone message earlier, to call in or drop in. George, or Willing Boy, as I had so aptly named him once in a moment of total clarity, was not only willing, like Sara, to take my hard-earned lucre for performing simple tasks for me, he was also the airhead's boyfriend. And thus, of course, had been her late accomplice in the highly unamusing Born Again number. And what Willing Boy was doing, I hoped, was following Miss Ruth Braukis to wherever it was Miss Ruth Braukis was going.

Willing Boy and I had invented our own secret code for use when I had company in the office and couldn't speak to him openly on the phone; rather, I invented it and taught it to him. For security reasons I won't reveal all the complexities of the code at this time; suffice it to say that the message I sent to him about changing it from three o'clock to an hour later can be roughly decoded to mean, "Get your skinny ass over here on that silly, noisy oriental motorcycle of yours pronto and follow the woman in the case." Which, as I just mentioned, I dearly hoped he was doing, although I hadn't spotted him outside when I escorted my client to the door, which was the other reason apart from gallantry that I'd escorted her to the door.

I retrieved my Apple II from the safe, set her up, and switched her on. My computer has always been a she to me, why should boats have all the luck? I called her Betsy, actually, the same name Davy Crockett gave to his rifle. Were feminist groups against the practice of calling ships "she"? Probably. It is not untrue to say that Evonne and I did not always see eye to eye on the complicated subject of women's rights. I had—perhaps wisely, perhaps cravenly—some time ago adopted a simple strategy to deal with any potential fireworks: I agreed with her. I do not know why this makes her even madder.

Betsy, that nosy know-it-all, couldn't wait to inform me of what I was already well aware of—I was broke.

I wasn't always broke. I wasn't one of those gumshoes who made their breakfast coffee from yesterday's grounds and never could come up with the rent on time and had to drink cheap booze; I drank cheap booze because I liked it and usually made a pretty good living; all things considered, my per annum was certainly that of a carhop or a one-legged waitress, counting tips. But my good pal John D., owner of the Valley Bowl, had called me at home Sunday saying he needed some heavy bread for a couple of months and could I help. I said sure. He was due by Tuesday morning sometime to fill me in and pick up my check, which would pretty well clean me out. So I could certainly use a lucrative job or two right then and whatever else Miss Insanely Gorgeous

Ruth Braukis was, she wasn't short of readies, as the Limeys put it, the traveler's checks she'd given me had hardly disturbed the wad she was carrying.

I waited.

I got out the typewriter and answered some mail. I could have used the computer's perfectly adequate printer, except every other time it started printing halfway down the !!#%$! page instead of at the top, and I couldn't figure out why. And I was too embarrassed to ask young Mr. Nu, who ran the TV, radio, VCR, and what-have-you emporium next door to his cousin's Vietnamese ricery, which was right next door to me, for help yet again.

I answered a sad, xeroxed letter from an ex-cop who wanted to know if I needed any part-time assistance, which I didn't; the sad bit came at the end and said, "PS: Haven't touched a drop for two weeks!" Talk about a giveaway. Maybe my memory was going but didn't I once get the identical letter from him, some years back? Maybe it was from another ex-cop who drank—who could blame them? I answered a letter from a potential new client, a department store in one of the nearby malls, wanting to know if I offered a debt collection service and if so, could I please supply details. I wrote back saying regretfully I could not offer such a service as all my manpower was tied up at present. I'd done a spot of debt collection in my time, though, back east. I worked in tandem with Mickey, who was so tough that when we went a-calling on creditors, huge, scarred, and battered old me played the good guy, the one willing to give the poor sap a break, and him the heavy. Debt collecting can pay off as you usually get about a third of what you collect, but the work does have its perils as the kind of debts we collected on, like shylocking and gambling IOUs, being themselves illegal, had to be collected *hors de* law. Which, in practice, meant threatening to do serious physical damage to every bone in the creditor's body except his check-signing hand. And often, of course, it does not need underlining, doing more than threaten. I finally had enough of it one winter day and coldcocked Mickey from behind, using the same baseball bat he'd used on some poor welsher's kneecap, and then it was "Feets, do your stuff!" I was on a fast train west before he came to.

Then I thumbed through an interesting tome my pal Benny had left behind one day, *Why SOBS Succeed and Nice Guys Fail in a Small Business*, paying particular attention to chapter 5: "How to Teach Legal and Financial Vultures Humility." Lotsa good ideas there. . . .

After a while I closed up and nipped in next door but two to Mrs. Morales' Taco-Burger stand and tucked away some chewy burritos and a bowl of refried (more than once) beans and a bottle of Corona, left my customary generous tip, then went back to the office and waited some more.

Willing Boy finally showed up about a quarter to two. He stopped just outside my plate-glass front window, swung his Yamaha up on its stand, locked it, then came in, swinging his helmet by the strap.

"Greetings, Prof," he said with a wave of one black-gloved hand. Ever since I'd started wearing glasses a few months back, he and noodlehead had derived considerable humor by calling me Prof, as if I cared one way or the other.

"Likewise I"m sure, Willing Boy," I said. "Take a pew." He threw his lanky, leather-clad frame down in the spare chair, grinned at me, got his foot-long plastic comb from a back pocket, and gave his gleaming blond shoulder-length locks a good workout. Willing Boy was so handsome he could have had tresses down to and including his waist and still be handsome; no wonder the twerp was so dippy about him.

"So how's it going, Prof?" he said, tucking his cootie-catcher away again. "Haven't see you for a couple of weeks." It had actually been ten days ago when he'd spent two extremely profitable (for him) hours in my employ got up as a chaffeur, driving me around. In a fifty-dollar-per-hour rented white Daimler, too, I might just mention in passing, as my own pink-and-blue Nash Metropolitan didn't seem the appropriate wheels for the occasion, which was a get-together of me, two Italian gents, a county sheriff, and a Canadian "businessman" in a bonded warehouse down near the convention center in Long Beach.

"Weird," I said, "is how it's going. Most bizarre. How did you get along with the little lady?"

"What about her!" he said. "Pheew. Did you see that mouth?"

"I was too busy looking at her lips," I said. "So where'd she go?" I would have bet my last Mexican dollar she didn't go shopping for grapes and then go to the Hollywood Kaiser.

"Around the corner," Willing Boy said, stretching out his long legs. "She walked right past me."

"Then what?"

"Then she gets into a blue Ford driven by an older guy, then they talk for a bit, then they drive away."

"I don't suppose the car had a license plate."

He reeled the number off from memory.

"Where did they go?"

"Eighteen forty-three South Vermont," he said, again from memory.

"And what is there, Willing Boy?"

"An office duplex," he said. "The Vineyards of Bourgogne on the ground floor, something called ITC on the top. I didn't want to go in, I thought the guy driving might have made me, or maybe the little lady, she was looking back over her shoulder."

"She shouldn't have," I said. "Willing Boy, attend. If you ever have cause to suspect someone is following you, what you don't do is look back because that tells the person who is following you that you have cause to think someone might be following you, which is not an activity innocent people indulge in."

"Truly words of wisdom I shall ne'er forget," he said humbly.

"What did the guy driving look like?"

"Short," he said. "Full of energy. Looked like he could take care of himself, dunno exactly why. Chinos, white shirt, sandals. Crew-cut blond hair. Sunglasses."

"Anything else come to mind that might be helpful?"

Willing Boy thought it over for a moment, then said, "Nope. That's all she wrote."

"I hope you will not refuse this token of my gratitude," I said, fishing out two twenties and a ten.

"It would be uncouthness itself to do so," he said, folding up the bills and putting them into one of the myriad of zippered pockets in his leathers. He arose and made to leave.

"Speaking of that's all she wrote, and I wish it was," I said, merely to be polite, "how's Sara?"

"How would I know?" he said. "I haven't seen her since last night. She sounded OK on the phone this morning." He grinned again and departed. I watched him start up and chug off, wondering briefly what hidden qualities Miss Sara Silvetti, poetess and total nerd, could possibly have to attract a gorgeous hunk like that. Maybe he was teaching her how to spell. Maybe he was enlarging her vocabulary all the way up to two- and three-syllable words. Yeah, that was probably it, the old Pygmalion game.

The Vineyards of Bourgogne—what the hell. I got down the atlas again. Maybe that's what Ruth Braukis was, a purveyor of overpriced French rotgut with fancy labels saying things I didn't know what they meant. I thought labels were supposed to be helpful these days and list all the poisons within and generally be of some use, it was time the Frogs woke up and started communicating in good old U.S. of A. And that stuff called French bread you get in supermarkets now? Awful.

I located the administrative district of Bourgogne right in the middle of the map of France. I'd never heard of any of the towns in it, except maybe Limoges, which almost rang a bell. Was it beer mugs they made there, or soup tureens . . . *zut, alors.*

I looked up ITC in the phone book. There were quite a few, but only one at 1843 South Vermont. Holy shit.

Yes, holy shit, I thought. I may even have said it aloud. Give me the Vineyards of Bourgogne any time. Give me the Industrial Tools Cooperative, the International Turbine Corporation, the Instant Ticket Company, give me any of the other ITCs but don't give me the Israeli Trade Center.

Oh, I had no doubt that down there on South Vermont the Israeli Trade Center was busily polishing a million oranges at that very minute, then squeezing them into little cardboard cans. I had no doubt their grapefruit salesmen who were out scouring the country were continually phoning in with new orders, and that teams of Sabras were busy giving thousands of avocados a final green rinse. I also had no doubt, none at all, that in a small back room protected by a heavily locked door, a group of the most respected and/ or feared secret service agents on earth, members of the dreaded Israeli Mossad, were gathering to plot the downfall of one harmless, innocent, still boyish-looking in the right light—and not an eclipse, either—private investigator.

Why oh why couldn't ITC have been the Italian Tagliatelli Connection? Give me the Mafia anytime.

And what did Mossad want with me, anyway? What were they up to these days? They couldn't still be trying to track down guys with hankies on their heads for what they did to the Israeli athletes at Munich, that was ancient history, come on, and so was Entebbe. Of course, there were probably a few of the most ruthless, most dedicated, and most unforgiving still out there, scouring the globe for ancient Nazis. . . .

Oh no.

Not them.

Say it ain't so, Ruth.

CHAPTER THREE

I muddled through the rest of the day somehow, and grad- ually my fears began to recede somewhat. Ruth Braukis mixed up with Nazis—ridiculous, almost as ridiculous as me being involved with those nightmare goose-steppers. Anyway they were all dead years ago or else hiding out in Brazil cloning new baby führers from strands of his pathetic mustache or else down in Argentina tossing the bolas and gauchoing across the pampas. Grow up, Daniel, and about time, too.

So it was a moderately carefree and footloose PI who locked up the office, drove home, changed into suitable fin- ery, including dress holster and .38-caliber revolver, caught the day's news on TV and then, just after seven o'clock, headed over to a certain blond-tressed secretary's apart- ment to pick her up for our date. Don't get me wrong, I didn't always tote the armament when I went out with gor- geous women, I could defend myself perfectly adequately with my bare hands, it was just that our date was only half a date, the other half was business.

My friend and near neighbor, Mr. Aaron Lubinski, of Lubinski, Lubinski & Levi, family jewelers for over twenty years, had, as a partner, his cousin Nate Lubinski. The lugu- brious Nathan had an equally gloomy, unlovely daughter, Rachael, whose oft-postponed marriage, it appeared, had finally taken place that afternoon, to her family's intense relief and, no doubt, hers as well. Every few months, for years now, it seemed like, I'd get a call from Aaron Lubinski to see if (a) I had a presentable suit, (b) if it was clean, and (c) could he book me to attend the wedding reception, partly as a guest and partly to keep an eye on both the family silver and the wedding presents, which, given the business he, most of his family, and many of his friends were in, would be of considerable value. As would, no doubt, the bijoux some of the guests would be wearing.

As I recall, the nuptials were once postponed when the groom ran off to join a kibbutz in the Negev, once when he ran off to try and teach Cambodian peasants to grow potatoes instead of opium, and once when he just ran off. Anyway, it looked like Rachael had finally snagged her man, or maybe his legs just gave out. And that is why Evonne and I, attired in our wedding-reception best—Mr. Fashion Plate in a stunning ecru Indian-cotton suit with complementary accessories, her in something white, silk, and clinging— were on our way, via the San Diego freeway, to Bel Air and smoked salmon on toast instead of West Holly wood and sauce Alfredo on fettuccini at Mario's. And if I didn't look like your typical wedding-reception guest, I didn't think I looked like a typical security type either, especially with Evonne on my arm, so maybe it would all even out. It was the first time I'd ever been on any kind of a job with her along; she'd offered to help once or twice in the past but it hadn't happened, mainly because I always came up with a good enough excuse to prevent it happening. She had been in on the tag end of one escapade, though, and had seemed to enjoy herself.

Bel Air. Lots of money in Bel Air, which is just west of Beverly Hills, which, as we know, is not without a few bucks of its own. Both the residences and the fortunes tended to be older in Bel Air, but one could find the occasional upstarts, like the Lubinskis, installed there in the green hills behind ten-foot, barbed-wire–topped walls and heavily barred front gates.

Aaron and Nathan had adjoining properties on St. Cloud, which is off Bel Air Road. We located the right house without any trouble, as there were three uniformed valet parkers, hired by me as part of my chores, waiting patiently outside the front gate to take care of the overflow once the interior driveway and parking spaces in front of the house were full. On the way there I did not mention a word to Evonne about the Israeli Trade Center, agents not only licenses, but encouraged, to kill Gestapo swine, or come to think of it, Miss Ruth Braukis. Yet more proof, if indeed it be needed, that I have not as yet lost the last of my marbles, amigos.

I pulled up outside the gate, got out, traded friendly quips with the youthful carhops, complimented them on their neat appearance, warned them severely against any teenage antics like drag racing or playing chicken with the visitors' wheels, then strolled through the now-open gate to have a word with the guard who came out of his little hut to greet me. He was an old pal of mine, an ex-cop name of Frank O'Brien who I got to know years ago upstate before I started up on my own when I was doing more or less what he was doing these days—standing around a lot keeping an eye on other people's property.

Frank was a fit-looking, stocky man a few years older than me, dressed in his working clothes of black shoes, blue trousers, short blue jacket caught at the waist, blue cap, and holstered weapon. We shook hands; I introduced him to Evonne, and he shook hands with her too, then he raised his eyebrows at me in that man-to-man look that means "You lucky old dog, you."

"All quiet on the western front?" I said.

"Yep," he said.

"Annie up at the house with the guest list?"

"Yep," he said. Annie was his wife, a tiny powerhouse who looked, and was, just as fit as her old man. She talked about as much as him, too, which was hardly at all, except when she was squiffed.

"OK, pal," I said, getting back in the car. "Any problems, give me a call."

"Yep," he said. "Anythin' particular I'm lookin' for?"

"Nope," I said. I proceeded slowly up the curving tree-lined drive, waving once in a casual fashion to a gardner who stopped work to admire my classic wheels as we passed, then I was directed by yet another valet parker toward the side of the house, where I slipped in neatly between a caterer's van and a stretch limo. The catering van's rear doors were open and two youths in T-shirts were busy unloading large, foil-covered trays and serving dishes and, I was pleased to see, cases of liquid refreshments, and then toting them down a path at the side of the house to the kitchen. The house itself was huge, sprawling, and utterly gorgeous. It was Spanish in design, with white stuccoed walls and terracotta roof tiles, also with decorative tiles outlining all the windows and doors. My friend Mr. Aaron Lubinski, looking very sharp indeed in a dark blue tux, ruffled shirt, red cummerbund, and red rose in his lapel, was standing at the front door waiting for us.

"Hum, a regular clotheshorse suddenly," he said to me as we shook hands.

"Look who's talking," I said, grinning down at him. "So how are you?"

23

"How should I be on such a day, heartbroken?" he said.

"You will no doubt remember Miss Evonne Shirley, who came to your reopening party with me," I said.

"Could I forget such a vision?" He took her hand and kissed the back of it gallantly. Then he led us into the house, through the large living room, and then out through open French doors into a spacious courtyard enclosed on all sides by the various wings, ells, projections, and abutments. There we discovered other members of the catering crew busily putting the final decorative touches that mean so much on rows of linen-draped trestle tables. Three additional tables at the rear, under some arches next to the kitchen, groaned under the weight of enough high-class comestibles to relieve the famine in Somalia overnight.

The booze—plus all the soft drinks, fruit juices, ice buckets, Maraschino cherries, and cunningly cut slices of assorted citrus fruits—were temptingly laid out on yet more tables right next to the food.

I raised my eyebrows. "Quite a spread. Quite a joint, too. I never knew there was so much money in ankle bracelets and mood rings."

"Don't mind him," Evonne said. "He's just jealous."

"You better believe it," I said. "Mr. Lubinski, how about you entertaining Evonne for a few minutes while I have a little snoop around."

"A rare pleasure," he said, taking her arm and leading her toward the drinks table. "I think there's a bottle of champagne already open, my dear, and if not, there soon will be."

"What a treat to meet a real gentleman at last," my beloved said over her shoulder so she'd be sure I heard it. I winked at her and wandered back into the front of the house. As I was admiring the artwork in the living room,

Frank's wife Annie called to me through the open door of an adjoining room.

"Peekaboo, I see you," she said, raising a glass of cheer in my general direction.

"Likewise, I'm sure," I said. I went in and patted the top of her head. She blew a kiss up at me. She was sitting at a desk in what turned out to be Nathan's office or study or den or all three, two pages of guest list in front of her and in front of them, a complicated-looking telephone setup, almost a junior switchboard, also a FAX machine.

"How's it going, shortie?" I asked her.

She shrugged. "Could be worse." I took a quick look around. In the walls were framed pictures of various Jewish leaders in all fields—political, artistic, business—and in many of them the tall, stooping figure of Nathan Lubinski also appeared, to my surprise. There were also several framed letters of thanks from various Jewish charities which Nathan had either donated heavily to, served on the board of, or in one case, chaired. The walls were otherwise lined with bookshelves; from my brief examination, all seemed to deal with some aspect of Jewish history. One, Hugh Trevor-Roper's *The Last Days of Hitler*, I'd even read part of once. Or maybe I just saw the movie. I have to confess my ignorance of works by Shirer, Spicehandler, Mann, Speer, Rabinowitz, and all the others.

"Looking for something to read in the john?" Annie said.

"Not in this library," I said. "Unless he's got some Elmore Leonard westerns tucked away somewhere."

Oh. There was one more item on the walls aside from the ones I've mentioned—a large and elaborate family tree, done with exquisite penmanship—by Nathan, I found out later. I noticed that one whole branch of his family, those

living in and around Riga, were marked by an asterisk, signi-
fying they had been killed in 1941 in the Holocaust. I wondered if Riga was anywhere near Estonia, and made a mental
note to look it up next time I was in the office. I did—it
turned out to be the capital of Latvia, Estonia's neighbor to
the west. I also wondered briefly if Miss Ruth Braukis just
happened to be an acquaintance of the Lubinskis, too, as
she was of the Lewellens; maybe the whole wedding was
merely an Israeli intelligence ploy to get me into Nathan's
office for nefarious purposes as yet unrevealed.

Before I got out of there, I asked Annie how may guests
were expected. She said about 120, and thanked me for getting her in on the act as there was no reason Frank couldn't
have retained the guest list and done all the vetting by himself. I said, "What are friends for," told her to hang in there,
and departed.

I was outside admiring the rhododendrons when a dul-
cet voice I'd heard before once or twice in my life called
out from somewhere above me, "Yoo hoo!" I looked around
and spied Evonne waving at me from the sun roof above
one of the bedrooms, from which from time to time came
the sound of female laughter. I climbed up the spiral stair-
case nearest to her—there were four in all, one in each corner of the patio—and stole a sip of her champagne. Aaron
Lubinski was twirling the rest of the bottle in an ice bucket
on the counter of a small wet bar that was nestled under a
striped awning in one corner.

"It's lovely from up here," Evonne said, "except for
champagne thieves who are too lazy to get their own glass."

"Here, enjoy," Mr. Lubinski said, pouring me out one.

"When are the guests due?" I asked him.

"As soon as they uncover the chicken liver," he said.
"Like vultures they'll gather."

"Let me ask you something," I said to him. "Do you put all the wedding presents on display, like they do at Italian weddings, I think it is?"

"It is, and we don't," 'he said. "A lot of the guests, though, will be giving the happy couple, I hope, money, like our Italian friends also do at a wedding."

"Money money?"

"More likely check money," he said, refilling all our glasses.

"Did your cousin call his insurance guy like I suggested?"

"He did," Mr. Lubinski said. "I was there."

"What was that for?" Evonne wanted to know.

"Normal precautions," I said. "Although it's not likely anything will happen with me and you and Frank and Annie here, you never know. There's going to be over a hundred guests all dressed up in pearl chokers and gold cuff links and there's a roomful of wedding present loot somewhere, to say nothing of the Renoirs in the living room."

"Renoirs they're not," Mr. Lubinski said. "They were painted by a Jewish artist who died in one of the camps. I forget which one, Nate would know."

"About how many were there, just out of curiosity?" I said.

He shrugged. "Auschwitz, Chelmno, Sibibor, Majdanek, Belsec, Treblinka, of course, there was Belsen, Stutthof, Neuengamme, Dachau, Flossenburg, did I say Buchenwald? There was Sachsenhausen, there was Mauthausen, Riga, Theresienstadt, Ravensbrück. Enough? You want more, ask Nate, or the rabbi, when he comes, they're the experts."

"No, no," I said hastily. "That's more than enough, thanks, Mr. Lubinski."

"So why all this interest all of a sudden?" he said, looking up at me.

"No real interest," I said. "I was just in his den, that's all, having a word with Annie, and saw all the stuff he had on Jewish history. Anyway, Evonne," I said, changing the subject rather clumsily, "aside from all the guests wandering around and dancing the hora you've got all the catering staff, plus a bunch of chaffeurs, no doubts, maybe some kids breaking things, plus those valet parkers—"

"—Plus the band," said Mr. Lubinski. "All five pieces."

"Plus all five pieces," I said, "of zonked-out accordian players, so why take a chance? Better get temporary coverage for everything and everyone including God knows how many Rolls-Royces and Mercedes-Benzes, let alone guests who choke on a bone in one of those cold fishballs I saw piled up on the goodies tables. Frankly, I was hoping for chicken a la king, its got more class."

"Oh, oh," said Mr. Lubinski then. "Action stations." He gestured with a thumb over the parapet where a white Cadillac was pulling up in front of the house. He downed the last of his champagne and left us alone with the rest of the bottle of Mumm's.

"What a sweet man," my favorite blonde said.

"Yeah," I said. "But not as sweet as you." She gave me a quick kiss.

"I wonder where the blushing bride is," she said. "And what she's doing."

"Ask me a tough one," I said. "She's in the room directly under us where all the giggling is coming from and what she is doing is telling dirty jokes with the bridesmaids." I poured us out the last of the bubbles.

There was a pause, then she said idly, "You ever think of getting married, Victor?"

"Sure," I said promptly.

"You do?" She seemed surprised.

"All the time. I just can't decide who to get married to."

"Ha-ha," she said.

"OK," I said. "I have, from time to time, thought about walking down the aisle with you, Evonne Louise Shirley."

"And?"

"That's all," I said. "I have, from time to time, thought about marrying you." She turned away. There was just enough breeze to disturb the tendrils at the back of her neck. I disturbed them a little more with my free hand, took a big drink, then a bigger breath, cleared my throat, then asked her ever so casually, "What about you, do you want to get married? To me, naturally."

"Naturally." She turned and gazed at me for a long moment with those blue, blue eyes of hers. Finally she sighed and said, "Almost."

I said, "I know exactly what you mean, honey," although I wasn't at all sure I did. She put her head against my shoulder and hugged me. I hugged her right back. After a moment or two she disentangled herself, then shook out her coiffure.

"Come on, babe," she said. "Time to mingle."

"Right here?"

"Down there." She pointed to the patio where fifteen or twenty guests were already mingling pretty well without us. As we watched, the bride, Rachael, and her six bridesmaids made their entrance from the room below us while at the same time from the room facing theirs the groom and his six ushers or whatever you call them made their appearance. The bride wore white, her attendants identical pretty, long white summer coats over their dresses. The groom wore black, while his team sported white tuxedo jackets worn with navy blue trousers, and with a red carnation in each lapel.

I forgot to mention the bridesmaids all had red carnations pinned in their tresses.

Down we went.

Mingle we did. While we were so doing I borrowed a couple of red carnations from one of the vases for me and Evonne.

During the next couple of hours we ate, drank, mingled, even danced, when the band finally struck up after the speeches, wandered, and met people. We met Yoav, the groom, whose suit was too big for him and who looked like he'd been dragged to the reception by his hair; Rachael, the bride, who looked like she'd been crying and drinking; Rebecca Lubinski, the bride's mother, who said her feet were killing her; assorted guests; the perspiring head of the catering team; and during one of their breaks, three members of the band, two out back who were sharing a companionable reefer and one up on the sun roof. I even met the elderly rabbi, and Mrs. Rabbi,

"Try the potato salad," he said. "It's delicious."

"Is it kosher?" I said.

"If it isn't, don't tell me," he said.

I did try it; it was delicious, it had capers in it. I also essayed the chopped liver, the pastrami, the lox, the cole slaw, and the cold tongue. The horseradish was red, also red hot. I gave the fish balls a miss. I kept my eyes as well as my mouth open.

At one stage I strolled down to visit Frank, taking with me, in a glass in one pocket, a hefty slug of bourbon, which Annie had told me would be much appreciated. I noticed she was appreciating a tall tumbler of something refreshing as well. Frank reported that all was quiet at his end. I said, "Likewise."

Shortly thereafter, back up at the house again, I was standing near the band watching the dancing and sipping a brandy and ginger ale without the brandy when the little rabbi popped up beside me.

"Aaron tells me you are a private detective, Mr. Daniel," he said. "Hum, interesting. I never met anyone in your line of work before."

"Can't say I've met many rabbis, either," I remarked. "Is it true that to be Jewish your mother has to be Jewish, not your father? That always seemed a little strange to me."

"A lot of our laws seem strange at first," he said, "until you know the thinking behind them. Then it is highly possible they may still seem strange, of course. But in this case, the logic is clear enough. While it is not always possible to tell who the father of a particular child is, it's usually highly obvious who the mother is."

I laughed. He peered innocently up at me through his bifocals.

" 'Daniel,' " he said reflectively. "You have the same name as one of our greatest prophets, as you no doubt know."

"No, I didn't," I admitted. "Was that the same Daniel who I heard had all kinds of problems with some lions once somewhere?"

"In Babylon," he said, nodding.

"Yeah, well," I said. "Always was a lively town, Babylon, especially on Homecoming Week."

He smiled, then waved to Mrs. Rabbi, who came sedately fox-trotting by with Yoav.

I looked around to make sure Evonne wasn't within hearing distance, i.e., a nautical mile. "Rabbi, can I ask you something?"

"Why not?"

"Did you ever meet a Nazi?"

"Yes," he said. "I did."

"When?"

"This morning." I stared at him.

"What was he doing?"

"He was scrubbing off a swastika someone had sprayed on the door to our temple. He shows up every time there's been vandalism, with his bucket and Vim and paint remover and whatever, rolls up his sleeves, and goes to work."

"How do you know he was a Nazi?"

"He told me," the rabbi said. "The time I took him out a cup of coffee. 'Why are you doing this?' I asked him. 'Because I was a Nazi,' he said. More than likely he was SS as well."

"And why is that, Rabbi?"

"They were the only ones with the money and the resources and the organization to be able to leave Germany before the end," he explained patiently. "Of course, they had the most reason to leave, as well, as it was estimated they were responsible for something like ninety-five percent of all the atrocities."

"And where'd they go? South America?"

"South America," he agreed. "Uruguay. Argentina alone gave them seven thousand blank passports. South Africa."

"Here?" I asked uneasily.

"In Mr. Allan Ryan's book, he estimates ten thousand came here. Naturally, they'd all be trembling old men now in their middle seventies, like me." He took off his skullcap, looked at it, gave it a little shake, then put it on again. "Not a particularly cheerful subject for such a festive occasion, if I may say so, Mr. Daniel. Have you some particular interest in the subject? A professional one, perhaps?"

"I sure as fuck hope not," I said, but under my breath. To the diminutive rabbi I merely repeated what I had told

32

Mr. Aaron Lubinski, that a passing interest, nothing more, had been aroused by Nathan's library.

"Oh, yeah," I said, snapping my fingers. "I know what I did want to ask you about. Did you ever happen to come across those rabbi mysteries? *Monday the Rabbi Slept Late.* Tuesday he did something else and Wednesday I can't remember what?"

"Indeed I did," he said, nodding. "I have the whole series. My son, the well-known comedian, sends me one every time I have a birthday. He thinks he's shocking me."

"So what do you do?"

"I pretend to be deeply shocked," he said. "Who am I not to give my only son what he wants most?" He went off to rejoin Mrs. Rabbi, who was beckoning energetically to him from a nearby table, one of two that had been left in place when the rest were dismantled to provide space for cutting the rug. I went off, rather hastily, to put the merest splash of booze in my ginger ale.

It was a little after eleven when the party started running down; some of the more elderly of the guests had already left, as had some of the ones with young children. I tracked down Aaron Lubinski and asked him to please join us in his cousin's den in five.

"Why not?" he said.

I cut in briefly on Evonne, who was dancing a spirited cha-cha-cha with the best-looking of the ushers, and asked her the same thing.

"Sure, toots," she said.

When we had all gathered, Annie got me Frank on the phone.

"Anything?" I asked him.

"One fender," he said. "Annie took care of it."

"OK, roger and out," I said. "Tell the head hot-rodder I'll be down in a few minutes to pay him off."

Frank said, "OK, pal," and rang off.

"What fender?" I asked Annie.

She looked at a slip of paper in front of her.

"Fender of some kind of a technicolor circus car," she said. "Completely totaled."

"Very funny," I said.

"Fender of a dark green Buick Le Sabre," she said. "The name on the keys was Jacob Vineberg. Couldn't find a Jacob Vineberg. Was directed to a Samuel Vineberg. Told him his fender had been slightly dented by one of the parkers. He laughed. I said, 'What's so funny?' He said, 'It's not my fender, it's my brother's, so let him worry.' "

"How about you, babe," I said to Evonne. "See anything untoward?"

"Well," she said, frowning prettily, "I don't know if it was untoward or not but I saw a man in one of the bedrooms smooching with a lady who wasn't the one he came with."

"Well!" I exclaimed. "Did you ever!"

"I saw something," said Mr. Lubinski. "I witnessed an outright act of theft." He unloosened his bowtie with a sigh of relief.

"No kidding?" Annie said. "What was stolen?"

"Two red carnations," said Aaron Lubinski severely, winking at Evonne.

"So take a buck off my bill," I said. "Let me ask you this, Mr. Wise Guy. How do you pay for the booze?"

"Meaning what?" said Mr. Lubinski, looking slightly baffled.

"I mean do you pay the caterers a flat rate per head, or do you pay them a flat rate per head just for the food and then, on top, pay for whatever booze was drunk?"

He shrugged. "Who'd pay for undrunk booze?" he wondered. "Also, what caterer in his right mind would give you a flat rate for food and drink ahead of time, anyway, is he suddenly Bet-A-Million Bates? So he wins if he's catering the Pasadena Grandmother's Bridge Club, but what if the party's for the twentieth anniversary of the Private Investigator's Social Club? You pay by the empty bottle—my wife's out there now counting them up with the barman."

"Yeah," I said. "That's what I thought."

"So?" said Mr. Lubinski.

"So this," I said. "I knew a barman once."

"No!" exclaimed my darling. "Did you ever!" She and Annie shook their heads in disbelief.

"The owner of the bar where he worked personally supervised the delivery of all booze, that was like once a week. So then all he's got to do, at the end of the week before reordering, is count the number of empty bottles, multiply by the number of shots in a bottle, and multiply that by the price per shot, and that's how much money he wants in the till. OK, roughly. The barman can't sell a bottle of his boss's booze and then chuck out the empty in the garbage because the boss is going to say, Where's the empty that belongs in this case of empty Johnny Walkers?"

"Good question," said Mr. Lubinski.

"Gee, it just slipped out of my hands and got broke," said Evonne. "I always been a butterfingers."

"I gave it to an old lady who wanted to make a lamp out of it," said the other comedienne, who then hiccupped delicately behind one palm.

"You two probably finished it off yourselves," I observed.

The ladies giggled.

"So what the guy does," I went on, "is bring in his own bottle of booze, bought at Cut-Rate Charley's Cheap Booze

Emporium, and pours the customers' drinks out of it. He chucks out the empty and pockets the difference between his cost at Charley's and what he nets selling it at a buck and a half a shot, and unless the owner's got a permanent spotter in the place making sure that every drink sold gets rung up in the till, there's not much he can do about it."

"Aw," said Annie. "The heart bleeds."

"So?" said Mr. Lubinski again.

"At a gala soiree like this," I said, "there's no percentage in the barman bringing in his own booze, because he's not the one who gets paid for it. But when we were parking outside, I spied with my little eye something curious. I spied two guys, a little guy and a big guy. Each was carrying a case of champagne. Guess which one was having the most trouble?"

"The big guy," said my beloved. "I saw him, too."

"And the little guy wasn't a secret weight lifter, either," I said, "because all he was wearing was a T-shirt and Mr. Universe he wasn't."

"So what if what he was carrying was a case of empty champagne bottles, right?" said Mr. Lubinski. "Which my good wife is out there counting and which will be charged to Nathan at forty bucks a bottle, right?"

"It could be," I said. "There's no way we can prove it now one way or the other, but next time tell your good wife to count the bottles on the way in, too."

"You better believe it," said Mr. Lubinski grimly. "You better believe it's the last time we use that caterer, too. So what else did anyone notice although I hate to ask, a pickpocket maybe, a blackmailer?"

"One of the musicians," Annie said. "The guitarist. I saw him wandering around the living room."

"Me, too," said Evonne. "Only it was up on one of the sun roofs."

"Me three," I said. "Only it was out back by the garage."

Mr. Lubinski sighed and rolled his eyes skyward.

"Curiouser and curiouser," Evonne said. "Eh, gang?"

"What's so curious?" said Mr. Lubinski. "That little momser was—what's the expression, casing the joint?"

"That's the expression," I said, "Could be. We'll have to find out for sure. What I don't like is, he was out by the garage, which is often easier to break into than the house, which it is often connected to. He was also up on the roof, which can be another comparatively easy way in."

"So what'll you do?" asked Mr. Lubinski.

"Maybe I'll have to case the momser's joint," I said.

CHAPTER FOUR

I went out into the living room and took a quick look at where the band had been set up. They must have unset themselves because they weren't there anymore. I hastened back into the den and asked Annie to get me Frank on the phone pronto. When she did, I said, "Frank?"

"Yep."

"Any of the band still on the premises?"

"There equipment van hasn't shown yet," he said.

"If it shows before I do," I said, "don't let it out. Tell whoever's in it they got a surprise bonus coming or whatever, but don't get them all het up. Got it?"

"Yep. Anythin' else?"

"Nope." We both hung up. I turned to Evonne, who was exchanging some girlish confidence with Annie in a whisper. Oh, darn, there I go again, being male and chauvinistic; maybe they were discussing philosophy, maybe even that hopeful remark by I forget who—"There is more felicity on the far side of baldness than young men can possibly imagine." Anyway, I turned to her and said, "I hate to interrupt but it's show time, babe. Let us be on our way."

"I'm with you," she said. "What are we on our way to do?"

"With any luck I'll think of something clever." I got out my wallet, dug out two hundreds, and passed them over to

Annie. "For the hot-rodders. Tell them thanks from me. I don't want whoever's in that van to catch me paying them off. You might as well come with us, you're done here. Oh." I passed her over several more hundreds. "For you and Frank."

She bounced out of her chair, kissed my chin, gave Mr. Lubinski a hearty handshake, then tucked her handbag, which was shaped like a twenty-six-inch TV set and only slightly smaller, under her arm, ready to go. I told Mr. Lubinski I'd let him know what happened as soon as something did. Evonne patted him on the cheek, said, " 'Night, you all, and thanks for the party," then patted him on the other cheek.

"It started as a party," he said. "What it turned out to be was more like a Mafia reunion." He escorted us to the front door and watched us drive off.

"What a swell party, what a swell party, what a swell party that was," Annie sang loudly as we tootled back down the drive toward the front gates. I patted my breast pocket to make sure I had a memo pad and pen; I did. I asked Evonne if she had one. She rummaged in her purse and held up her address book, the kind that has a small pencil attached.

"Why?" she wanted to know.

"Couldn't hoit," I said, "which is what Mrs. Rabbi said to me when I asked her if chicken soup was really any good for sick people."

When we arrived at the gates, the equipment van was already pulled up on this side of them waiting for us. I parked behind it. We all got out.

"See ya," Annie said, and bustled away to pay off the boys. Evonne and I strolled up to the front of the white Volkswagon van, on the side of which was painted in wavy blue script, "Ron's Rhythm Kings," with a few musical notes added here and there as decoration.

There were two gents in the van, a chubby one with round granny glasses and a goatee, who'd doubled on sax and clarinet, and a large, fully bearded one, drums and the occasional backup vocal. The group's amps and speakers, mikes and instruments and coils of wire and whatnot were neatly arranged behind them in the body of the van.

"Hi!" I said brightly to the one nearest me, the chubby one, "One of you wouldn't be Ron, by any lucky chance?"

"I don't know how much luck is involved," said the chubby one, "but you are looking at Ron the Rhythm King himself."

"Star of three continents," the bearded one said. "Iceland, Greenland, and Tasmania."

"That unspeakably hairy thing there," said Ron, "is Rufus, and Buddy Rich he ain't."

"Don," I said, with a warm smile. "Don Upton. And this here living dream is the future Mrs. Upton."

"Oh, Donny," said Evonne, fluttering her lashes. "You don't have to go round telling everyone."

"Sorry to keep you good boys waiting," I said, "but, well, me and honeybun here were kinda looking for an orchestra to play at our wedding next month sometime . . . gee, I forget the exact date." Evonne rolled her eyes heavenward. "Just funnin', honey," I added hastily, and we all had a good chuckle.

"Rufe," said Ron. "Take five. Go talk to the buttercups for a while, would you? This gentleman and I will shortly be discussing money, and I know how the subject distresses you."

"OK if I look for mushrooms instead?" said Rufe. He clambered down his side, stretched, moved off slowly about twenty feet, collapsed under a tree, and apparently fell asleep immediately. Ron opened up the glove compartment, took out an exercise book, then he climbed down to join us.

"What is that?" I inquired. "Your fake book?"

He grinned. Evonne wanted to know what a fake book was. I said I'd tell her later, I didn't want to embarrass the mighty rhythm king himself in front of a lady.

"It's my gig book," he said. "In which, as the name implies, are neatly listed all our gigs."

I gave Evonne a deeply meaningful glance that she pretended not to see.

"Gee!" she exclaimed. "Can I have a peek? I wonder if I know any people you've played for. Do you do a lot of weddings round here?"

" 'A fair share,' he said with becoming modesty," Ron said. "Help yourself. Fill your eyes with our recent triumphs on the bar mitzvah circuit. All the incriminating details, like how much, are penned in my own private unbreakable code so the two members of the group who can actually read cannot figure out how much I am not paying them. Oh, dear, I've lost me testimonials, hang on." He got back up into the cab again.

I nuzzled up to Evonne.

"Names," I whispered between nuzzles. "Rough addresses. Starting a few months ago. Get all you can."

"Oh, Donny, you're so masterful," she whispered back.

Ron got down again and handed over three or four envelopes, bowing from the waist as he did so.

"Me testimonials, monsieur, and if I do say so myself, rave reviews every one." I gave them to Evonne.

"You have a look, buns," I said. "Business is a-calling me, and the maestro here." We strolled off over the sward. I asked him what he charged for an event like a wedding reception. He said it depended on the size of the group.

I said, did it not take the same amount of playing whether he was playing for a group of two dozen, or a hundred? He said, not the size of my group, the size of his group. He also said the price naturally depended on the number of hours they played. I asked him if a deposit was required. He allowed that he would not take it adverse in the slightest. I asked him if he charged more for playing some types of music rather than others.

"You better believe it, my man," he said. "Polkas cost double."

"And naturally," I said, "as consummate artists in your field, your orchestra members would expect to be treated as such and be fully wined and dined."

"And boozed," Ron said. "Don't forget that." I saw, over his shoulder, the satisfactory sight of the future Mrs. Upton scribbling away furiously in her address book.

After a spot more badinage and a smidgen more bargaining, we amicably settled on a price for the would-be Upton wedding reception, discussed briefly the contents of the intended musical program—no polkas, no punk, no Mexican hat dances—then we headed back toward the van.

"One thing," Ron said apologetically on the way. "I of all people do not want to seem pushy, greedy, or indeed, needy. I am a musician, after all. I do have a certain reputation to uphold. But was there not some talk of, ahem, a bonus of some modest kind?"

"Golly," I said, slapping my leg. "I forgot all about that, Ron. Did you meet your host, by any chance? Nathan Lubinski?"

"Briefly," he said. "He came up to thank us all when we were packing up. It was his missus who took care of all the details, including the main one—the big payoff. Isn't he like a jeweler?"

"Is he ever," I said. "Miss me, Precious?" Precious blew me a kiss. I pretended to catch it and tuck it away in a pocket. She simpered back at me.

"He's got a lot of class, too, old Nate," I said. "He gave all the ushers gold cuff links with their initials on them and the usherettes gold charm bracelets and his daughter and new son-in-law a car with their initials on it, and moreover, he must be tone deaf is all I can think of, he wants to send all you musical vagabonds silver tie clips or something, with all your initials on them."

"A thoughtful gesture," said Ron.

"Indeedy," said I. "So. If you and the boys actually happen to have homes these days and aren't still sleeping out on Manhattan Beach, let me have the addresses, please, and Nate'll have them made up and have them hand-delivered in his own company van"—nonexistent, needless to say—"which is not a tarted-up old Volks, either, like some I could name."

Ron was only too happy to oblige. He retrieved his gig book from Precious, flipped to the back pages, copied out the names and addresses of his brother musicians on a pad I happened to have at the ready, then dug out one of his business cards to cover himself.

"Which one was the guitarist?" Evonne asked him ingenuously. "He was cute as all get-out. I loved his riffs."

"You keep your hands off his riffs," I said sternly.

"That one," said Ron, pointing to one of the names. "D. Gresham the Third. Also known in the trade as 'Finger-Lickin' Good.' "

Evonne let out a trill of high-pitched laughter. Ron penciled in his book what he thought was my name and what he thought was my address, plus a phone number that wasn't mine, under the appropriate date. I said I'd get on to him within a day or two about a definite commitment and that the deposit check was practically in the safe hands of the U.S. Postal Service already.

"All right already!" he said to me. We exchanged high fives. "Adiós for ahora, sweet madam," he said to Evonne.

"Adored your testimonials," she said to him.

Ron climbed up into the driver's seat, started up the van, then shouted out the window, "C'mon, Rufe, you'll miss the bus."

Rufe came, Frank opened the gates, and off they drove, giving us a farewell *toot-toot* on the horn.

" 'Bye!" waved Precious.

As soon as they were out of sight, she dived into her purse, got out her address book again, and began scribbling furiously again, muttering under her sweet breath as she did so. When she finally came up for air, Frank and Annie had wandered over to join us.

"What was that all about?" Annie asked me.

"Kim," I said. "She was being Kim."

"In what movie?" she said.

"Not that Kim," I said disgustedly. "Haven't you ever read any higher literature?"

"He has," she said, referring to her hubby. "He gets *Guns and Ammo* every month." Frank looked away sheepishly.

"Rudyard Kipling's *Kim*," I said. My pop loved Kipling. He had his complete works, along with those of O. Henry. Otherwise, his only other literary interests, as far as I could recall, were *The Saturday Evening Post*, the *Police Gazette*, *Look*, and *Life*, although once, in the basement, I came across a tattered copy of something called *Sun 'n' Sport*, which surprised me because I never knew my pop was at all interested in ladies' volleyball.

"Kim," I said, "was some English kid who trained to be a spy in India by practicing memorizing. His teacher would lay out thirty or forty assorted items on a tray and the kid would have say thirty seconds to try and remember them all. And that is what Precious was doing, remembering all the ones she didn't have a chance to write down."

"Oh," said Annie. "That clears that up, I don't think."

"Sure you do," I said. "Frank told me he caught you thinking only last week."

"Did not," said Frank.

"So how did you do, Precious?" I said.

"You tell me," she said airily. She showed me her address book; two whole pages were full of entries like, "Jacobson, BH"; "Martin, WH"; "Tuaber, BA"; "Hall, SO"; "Flint, PA"; and so on. I quickly deduced that the letters stood for Beverly Hills, West Hollywood, Bel Air, Sherman Oaks, Pasadena, and so on; the little dumpling had managed to list about thirty names altogether.

"Brilliant," I said.

"Thank you," she said. "I naturally didn't bother with any of the ballrooms or restaurants or clubs the band played in."

"Excellent," I said.

"Now what, Donny-poo?"

I shrugged. "We'll have to see. Frank, you know anybody working out of Robbery? I used to know this midget lieutenant, he was about the size of Little Orphan Annie in flats, but he moved to Vice last I heard."

"What about Jasper?" said Annie. "Jasper Johnson."

"Yeah, right," said Frank. Jasper turned out to be a cop Frank had once shared a patrol car with who'd since made detective; he worked out of the same LAPD station downtown as did my beloved brother Tony, but Tony toiled in the basement in Records, and Jasper would be up on the fifth or sixth floor somewhere. Anyway, there was nothing more to be done right then, in the line of business, that is, so we made our farewells and went our separate ways into the not-so-gentle California night. On the way back I told Evonne what a fake book was—a book containing basic chord charts for hundreds of standards, for use in emergency by unprepared bands. Too bad the same thing didn't exist for unprepared PIs.

And aging Casanovas.

CHAPTER FIVE

I cannot, nor will not, say I slept like the proverbial top that night. When I awoke not too early the following A.M., my sheets were soaked through and so was I. Luckily for Precious, I was in my own little bed; I'd driven back to my place to sleep because, although it happened from time to time, Evonne wasn't completely comfortable with my staying over at her garden apartment, and if there is anything worse than waking up to soaked sheets, it's waking up to sheets soaked by someone else. Evonne did not seem to mind spending the occasional night of love and laughter *chez moi*, though; she'd' even recently taken to leaving the odd bit of clothing or makeup behind. I wondered if it meant something Freudian, like she left articles behind to give her a reason for returning, but then I figured she already had good reason—my sweet and practiced caresses.

As I hadn't drunk at all the night before hardly, it couldn't have been the booze that caused the ooze, excuse the poetry, so it must have been my dreams that drenched the seams. Although, as usual, I couldn't remember anything about them, and I wonder if that means something. But they must have been your veritable nightmares, no doubt brought on by the company I had recently been keeping, like having your molars drilled without anesthetic by

Himmler or having to sit through all of *Waiting for Godot* again without a full hip flask and a portable opium pipe.

I used to dream a lot about islands, hence I would suppose my firm penchant for Hawaiian chemises, but I don't need Freud to tell me what islands stand for in dreams, they stand for islands, they stand for escape and planter's punches and sandy kisses and, dream of dreams, not one Boston Celtic fan within a million miles.

" 'No man is an island,' " someone once wrote, which always seemed pretty obvious to me, unless he's the Isle of Man.

" 'Little islands are all large prisons,' " someone else wrote, which is obviously rubbish. I think he meant to say, *some* islands, like Devil's Island, are prisons, but so what? Everyone knows that. My island, call it what you will, Daniel's Dunes, The No-Clothes-At-All Atoll, in whatever balmy southern sea it may lie, is no prison, believe me. I've been in prisons, and not to take a cake with a file in it for a wayward chum on visiting day either. Prisons are prisons, are what prisons are, and they tend to be a little short on fresh coconuts, fish barbecues, free bananas, and all the clams you can dig.

Morning thoughts, perched atop a porcelain bowl—mornings would be far more tolerable if they came later in the day, like just after Happy Hour. . . it was still strange not having Mom around, especially in the mornings, when we always had breakfast together. . . . Some people sing when they are happy; some when they are sad. When I was but a tiny, tiny tot, someone, I don't know for sure who, used to sing me toward slumberland with the old folksong "Down in the Valley," from which ditty, you may already know, comes the hopeful plea "Write me a letter." Well, I hope it was my mom who'd been doing the singing, is what I hope, and I also hope 'twas not the blues she was singing. . . .

Actually, I'm not sure I ever was a tiny, tiny tot—I have the feeling that even when I was small, I was big. . . . Remember that philosopher, whoever he was, who claimed that you could never arrive at a finite point because every time you traveled half the remaining distance to your goal, half was still left, and if you traveled half that half, that still left another half, and so on. Which, as we all know, is foolishness, because you can get somewhere, like I managed to get to the john. But he almost had it right. If he'd used toothpaste as an analogy, he could have convinced me—there is no such thing as a completely empty tube of Colgate. There is always a weeny bit left, even if it means cutting the tube open along the bottom and one side with nail scissors. Yes, A.M. bits and pieces, which don't seem to be that much different from late-night ones, come to think about it.

John D. was waiting for me when I got to the office, sitting out front in his car. I opened up and he followed me in. John was a trim-looking six-footer, an ex–pro bowler who'd bought control of a bowling alley just east of where I lived, after he left the professional circuit. As far as I knew, he was doing pretty good; there was always plenty going on at the Valley Bowl whenever I dropped in, which was at least once a month, as I had installed and looked after his building's security system for him. He looked a mite weary that Tuesday morning, though; he sank into the spare chair with a noise part sigh and part groan and rubbed his gray eyes tiredly.

I got my checkbook out of the safe, wrote out one for a cool ten grand, and slid it across the desk toward him.

"Thanks, Vic," he said, putting it away in his wallet without looking at it.

"Sure, pal," I said. "You helped me out with a modest sum once, remember?"

"I do."

"You lent me your office once, too, remember?"

"I do."

"And your car that time?"

"Guilty."

"You even lent me yourself that time I needed a Marlboro man type."

"I lent you a bowling ball once, too," he said. "Always wondered what you wanted it for. I figured it wasn't just to drop on someone's tootsies."

I gave him an enigmatic smile, but he wasn't that far wrong, actually. He made no move to get up and go, so I figured he still had something on his mind, so I said, just making small talk, "Don't get me wrong, I'm delighted to help, John, but how come you didn't go to the bank? Your business is booming and God knows how much equity you've got in your plant and equipment."

"My wife is an accountant," he said. "She does the books every quarter, along with our personal finances."

"Ah," I said, as if I understood. I did; partly, anyway. If he didn't want his wife to know about it, it was either the ladies or gambling or maybe drugs, but I knew John didn't gamble at all, ever, and he'd never shown any signs sat all of being into drugs, or them being into him, so that left the ladies. To narrow it down still further, as we professional deducers like to do, John didn't play around, and he had plenty of chances as he was a handsome man with a good line of chat and his place was buzzing night after night with lady bowlers from a dozen local leagues and many of them didn't mind a drink or two during the evening, or a few in the bar afterward, either. To me, that left but one possibility—love. Some purple-eyed knockout had transfixed my friend John D., who was one of the last two surviving true romantics to be found west of the Pecos. I don't believe I need to mention the name of the other, the somewhat taller, romantic.

"Well, that's handy," I said, "having an accountant in the family. I always wanted to have a masseuse in mine."

"It is, it is," he said. "Except once in a blue moon."

"Ah," I said again, nodding wisely. I took off my spectacles and polished them on a shirttail during the long pause that followed, which I finally broke by saying, "OK, pal, out with it, what else?"

"Money," he said. "What else. Don't happen to know any way I can legally put my creditors off for a month or two, do you?"

"Which ones?" I said.

"The usual," he said. "The ones I pay every month—my major suppliers, the cleaning company, the landlord, the other half-dozens. I don't want to blow my credit with them, though, no way."

"I presume you won't want to arouse your wife's curiosity either," I said, "let alone ire."

"Let alone World War Three," he said, ruefully. "Vic, what happened, happened. I'll never forget it, I don't regret it, and I'm willing to pay for it, it's the least I can do. As for the creditors, I just need a month or two, then no problem, I'm straight again. As for you, you know soon as I got it, you got it."

I waved that one off.

"The money will be there," he said. "You likely know my lanes, or most of them, are booked up months in advance by the leagues, so I can figure out pretty well to the odd buck how much I got coming and when, and it is a tidy sum, believe me."

I believed him. Before I got to bowl gratis at John's I used to have to pay for the dubious pleasure of missing two out of three spares. I well knew what a money-making machine those warped boards were for him. I also knew what beers cost at the Valley Bowl, and brandy and ginger ales, and hot dogs, mustard and relish only.

"John," I said to him, "if you put off your creditors for a couple of months because you need the cash now for what I assume is a one-time payout—"

"One-time for now, anyway," he said.

"OK, one time for now, how is your wife not going to know you've been holding out?"

"Because I got a short-term deposit she doesn't know about, as cover," he said. "Trouble is, it's got a ninety-day lock on it."

"I get you," I said. "OK, my friend, attend, as I recently said to a young Evel Knievel type in this very office: this one I got from Benny, who else? It's completely legal, although you wouldn't want to do it every couple of days. What you do is write checks in the normal way at the end of the month to all your regular creditors. You mail them. The next day you call up your bank and tell them your checkbook and various other bits and pieces got stolen out of your office. You might have to tell your wife the same. You ask the bank to please close your account immediately. You ask the bank for a letter confirming you have reported a stolen checkbook and thus your account has been closed. You tell them, to avoid any possibility of confusion in the future, you think it wiser to open a new account at a different branch. OK?"

"I'm with you," he said. "Press on, McDuff."

"So you immediately open another account, but better you do so at another bank entirely, because banks have been known to make mistakes and some employee might just run a couple of your creditors' checks through your new account in error. Anyway, so says Benny, and when Benny talks, I listen. I might yawn a lot, but I listen."

"Me too," my friend said.

"Then you make copies of the bank's letter, which you send, along with a heartfelt letter of apology, to the billing departments of all your creditors, asking them to kindly return your now-worthless checks and informing them that of course new checks will be in the mail as soon as the bank prints them up. All of which will take some time, which is exactly what you need. That cheer you up any?"

"No," he said. "It is in no way cheering, but it is distinctly helpful, and I thank you." He slapped the desktop lightly with both palms and got to his feet. He held out his hand; I took it.

"Thanks again, pard."

"Anytime, amigo." He left. I went to the window and watched him drive away, thinking, Ain't love the bee's knees until it gets expensive. I bet whoever she was, though, she wasn't half as cute as my latest heartthrob. But then I thought, what was it that didn't add up about the whole . . . affair, one might say? Although it had to be more than that, given the considerable sum of money involved (mine, thank you), and John having to cover it all up and lie to his wife and goodness knows what else. One might conjecture a spot of blackmail on the fair damsel's part, but (a) John, although not brimming with cheer, hadn't behaved like V.D.'d behave if he was being blackmailed, i.e., to name but three, going through the fucking roof, plotting for dire revenge, and swearing off the so-called "fair" sex (make that all sex) for life. And (b) I find it impossible to believe that any damsel, fair, brown, or red, would stoop to such behavior in the first place. So what did that leave a poor deducer to deduce? That a certain door-to-door diaper service might have a new client some half-a-dozen, say, moons in the future? Getting warmer, maybe . . . and maybe, like a lot of things, maybe it was none of my business.

Right about then, the phone rang, disturbing my sensitive reflections on such things as young love, not-so-young love, autumn leaves a-falling, and calendar leaves likewise. It was my least-favorite bail bondsman, a guy called Fats Nathan, and Fats wasn't called Fats using the kind of reverse humor hoboes and other noted comedians often employ wherein a midget will be nicknamed Lofty and a skyscraper like me Peewee, Fats was called Fats because he was fat. I suppose he wasn't really a bail bondsman anymore if one wanted to nitpick, and it's surprising how many do; since a fairly recent change in the law, the courts now accepted a person's personal recognizance bond, as in a check, which pretty much obviated the need for outside sureties that used to be supplied by guys like Fats for a hefty price. So Fats had moved more into loan sharking, but he also continued with his old lucrative sideline, which was acting as an intermediary between felon and fuzz.

Say, for example—perish the thought, dismiss instantly from your mind—you were a felon. You had a trial coming up. A key witness exists whom you would very much like not to testify against you. A friendly cop appears on the witness's doorstep, the one supposed to deliver to said witness his subpoena to appear in court. He bears the welcome news that the witness can forget the whole business, he won't have to go through the hassle of a long trial and getting off work and, who knows, putting himself in danger of retaliation, it has happened; his testimony is no longer needed. Merry Christmas. The cop reports back that the witness skipped town, or went back east to his sister-in-law's ordination as a Baptist minister, anyway he's done gone. The cop gets a healthy hit, the felon gets off, and Fats takes his middle-man's slice.

Or so the story goes; far be it from me to even suggest that such things really occur. I for one certainly hope not, and the fact that it is a board of police commissioners that has to yearly decide whether or not to renew my PI license has nothing to do with the matter.

"Vic?" Fats said. "Fats."

"Hey, Fats," I said, perching on the corner of the desk. "Still going to Weight Watchers?"

"Ha, ha," said Fats. "Listen, you want one?"

"One what?"

"A skip," he said. "Smart guy like you, should only take a couple of days at most."

"Maybe," I said. "How much are we talking?"

"Five plus expenses up to another five?"

"How about a grand plus unlimited," I said. "That's for three days max."

"So come on down," he said. "We'll talk it over."

"Let me check what I got on," I said. I held my hand over the mouthpiece for a minute, then said to him, "I might be able to get to you about three, or a little after. How does that grab you?"

He said it grabbed him OK, and we rang off.

All right.

Business was booming suddenly.

I'd done a couple of skip traces for Fats before, and gotten paid, but you did have to watch your step with him, he was brighter than he looked, which wasn't hard, and as crooked as a hummingbird's flight path. And besides, Fatso had connections, good ones, on both sides of the law, but especially below it. But could a fatty like that be any match for V. Daniel?

Unlikely, amigos.

I gave Jasper Johnson a call at the Downtown Station and luckily found him in.

"Johnson, Robbery," he barker.

"V. Daniel, likewise," I said.

"Who?"

"V. Daniel. I'm a friend of Frank and Annie O'Brien, I'm in the same sort of line as Frank. I saw them last night, they put me on to you."

"They OK?"

I allowed they seemed to be in tolerable shape, considering.

"Frank making a buck?"

"Getting by," I said.

"Good," he said. "Glad someone is. I should've gone in with him when I had the chance. So I made detective, big deal, I'm stuck at this goddamned desk and I'm gonna be stuck at this goddamned desk the rest of my goddamned miserable life."

"Maybe I can put a little color into your cheeks," I said. I explained briefly about the Lubinskis and D. Gresham the Third, who might just be acting as an inside man when he wasn't rifling his way through "O Mein Papa." I mentioned I was aware that it was standard practice for the rich to be extremely wary about letting photographs of their mansion interiors appear in newspapers or glossy magazines as it was obviously asking for trouble, so some inside information could be very helpful to the criminal element among us. I said I had a list of names and addresses that, if checked out, might throw a little more light on the subject.

"Better come on down," he said wearily. "Let's have a look. Anytime, I'll be here. If I'm not here, I'll either be in the canteen or the nearest nut house."

He hung up. So did I. Then, just for the fun of it, I called up the Lew Lewellens again and, adopting a thick Teutonic accent, asked if I could speak with Lew.

"Sorry, Mr. Daniel, they're still out of town," said the señorita at the other end. So much for the master of disguises.

I then locked up, with my customary caution, climbed into my classic and made my way downtown via the Ventura and Hollywood freeways with my customary caution, keeping to the inside along with the other geriatrics, old maids, Sunday drivers, and those with a modicum of common sense.

"I'm gonna get a wino to decorate our home," sang some guy on the radio. Then Emmy Lou Harris said she really had a ball last night, held all the pretty boys tight. Sometimes I wish I was a pretty boy, like the twerp's big pash. Sometimes I don't, but those times I've had so much to drink I'm convinced I really am a pretty boy. Such is life in the slow lane.

I talked my way into the For Officials Only parking lot out back of the old courthouse building downtown, announced myself to the lady cop receptionist, who checked my ID, then checked with Jasper, then watched me all the way to the elevators. Jasper I tracked down in a small office on the fifth floor that contained three desks, two of them unoccupied, and wall-to-wall battered green filing cabinets. Detective J. Johnson was not, apparently, one to beat about the bush.

"Daniel? Johnson. What've you got?" he said, without bothering to get up or shake hands or make small talk about the Dodger's chances. I gave him what I had, the pages torn out of Evonne's address book.

"Herein are listed thirty-two private functions at which a group called Ron's Rhythm Kings played," I said. "Do not ask me how I obtained them, it is a professional secret. Now, no one is going to be stupid enough to knock over a joint a day or two after their inside man tootled the flute there, the connection might be a little obvious, so my skilled assistant and I only began listing dates roughly three months old and going back from there. So I thought if you could kindly run this list through your user-friendly police computer and then run all major robberies during the last nine months or so, who knows, we might get a match or two. If we're lucky. If D. Gresham really is an inside man instead of just some pothead having trouble finding the loo."

"Yeah, if," said Jasper, scowling at the list.

"You being a trained detective yourself, you will without doubt have figured out by now the cryptic letters after each name refer to parts of this loveable, madcap town of ours."

"Really?" said Jasper. "I thought they was blood types," He got to his feet, rubbing his red hair in a harassed manner, then brushed ineffectually at the jacket of his rumpled gray suit. "C'mon. Let's go find a user-friendly computer outlet and someone who can work the goddamned thing."

"Not a computer man yourself, then?" I asked delicately.

"Not yet," he growled. "But I soon will be, goddamn it. I start next month—can you believe me going back to goddamned school at my age?"

"When you go, don't forget your apple," I said, following him out the door and down the hall to the next door but two, the sign on which read 516 CAPT. LORNA T. CHAPMAN. A & A. He rapped once on the door, then barged in, with me at his heels.

"Momma? Brought you a visitor. You busy?"

"Not for you, dear," said Momma, beaming up at him from behind a large and well-cluttered desk.

"V. Daniel," I said, crossing to her. "*V* for Victor."

We shook hands.

"Nice meeting you, dear," Momma said. She was a—to put it politely—Rubensesque woman, somewhere in her forties. Actually, large is what Momma was. Very large. All over and in every direction. She was wearing a huge, woolly, flowered caftan affair, a string of wooden beads about the size of kiddies' play blocks, large, brightly painted wooden earrings, a Mickey Mouse wristwatch, and sticking up from the back of her mop of unruly hair, two things that looked like wooden chopsticks.

"How do you do, Captain Momma," I said. "Or would it be Mrs. Momma?"

"Just call me Momma," she said, with a happy sigh. "Everyone else does, including the dog. Sit, sit, take the weight off and tell me what Momma can do for you today."

I lowered myself carefully onto a spindly-looking chair across from her; Jasper perched on a corner of her desk. She dug out a package of crumpled Winstons from somewhere under her horse blanket, offered them around, got no takers, then lit up one for herself and took a deep puff. "Candy?" She pushed a tin of assorted fruit flavors in our direction. Jasper took one and began sucking noisily on it.

I filled Momma in on the story so far and passed over Evonne's list. Momma thought for a moment, then switched on her PC and went to work. Jasper watched her flying fingers with a sort of reluctant fascination.

Almost immediately, it seemed, she said, "Two matches, kids."

"Finger-lickin' good," I said.

"I'll be goddamned," Jasper said.

Momma scrabbled through the mess of papers on her desk, found a clean sheet, then copied down from the screen "Ronald & M. Rubin, 1224 Lexington, Beverly Hills" and "Thomas L. & G. Gowan, 44 Wilkins, Westwood."

"No recovery from either place so far, it says here and it don't lie."

"Any chance of finding out precisely what was stolen?" I asked her.

"If it's art, antiques, identifiable jewelry over a certain value, stuff like that, sure," she said. "And I ought to know, because it's Momma who inputs it all. If it was just TVs, VCRs, stuff like that, no, you'd have to go downstairs and dig up the original responding officer's probably illegible report."

Momma tapped in another set of instructions, waited a few seconds, then whistled.

"Though so. Though I remembered that one. "Chinoiserie. Collection faience. Art deco lamps and figurines. Early American quilts. Paul Revere teapot. Rugs. More rugs. Bit of everything. Jackson Pollack. Two Hockneys." She shook her head; a few more strands escaped from her straggly bun. "Stupid. Who's going to buy a hot Hockney?"

"Not me," I said. "I don't know how to ride anyway."

Momma blew some smoke skyward. Jasper groaned and shifted himself off the desk.

"That let's me out," he said. "I'm not art or antiques, thank God. You want anything else, you know where I am. See ya, Momma. Hello to Frank and Annie."

He bustled out. I picked through the candies looking for a lemon, orange, or green one, but they'd all gone already.

"Now what?" I said. "What now?"

"Well, dear," Momma said, "one of us had better check that the Rubins and the Gowans who are on my list are the same Rubins and Gowans on your list."

"Use your phone?" I asked.

"Nine for an outside line," she said. "I'll get back to what I was doing before you two pests came in to upset my rhythm."

I obtained the numbers of the Rubins and Gowans from the phone company after a certain amount of trouble and a lie or two, as neither of them was, as usual, a listed number. Shortly thereafter I got Mrs. Rubin on the line. I told her I was calling from the Los Angeles Police Department Downtown Station, which I was.

"Oh, no," she said. "Something's happened to Ron."

"Not at all," I said hastily. "No bad news. It might even be the opposite. I just have a few questions to ask you about the robbery that took place on your premises earlier this year, it's possible we may have a line on the perpetrators."

"Ask, ask," said Mrs. Rubin. "Anything. We'd given up hope, after all this time. So who was it, the butler?"

"Not quite," I said, with a chuckle in my voice. "We think it's possible that one of the perps at least had some previous knowledge of your collectables, your Revere silver, your faience"—whatever the hell that was, old coins, maybe—"and so on."

"And so on is right," she said with some heat.

"In the months preceding the burglary," I said, "did you happen to have any large social functions in your home? The sort of affair that would require you to hire extra help? Valet parkers, for example, or extra serving staff?"

"Oh my goodness," she said. "We did. We had a party for our daughter Ramona who'd just graduated from USC, half of Beverly Hills showed up."

"Ah-ha," I said. "A catered affair, no doubt?"

"Are you kidding?" she said. "What else?"

"Then it was dancing 'til the wee small hours, I suppose?"

"The kids danced 'til breakfast," Mrs. Rubin said. "Us old fogies called it quits about three."

I had a thought. A potential money-making thought, one of the best kind. The thought was about insurance and the sensible practice of many insurance companies to reward with a percentage of the value of the recovered items anyone who aids in their recovery. Mrs. Rubin kindly provided me with the name of her insurers. I thanked her warmly for all her help and rang off.

I then had an almost identical conversation with a member of the Gowan family, a Mrs. Sybil George, sister of Thomas L., only in the Gowan case it had been a birthday party complete with caterers and dancing until the wee small ones. And she knew the name of her brother's insurance company, also, as she'd been in the house when their agent dropped by to verify the losses.

All right so far.

True, neither woman had actually come right out and said that the music their guests had been swinging and swaying to was provided by the rhythm king and his minions, but it did look odds on. I rubbed my hands with satisfaction. I noticed that although Momma hadn't stopped punching away at her keyboard for an instant, she had been listening with undisguised interest to every word I said.

Then I got on to Sun Life and Realty, the Gowans' insurers, fought my way past two secretaries and ultimately found myself communicating with an A. Prescott, Claims. Yes, he was familiar with the Gowan affair. Yes, his company was prepared to pay a reward in certain circumstances.

"Such as?" I said, arching my eyebrows in Momma's direction.

"Such as," A. Prescott said in a slightly pompous manner, "the claimant of the said reward shall be proven to have had no connection with the criminals involved in the theft and also that he or she's contribution to the recovery of the stolen items shall be proven to have been substantial and this fact so attested by either the arresting officer or, in case of a recovery of stolen property unaccompanied by an arrest, by the head of the department involved."

I said I thought I got it, thanked A. Prescott, Claims, and rang off. A Bill Lendon, Claims, at the Rubins' insurers, said much the same thing only in fewer words and in a friendlier manner.

When I hung up after that last call, I discovered Momma gazing my way inquiringly. I filled her in on the parts of the conversations she hadn't overheard.

"No problem," she said, waving away a cloud of cigarette smoke. "I'm the head of department. I might even be the arresting officer, too, that might be fun, I could use a little exercise."

"Why don't we take Jasper?" I said. "He's always complaining he's stuck to his desk."

Momma laughed.

"He wouldn't go it you paid him," she said. "It's just a number he does, he's been doing it for years. He hates it on the streets. He's about as comfortable out there as a cat at a dog show."

"Oh," I said.

"Why don't you call up D. Gresham the Third and see if he's in, dear?"

I did. After a couple of rings, a man's voice said, "Good afternoon."

"Good afternoon," I said. "Flo in?"

"I'm afraid you have the wrong number," the voice said politely.

"Ever so sorry," I said, breaking the connection. "Well, someone's home, but he doesn't sound like a musician to me, he didn't say 'man,' or 'dig' or 'bebop' once."

"Now, now," Momma said. "Shall we go calling, dear, anyhow, on the off chance?"

"Delighted, I'm sure," I said. "What about a warrant?"

"Not for a little social call," she said. She switched off her machine, arose, gave herself a good shake, poked her bun ineffectually a couple of times, and pronounced herself ready, willing, and able.

"A moment, madam," I said. "We have a slight problem. You are, excuse the expression, the fuzz. The fuzz needs just cause to enter a suspect's abode. We do not have just cause, all we have is just a suspicion or two. If you gain access as someone else, such as the gas man or a collector for the home for unwed mothers-in-law, that would be considered fraudulent entry and any evidence seized by you would therefore not be admissible in court. Thus spoke A. Prescott, Claims."

"H'um." Momma furrowed her broad forehead, and reached automatically for another gasper. "A pretty dilemma."

"How's about," I said, "you are what you are and I am what I am. Together we are investigating the case of the empty champagne bottles." I told her about the two guys in T-shirts who worked for the caterer and my subsequent misgivings. "I have a legitimate client. I have a legitimate right to put a few disarming questions to anyone who might be able to help, especially members of the band as they and the caterers set up so close to each other. And you have a right to just happen to be with me while I put these disarming questions, why not? Perhaps we had just come from an intimate lunch together and I had to make a quick stop before returning you here."

"The intimate lunch I don't mind the sound of," Momma said archly. "Do you know the name of the catering firm involved?"

I thought for a moment, then had to confess I did not.

"D. Gresham might," she said. "Seeing as the band and the caterers were set up so close to each other."

"Not just a pretty face," I said. "Un momento."

I called up Aaron Lubinski at his place of business. I revealed to him the latest startling developments and asked him for the name of the caterers.

He said they were called the '£!!//$**%+!! Kosher Katerers, with a *K*, and wanted to know why I wanted to know.

"They may be '£!!//$**%!!s," I said, "but you gotta admit their chopped liver was heaven."

CHAPTER SIX

Momma signed us out an unmarked police car—a two-year-old Olds Cutlass—downstairs, into which we strapped ourselves, and off we went, with Momma driving, and extremely competently, too. D. Gresham wasn't far away, he lived west of where we were, on Denker. During the short drive I asked Momma how she became a cop.

"What's a nice girl like me, eh?" she said. "I was just out of UCLA—major, art history, minor, phys ed. In other words, totally unemployable. I saw an ad, they were just starting to seriously recruit women to do other jobs than shitwork like filing and answering the telephone. So I went down one day, took the test, didn't make too many spelling mistakes, passed the physical, then went off to school with all the rest of the recruits. You can't imagine the crap they threw at me, I threw it right back with bells on it." She drew out to pass a city bus and got back in line with inches to spare, pretending not to notice my involuntary braking motions.

"Second day out," she said without any apparent rancour, "as a rookie cop, I was partnered with a foul-mouthed bigot of Polish extraction called Ski. Ski thought he was tough, which he probably was. He thought he could drive, too, a lot better than any stupid broad."

"Aren't men the worst sometimes," I said, shaking my head.

"So we get a call and take off," she said, "and he runs a light and wham, next thing I know it's sixteen days later. First thing I see when I come out of the coma is Ski, blubbering like a baby and holding my hand, he hadn't left the hospital once in all that time. Five months on my back. Year and a half in rehab. I've got so many metal pins in me when I go through one of those detector things at airports, it tilts. I must be the only person in the world who put on weight in hospital. Swimming is about all I can do now. Someone in admin with half a brain for once looked over my record, saw I had a background in art history, and as soon as I was more or less mobile again, shifted me to Robbery and then to what I'm doing now. I got interested. I started taking night classes. I'm still taking them, I'm taking one right now in African art, especially West African. Ashanti. Stuff like that."

"Ashanti, eh?" I said. "I heard it's nice there in the spring. Whatever happened to old Ski?"

"Blew half his pension by taking early retirement and moved to Arizona," she said. "By the way, there's Denker." We turned left off Exposition. "What number are we looking for?"

I told her. After a minute or so she pulled up in front of a modest, two-story, stuccoed building that was divided into four apartments, two up, two down. A neatly lettered sign on a wooden gate to the left of the building said D. GRESHAM THE THIRD, BY APPOINTMENT ONLY. SALESMEN, MISSIONARIES, MORMONS & MARIACHI BAND MEMBERS ENTER AT YOUR PERIL.

As we were none of these, as far as I knew, we entered without undue caution. The path led us around the side of the building to a freshly painted firehouse-red door. Through an open window came a sort of eerie keening, a moaning chant, if you will. Momma made a "who knows?"

gesture, then rapped gently but firmly on the door. After a minute it was opened by a tiny Asian girl with a recently scrubbed face and long, tousled black hair. She was wearing a lemon-colored robe that was split up one side and just failed to cover her bare feet.

"Yes?" she whispered.

"V Daniel," I whispered back. I handed her one of my business cards, one that told the truth for once. "I'm looking into possible misdemeanors by members of the firm who catered the wedding reception Mr. Gresham played at last night. This is Captain Chapman. I wonder if we might ask Mr. Gresham a couple of quick questions, it's possible he saw something that might help us with our inquiries. Is he all right, by the way?"

She giggled. "It's just his mantra."

"Hope it clears up," I said.

"Come on in," she said. "I suppose it's OK. He'll be done in a few minutes."

We followed her into D. Gresham's front room. D. Gresham himself was seated cross-legged on a small prayer mat in one corner, his hands, palm upward, resting on his knees, his eyes open but seemingly unseeing. Directly in front of him was an ornate mirror bedecked with a garland of flowers and in front of the mirror a tinny-looking shrine of some kind. Pungent incense burned in two brass ashtrays on either side of the mirror. The low-pitched moans continued. Whatever he was up to he sure didn't get from the *Anglican Book of Common Prayer*.

"Make yourselves comfortable," our hostess whispered. "Be right back." She padded out. We made ourselves as comfortable as we could on a settee that looked like it was made out of Meccano parts. The high-tech look, I do believe it's called. In fact the whole room was high tech except for

D. Gresham's devotional corner; it was also immaculate. The dining table was brushed aluminum; the four chairs around it of the metal, folding type, painted the same red as the front door. One whole wall was covered floor to ceiling with pegboard painted in a bright yellow gloss, against which were displayed five electric guitars in various futuristic shapes, and one conventional acoustic guitar. All the instruments gleamed with good health and regular polishing. I saw nothing that resembled a Hockney, a faience, or a Paul Revere teacup, not that I would have recognized one anyway, I am the first to admit.

D. Gresham was just winding up his afternoon service when our diminutive hostess returned, wearing embroidered slippers and with her tresses tidied up into one long braid. D. Gresham emitted one last moan, then arose lithely. We introduced ourselves. I apologized sincerely for disturbing his reflections.

"I was far from being disturbed," he said gently, blinking guileless blue eyes up at me. "Tin-Thieu, have you offered our guests some tea?"

"No, no, really," I protested. "We'll only be here a minute, please don't put yourself out." I spun him my yarn about Kosher Katering; he stroked his whispy Fu Manchu mustache reflectively as he listened. I asked him if he'd seen anything at all suspicious. He thought for a moment, then shook his head regretfully.

"I wish I could help," he said in his soft voice. "But I can't remember paying particular attention to anything about the caterers except they were perhaps a little short on vegetarian food."

"Oh, darn," Momma said.

"Ah, well," I said, getting to my feet. "*C'est la vie.* Thanks anyway, it was just a chance."

"May I pop into the ladies before I go, dear?" Momma asked Tin-Thieu.

"Sure," she said. She led Momma out of the room; I presumed that what Momma really wanted was a quick look around at the rest of the apartment. I told Finger-Lickin' Good how much I'd enjoyed his playing the night before.

"Thank you very much," he said with becoming modesty. "It helps if you enjoy what you're doing."

"How true," I said. We sat smiling at each other until the ladies came back.

"You should see the bedroom!" Momma gushed. "It's so chic! So uncluttered!"

"Take a bow, Tin-Thieu," D. Gresham said. "It's all her work."

Momma went on raving about the bedroom all the way to the door and then back up the path. As soon as we climbed into the Olds again, she unlocked the glove compartment and switched on the police radio inside.

"What's up?" I said. "Calling the cops?"

"Right on, dear," she said. She got on to Control, identified herself, and asked for a patrol car to meet up with us a couple of blocks down the street, and directed Control to direct the patrol car to take a route that did not have it pass, sirens blazing, directly in front of D. Gresham's uncluttered bedroom.

"It couldn't have been the guitars," I mused aloud, "although a couple of those Fender Rhodes looked like custom jobs to me and worth a small fortune." All right, I may not be a great connoisseur of faience, sue me, but guitars I do know something about. Back east one time in the long long ago when all things still seemed possible, I labored as a gopher/chauffeur/bodyguard for a pop star whose star ascended mightily for a brief span until its inevitable wane due to the old and trite reasons. However, thus it was that I gained what little expertise I had on the subject of custom Rhodes and one-off Martins, to say nothing of the customs of rising pop stars before, after, and sometimes during their gigs.

"Not the guitars," Momma agreed. She hooked up her seat belt, made me do likewise, and drove us off down the street to our rendezvous.

"No fair if it was something you saw I didn't," I said. "Like in the uncluttered bedroom you adored so much."

"You saw it, too," she said.

"Ah yes," I said. "The carpet he was sitting on. Mongolian. Early nineteenth. Fourth dynasty. Did you ever see such closeness of weave!"

Momma grinned at me.

"A silver, copper, and brass *gau*," she said. "Not too old. I suspect it was made by one of the Tibetans living in Kalimpong, West Benal. Elaborately repoussé. Chased silver face. Ornamented with the traditional eight Buddhist symbols of good fortune. Not enormously valuable but highly collectible."

"That there tinny shrine thing?"

"That there tinny traveling shrine thing." She pulled up at our meeting place and backed deftly into a parking space between two cars that obviously wasn't big enough. "Silly of him to keep it, really, but it is gorgeous and I guess he figured no one would ever spot it as the real thing and even if someone did, so what. It was on one of the lists I ran through before we left."

"Little did he reckon on Mighty Mom dropping in for tea," I said. Momma beamed and slouched down in her seat so she could keep an eye on D. Gresham's entrance in her wing mirror.

"I wish that bloody patrol car would get here," she said.

"What's the hurry?" I said.

"What if D. Gresham gets to thinking?" said Momma. "Wonder how they got my name and address, he thinks. Had to be from Ron, he thinks. He calls up Ron. 'Did you give my name and address to a private detective named V. Daniel or a Captain Chapman?' 'No,' says Ron, 'but I did give it to some mother called Don Upton who said he was getting married next month.' "

"Oh-oh," said V. Daniel.

"Adiós, amigos," said Momma. "D. Gresham is out of there pronto with that there tinny shrine thing tucked under his arm."

"And maybe a Hockney or two under his shirt," I said. "Why didn't you collar him then and there? You're a cop."

"One thing you learn, and you learn it the hard way," she said.

"As if there was any other way," I said.

"Always, always phone in for a backup first."

"What about me?" I said indignantly. "A girl couldn't want a better backup than me."

"An official one, dear," she said, patting my cheek. The cop car drove up right then and coasted to a halt beside us. "About time," Momma said. She explained all to the boys in blue. Off they went, with us following them.

Sure enough, like Momma said, we got back to D. Gresham's just in time to head him off at the pass, or the gate, in his case. And no bonus points, kids, for guessing what he had in a brown paper bag under his arm.

The oldest of the two cops took out a printed card and mumbled through the reading of the suspect's rights. The suspect responded by bestowing a beatific smile on the cop, and led the way meekly back to his apartment.

The forces of law and order, all three of them, gave the place a rapid but thorough shakedown. The only thing relevant to our inquiry they unearthed was, in a locked cupboard in the bedroom, a reference library of some twenty books covering all types of antiques and valuables from Russian icons to classic cars. I snuck a quick peek at something called *The Antique Encyclopedia*, and discovered that faience was a brightly decorated version of majolica, which was a big help. I didn't have time to see if there was a picture of my multihued darling in the book on classic cars.

Now I know I've mentioned it before, but beware of taking things at face value, kids. Who would believe at first glance that V. Daniel would own a classic anything? And Jasper, with all his rantings about being deskbound. Who would believe that a zonked-out guitarist studied things like Persian carpets in his spare time? Flying carpets, maybe. And the chances of one of the two people in the world who could spot a *gau* across an uncluttered room, the other being the Dalai Lama, dropping in, we have already discussed.

It was about a half an hour later, I suppose, when we took our leave. Tin-Thieu slammed the door behind us. As D. Gresham the Third was climbing into the back seat of the patrol car, he said to me over his shoulder, "*Namaste.*"

I figured that meant something snappy, like "Up your enchilada" in Nepalese, and was about to reply "And from what teaching of the great Buddha does that come from, o humble seeker after truth?"

But no, D. Gresham immediately translated it as, "I salute the God within you." He even waved at us as the cop car pulled away.

So like I said, watch those prejudices, especially when there's someone listening.

Momma drove us back downtown. She turned in the Olds, I retrieved my Nash. She promised to let me know how things developed. I said great. She'd also get off an official letter for me, stressing my valuable contribution, in case I ever needed it. I said terrific. She patted me on my downy cheek one last time and disappeared into the station by the back way. I checked the time, noted that I was a little early for my rendezvous with Fats, so I took a short drive down to MacArthur Park, where one went to observe dope peddlers, winos, bums, and crackheads in their natural habitat. Thought I also might drop in and say howdy-do to an ambulance chaser of my acquaintance, Mel ("The Swell"), whose one-and-a-half-room office overlooked the park, and who might perchance have something for me in the work department. But no dice, no one was at home, so I continued on downtown, finally found an almost-legal place to park behind the old courthouse, then strolled around the block to Fats' first-floor place of business, getting panhandled a mere three times on the way.

Fats still had his old neon sign hanging outside: INSTANT BAIL—WALK IN—WALK OUT—EASY TERMS. Well, I guess you could call an arm and a leg easy. There was a squawk box beside the downstairs door; I pressed the appropriate button, announced myself, and it squawked at me to come up.

Up I went. Fats had two rooms; in the outer, the waiting room, an acned, two-bit hood was lounging on the wooden bench attending to his cuticles with a foot-long switchblade. How amusingly passé, I thought. He looked up briefly as I entered and gave me a sneer. I smiled at him graciously and passed into the inner room where Fats was leafing through the latest *Playboy*.

"Got some real inneresting items in it this month," he said around a gold toothpick.

"I hear the stories aren't bad, either," I said.

Fats' place of business was surprisingly comfortable, almost opulent, especially compared to the bareness of the waiting room. It was thickly carpeted, had a plush sofa with matching occasional chairs, in one of which Fats was sitting in front of a low, glass-topped table he did his business from; I guess he'd read in some childish "how to succeed in business" rag that the way to make a potential client feel at home isn't to put him on one side of a huge desk and you in a taller chair on the other. And tally ho! if he didn't have fox-hunting prints on the walls.

There was a booze cabinet in one corner disguised as a tallboy and an old-fashioned wind-up gramophone complete with horn in another. Fats himself, like I said, was fat. He was wearing a sleeveless white shirt with his initials monogramed on the pocket; it was unbuttoned enough so the observant could detect he was wearing an off-white string vest underneath. His dainty feet were clad in highly polished snakeskin loafers, the tassles of which had little brass bits on the ends. He had a gold wedding ring on the appropriate pinkie but otherwise no jewelry except on one pudgy wrist he wore that kind of very expensive, aluminum-looking chronometer pilots wear even in bed that tell you everything including when your matzoh balls have boiled three minutes.

"So what you got for me, Fats?" I inquired, sitting on the arm of the spare chair.

He arose in a surprisingly spritely fashion, considering his bulk, crossed to a set of wooden drawers, on top of which sat a small, compact TV–radio–tape deck, unlocked the top drawer, took out a sheet of paper, crossed back to me, and dropped it in my lap.

"You drinkin'?" he said.

"Maybe later," I said.

"Just holler," he said.

"William Gince," I read off the top of the piece of paper. There followed an address on Lynwood Gardens, which I surmised was in a part of L.A. called Lynwood, which I knew was east and a bit south of LAX, the main L.A. airport. There followed after that a phone number, which I took to be that of the missing William Gince, then the words "mother/sister, s.a.," then the initials "B.F" and that was all. I turned the paper over to see if there was anything helpful on the back, like a map with a line saying, "I am hiding here," with an arrow pointing to a house of ill repute in West Texas. No such luck, needless to say.

" 'Mother/sister, s.a.,' meaning same address?"

"Brains," said Fats. "Wish I had 'em." He took a bottle of soda water out of the booze cabinet, uncapped it, and poured the contents carefully into a blue-tinted tumbler, then took a sip.

"Not a lot on paper, is there," I said. "Not even an IOU."

"We go a lot on trust in my business," Fats said, poker-faced.

"I bet," I said. "You big Boy Scout, you. The initials 'B.F,' what do they refer to?"

"Nothin' that concerns you," Fats said. "That's the guy who recommended him is all."

"I'm surprised he hasn't taken off for the Outer Hebrides, too," I said. "So how much is this guy into you for?"

"Six grand," he said. "It'll be seven Saturday. Eight a week Saturday."

"You make the Bank of America look generous," I said.

"So why didn't he go there?" Fats said. "He knew the score. I didn't drag him up here, he just walked in. If you don't like the odds, stay out of the game." And six to five is what the odds in that game are, rather six for five, you borrow $100 bucks, you pay back $120 seven days later, amigos. In five weeks the interest, or vigorish, equals what you borrowed to start with. And if you don't come up with at least the interest, pleasant types like myself and Mickey come a-calling just as you're heating up your Swanson's TV chicken dinner with peas.

"Why me, Fats?" I asked him, as I had not so long ago put to someone a lot prettier than him. "Why not the boys in blue or one of your regular collectors or even that punk outside who's lowering the tone of your waiting room?"

Fats shrugged. "I don't like to bother them with penny-ante shit like this," he said. "Besides, I'm gettin' soft, I guess, I like to help out the needy and the unemployed from time to time."

"Touché, Fats," I said. What I thought was, Fats, you're not only fat, you're a liar. It seemed to be my day for them. Why pay me a grand or so when he could get some amiable cop to take on the chore for a case of Four Roses and a jar of Hot-Styx? Something was no doubt up; maybe I'd find out what it was somewhere along the way. I figured I'd take the job, what the hell. It has already been established that I could use the work; also, having something to do might drive away any lingering apprehension I still had about storm troopers lurking in the offing and Estonian beauties lurking everywhere else. At least for a while—better than nothing.

"If I do find him, then what?"

"Then nothin'," Fats said. "You just find him, that's all, and without rousting him, either.' "

"Nothin'?" I said. "Nothin' at all? Not even a phone call to you letting you know where he is?"

"Said you was smart, didn't I," Fats said. He finished up the last of his tipple, burped delicately behind one cupped palm, put his glass back in the cabinet, and closed it up again.

"Do you know where the guy worked?"

"In a garage down on Wilcox somewhere, he said," Fats said.

"And what does this guy look like?" I said. "Don't suppose you got a picture or anything useful like that."

Fats shook his head.

"What's he look like? A nobody. A nebbish. Skinny, pale face, glasses, losin' his hair, what can I say?"

"A grand," I said. "Five now. Plus expenses. If I don't trace him in three days, I'll deduct my expenses from the grand and give you back half of what's left. Deal?"

"Deal," he said. He got out his wallet, counted out five crisp hundred-dollar bills, padded over to me, dropped them in my lap, then seated himself again in his chair. I got out my memo pad, copied what was on the sheet of paper, then got up and dropped the sheet onto his lap.

"I'll let you know how it goes," I said.

"That would be nice," he said.

I went out into the waiting room. The kid was still working on his nails.

"Frosted scarlet," I said to him on the way past. "That would be a divine color for your nails. Go great with your complexion." I blew him a kiss and opened the door. His knife thudded into the door jamb an inch from my left ear. I picked up the water cooler, complete with stand, which was right next to the door, and threw it none too gently into his lap. He said a dirty word. I crossed to him and cuffed him, hard, with cupped palms, on both his ears. (Be careful when you try this one, kids, it's all too easy to pop someone's eardrums.) Then, just to make sure I had his attention, I let him have a short but solid left hook right on his temple.

Fats came out to see what the commotion was all about.

"Poor kid came over faint," I said. "I was just giving him a drink of water."

"You didn't have to give him the whole cooler," Fats observed mildly.

"So I got carried away," I said, tugging the kid's blade out of the wood. "Sue me." I propped the knife up in the angle where the floor met the wall and gave it a healthy kick in the middle with one heel, just the way my pop taught me to break kindling many a moon ago. It broke cleanly into two pieces. "Where's he from, anyway?"

"South Chicago," Fats said. "Why?"

"I knew he wasn't local," I said. "A true Hollywood type would have asked me to recommend a good manicurist."

CHAPTER SEVEN

On the way down the stairs I figured that the first task ahead of me was to ascertain whether or not William Gince had ever done time—for example, for shooting at people—which would be a useful tidbit of information to know if I ever got within a hundred yards or so of him. It would also mean there'd be pictures of him, full face and profile, on record. His arrest sheet might also mention other potentially helpful items like his last place of work.

There were two main ways of finding out whether William had ever been in the clink. One was to find him and ask him, but then of course he might lie about it. The other, slightly simpler way, was to ask Sneezy, an irascible little geezer who worked in the Records Department in the basement of the LAPD's Downtown Station with my younger brother, Tony. You might ask, why not ask my brother, isn't that what brothers are for, to help one another, as in brotherhood? Not mine, especially for favors like tapping the police computer for me, and I'll spare you the details why, but I might just remark it is strange how jealousy can affect a human being sometimes.

Actually, if you want to know, if you don't already—and even if you don't want to know, frankly—it wasn't really jealousy that was involved. I was in no way jealous of my little brother, Anthony, and he sure never showed any signs of being jealous of macho old me. What he did show to me was hostility, because way back in the olden and supposedly golden days when we were kids, back when the Dodgers played in a stadium that hadn't been designer-decorated in fetching pastels, when the crunch came, he chickened out, while I, for once, did not.

The tale of woe is briefly told. Tony imbibed an alcoholic beverage, stole a car, then went a-joyriding, unfortuantely knocking over an elderly female pedestrian en merry route. For reasons I will not go into at this time, I took the can for him and did a couple years subsequently in a charming juvenile detention center in glorious upstate Illinois. So: if one accepts the far-from-highfalutin proposition that a long-standing guilt complex might just conceivably produce hostile behavior as a pathetic cover-up, the rest is silence.

So, from the first phone booth I found that hadn't been razed to the ground, I called the Downtown Station and in a moment of forgetfulness asked the lady cop at the switchboard for Sneezy, instead of using his official name and rank. She laughed, but knew who I meant all right, and put me through.

"Yeah?" he barked into the phone.

"Want a picture of Andrew Jackson for your very own?" I asked him.

"Who doesn't?" he said. "What do you want, Daniel, and whatever it is, why don't you bother someone else about it once in a while, like your brother?"

"Because he's my brother," I said. "Didn't you ever have a brother?"

"No," he said. "My family was so poor we could only afford a dog once a week."

"William Gince," I said, spelling out the last name. "LKA in Lynwood Gardens. See if he's got a sheet for me, will you,

Sneezy, there's a good chap, and that twenty is as good as in your hot little hand right now." He hemmed and hawed awhile but I knew he'd do it eventually because Sneezy hated felons and therefore was partial to folks that got them their just deserts, even lowlife private types like me. Also, he adored money, because he had one of mankind's most expensive habits—listening to wedding bells.

The line went dead. I waited. After thirty seconds or so he came back on and said, "No form under that name. You owe me," then he hung up.

"Adiós," I said. Then I said, "Damn!" and hung up, too.

I made an entry in my memo pad: "Expenses: For Info. Received, $25.00. Phone, .25." Then I strolled back to my car, put the top down, and leisurely made my way via the Long Beach freeway south to Lynwood, or at least as leisurely as one can on a California freeway, which is hair-raising. I defreewayed at Century, by mistake, asked someone, then drove around for a bit, then found Lynwood Gardens more or less accidentally, then proceeded along it to the number I was looking for, 947½. Fractions mean as little in L.A. as they did to me in school; 947½ turned out to be an apartment building twice as big as the one at 947, which might tell you something about real estate in this part of the world. Then again it might be completely meaningless, like real estate in this part of the world.

I parked down the street aways out of view of 947½ and had a brief ponder. I prefer pondering in dimly lit establishments that have signs in front of them that flash on and off like Fats' but that say COCKTAILS instead, but I can ponder in other locations if I put my mind to it. My problem was I wanted to put the wind up William's mother, or sister, or both, slightly. Not too much, not too little. I came to the honest conclusion that if I, V. Daniel, put in a personal appearance, there was no chance Mom or Sis or both would be scared only slightly; even, say, in parson's garb, reciting Proverbs IV:2 in a hushed voice, I'm hardly a reassuring sight. There's my size, of course, and then there's no denying Time had left its brutal traces on my once fair-complected visage, someone else a couple of scars, and several someone elses a broken nose.

So, although reluctant as a small boy being dragged in the direction of soap and hot water, I decided it looked like a job for punk power, or ex-punk power, yet again. OK, I'll give you that the lamebrain was useful from time to time, but how much suffering can a guy take, even in the course of justice? I did amble back to 947½ to check if there was a listing for Gince in the register of tenants beside the intercom-buzzer affair; there was. On the way back to my side of town I stopped at a hamburger stand for two chili dogs and a root beer, then I called the twerp.

The twerp was in. Not only in but hovering over the phone; she answered it almost before it started ringing.

"Hello?" she said eagerly.

"Hello yourself!" I said warmly. "Waiting for a call, were we? From anyone special?"

"Oh shut up," she said.

"How are we this fine afternoon?"

"Bored out of my skull," she said. "And you're not helping."

"What?" I exclaimed. "Are we not working? Are we not laboring over some sonnet writ in the Italian mode? Or leafing busily through our rhyming dictionary trying to find the perfect rhyme for pepperoni pizza? What is it, dear, writer's cramp?"

"No," she said. "And it's block, stoopid, not cramp."

"Pardon me ever so," I said. "I knew it was writer's something. I thought it might be knee. Anyhow, as you're not doing anything, how about meeting me at the office in a half-hour or so, I just might be able to put you out of your misery, for a while, at least."

"I'll think about it," she mumbled, then hung up. I did likewise. She'd show up, all right, like spring in springtime, like a crowd at a disaster, she was probably already circling over my office like a vulture waiting to dive on some hapless baby gazelle. And why not? Even doing simple chores for me must be more fun than scribbling odes in her bedroom; anything must be more fun, even eating beets.

Sure enough, she was sitting on the bench outside Mr. Amoyan's shoe repair establishment when I turned in and parked in front of the office. Mr. Amoyan was beside her, taking a breather and casting his experienced and appreciative Armenian eye on everything feminine that passed; his store was next to the laundromat that was next to Mrs. Morales' Taco-Burger counter joint. For some obscure adolescent reason Sara professed not to notice me although I both waved and called out "Yoo-hoo" as I passed.

I opened up. I looked up William Gince in the phone book; there was no entry for him. Nobody was in the L.A. phone book, I'm surprised they keep putting one out. After a while, in her own good time, the twerp meandered over and came slouching in, then sat on a corner of my desk, then gave my locks a tousle, two things she knew got my goat.

"What's up, Prof?"

"A small job," I said. "Just a trifle. I'd do it myself but you know how I like to give work to the needy and unemployed, and try and find a better definition of a poet than that."

"Doing what?"

"What I tell you," I said, "for once, and without any of your brilliant improvising, either."

"So tell," she said. "What am I, a mind reader?"

"No, but you're curly as a little lamb today," I said, running my hand over her head for a change. She'd had all her hair cut off a while back, in the line of duty, I must admit, and it had grown back in its natural color, Guinea pig white, in a tangle of tight curls. It didn't look that bad, actually, and anything was better than the way her hair shrieked during her long, tedious years of punkness. As for the rest of her, she was about five foot high on tiptoes, skinny as a billiard cue, with about the same number of curves, and tough as dried beef jerky. Her eyes were bright blue and cheeky, her mouth small, with an ironic twist at one corner. She had the usual number of ears, noses, teeth, and limbs, and the latter of which were attired in tight short-shorts and a pair of those Spanish rope-soled sandals, with red laces that came up and tied behind the ankles. Over a T-shirt that was clean, all in one piece, and that didn't say anything insulting, unlike the old days, she wore a man's zip-up suede jacket, borrowed without a single doubt from Willing Boy's cupboard. In case anyone from *Gentleman's Quarterly* is interested, I was attired in my usual workday outfit of cream cords, a Hawaiian short-sleeved shirt not altogether lacking in striking pigmentation, socks that matched, and brown moccasins that did likewise.

"We're looking for a skip," I said. "Which is someone who has skipped, and I don't mean rope, I mean town."

She raised her eyes heavenward for some reason. Seeking the poetic muse, no doubt.

"He could be anywhere," I said. "Narrowing that down, he could be far away or he could be not far away, but still not here."

"That's a big help," Sara said.

"If he isn't that far away," I went on patiently, "I don't want to frighten him into taking off on a camel overland to Timbuktu. Which is probably what will happen if I drop in on his mother or sister or both, who seem to still reside where our skip, one William Gince, resided until a few days ago when he took off with a lot of money that didn't belong to him. Anyway, that's the story, although I think there's more to it than that."

"How would your visiting his mother and sister frighten him?"

I sighed.

"It's called the telephone, dear," I said. "Which they use the moment I leave, saying the heat is on."

"Presuming he's got a phone number and they know it," she said.

"I've got to presume something," I said. "I've got nothing else to go on."

"Also presuming they know why he split and that they connect you with it."

"Also presuming," I agreed.

"What if they write him instead of phoning?"

I shrugged.

"I'll try something else," I said. "Look. Let us assume they know where he is. Let us assume they will call him, given sufficient reason. I can give them sufficient reason, or you can give them a less-sufficient but still-sufficient-enough reason. Either way, he gets called. And if he gets called from his old apartment, I can find out where he is now."

"How?"

"You'll find out, maybe. If he's already in Timbuktu, it doesn't matter who goes calling, me or you. We still win because we've found out where he is, assuming what we've assumed, and can take it from there. But what if he's somewhere relatively close like San Diego or Disneyland? Last thing in the world we want to do is frighten him into taking the first plane out, we want him right where he is, close. And that, noodlehead, is where and why you come in."

"I get it, I get it," she said. "You don't have to go on and on forever. I drop in instead of you. I've got no connection with the reason he split, but I do give them some other reason for calling him. Like what, for instance?"

I told her.

She groaned theatrically. "Is that the pathetic best idea you could come up with?"

"Hers is the tale you spin the ladies," I said. I told her the tale. "And here is what I want you to do while you are talking to them, and after you have finished talking to them." I told her that, too. "OK? All clear?"

"Yeah, yeah," she muttered. "When does all this happen?"

"As soon as you go home and don some apparel more suitable for the job," I said. "Not that you don't look most fetching in what you have on, which is a welcome change."

"It gives me the creeps just thinking about what you probably wore back in the twenties when you were my age," she said. "So what should I put on?"

"How do I know what sartorial splendors lurk in your walk-in closet," I said. "Something respectable."

"You gonna drive me down there?"

"No way," I said. "I got a small sum, a token, really, up front for expenses, it should just about run to a cab for you."

"Both ways," she said.

"Of course!" I said. "Really, Sara, you do disappoint me sometimes. Don't forget to get a receipt."

"Get the big spender suddenly," she said. "How about something up front for my expenses?"

I handed over forty dollars without further ado.

"And there's fifty more when you come up with the goods," I told her. "Hell, make that seventy-five."

She whistled in mock amazement and rolled her eyes.

"Are you sure you're feeling OK?" She leant over and touched my forehead, then blew on her fingers as if they were red hot.

"Now that we've had our little laugh at ol' Vic's expense," I said, "can we get on, lambie-pie, unless you'd like to pop round to the pharmacy, steal a rectal thermometer, and double-check my temperature." I remembered to scribble the Gince's address down and passed it over. She grinned, gave my specs, which I was wearing, an unnecessary wiggle, then hastily removed herself from the premises before I could retaliate by tickling her, which she hated, or whatever. As if I'd even bother.

She came back into my life late that afternoon, it would have been about five-thirty. I was still in the office running a chess program for beginners Benny had given me, on the computer. For beginners—I like that, most amusing. I did actually know that bishops moved one way and the guys on horses another. I switched off speedily when Sara appeared, wanting to forestall any comments she might have about grown men wasting their time on silly games. She handed me the following, hot off her typewriter, then paced around nervously as I scanned it. Writers can be such a pain sometimes, if not usually.

April 5, 1988
Confidential Report No. 17.
From: Special Agent SS.
To: V.D. (ha-ha)
Homeward I bound
Suitable gear I found

Trousers top low heels and granny glasses
(Men seldom make passes
At grannies in glasses
And hair that's rinsed bright blue
Except maybe old farts
With lonely cold hearts
Who have to wear glasses too)
Called a cab
Stow the gab
I sed to the loquacious driver
And there's an extra fiver
If you hang around for me
The driver he say sí
With worried look on face
White lies all in place
Buzzed le buzzer of le family
Explained my needs most humbly
Was told direct my feet
Back out into the street
No not back into the cab
T'were so the girls could grab
A look at me through a third-floor pane
Then the buzzer buzzed again
The front door ope'd to let me in
In went the erstwhile heroine
Up went the plucky Sybiline
Pumpin' lotsa adrenaline
    If 'tis St. Elmo who protects the tars
    If 'tis St. Christopher those in motor cars
    St. Veronica the gallant matadors
    Who
    Watches
    Over

Those who go a-tap-tap-tapping
At locked unfriendly doors question mark

"I like that bit," I said to the twerp, who was by then reading it with me over my shoulder. "About the doors." She went pink with delight. What the hell. My mother always used to say a lie isn't really a lie if is gives someone (other than the liar) pleasure. With a concealed sigh, I resumed:

Mother and sister awaiting I
Mother and sister awaiting by
Their open porte inside I go
Inside I spin my tale of woe
Of the end of innocence
Plucked by that dastard Gince
At the garage where I cashiered
And where toiled he and how I feared
A girl alone what's she to do
Does not the père have duties too
They are surprised They look askance
Could their Willy had led me such a dance
    And now he's gone suddenly
    Without a word suddenly
    Without farewell without a final kiss
    Surely surely it would not be amiss
    For the ladies to put me in touch
    Would that really be asking so much
    An address, phone number, PO box would do
    Somewhere I could sent him a tear-stained
        billet doux
Sorry, sed the ladies
Sorry, sed the girls
Lying through their twin sets

And their imitation pearls
No way Nada Forget it Blow
Don't get up I sed I'll go
Exactly where I do not know
So out I went into the snow

The time she was precisely 4:22.
Their phone number is 477-2063.
The cab cost $44.50-receipt available.
    $44.50 (cab
  - $40.00 (advance)
    $4.50
  + $75.00 (wages)
    $79.50 (balance owed me)

  Luv,
  Sara

"Well?" she demanded as soon as I was done.

"It won't do, Sara," I said. "It just won't do. You can't leave out all the punctuation in the desperate hope it'll make it appear more poetical."

"That's not what I meant by 'Well,' " she said.

"Ah," I said. "Well, it was a commendable piece of investigatory work."

"Not that 'Well,' either," she said. "Well, what about my bread?"

I extracted the required sum from my wallet and handed it over without further comment, although I did remark to her that I happened to be extremely familiar with the old cab receipt ploy—you got the cabby to give you a receipt for ten bucks more than it cost, and split it with him—and she'd better not even think of trying it on me.

"And fifty cents," she said.

I gave her fifty cents, mostly in nickels. Then and only then did the suspicious, grasping creature hand over the receipt.

"What were the ladies likes?" I asked her.

"Ordinary," she said. "Not a lot of life to them. They looked and dressed alike, they could almost have been sisters."

"Were they relaxed, were they frightened, what?"

"They sure weren't relaxed," she said. "As for frightened, maybe."

"Good," I said. "Any pictures of William around?"

"Yeah," she said. "A big one of him and his sister. Only trouble is, it was taken when they were like two."

"Ah well," I said philosophically. "You can't win 'em all." I gave the twerp's curls an affectionate rub. "But you did pretty good, pal." She looked pleased. "Now watch a real pro in action."

I retrieved an innocuous-looking scrap of paper from one of my desk drawers, the one under the one where my firepower was whenever I was in the office, otherwise it went into the safe out back. Written on the paper in my untidy scrawl were a seven-digit number with two other numbers tacked on, a five-digit number and one of four digits.

"What's that, Prof?" the twerp wanted to know. "The combination to the safe?"

"In a way," I said. Telephone companies, including the one that sent me my bill every month, Pacific Tel, have a special number. If you're fuzz or belong to one of several other accredited law enforcement agencies, which includes me out, and call that number and identify yourself correctly, you can obtain, among other things, a read-out of a suspect's phone bill for whatever time span you require.

Unfortunately, the procedure for obtaining unlisted phone numbers is more complicated, which is why I'd asked Curly to obtain the Ginces'. I dialed the special number, then asked to be put through to the appropriate extension. A lady answered. She said her name was Miss Hanoran and wanted to know how she could help me. I read off my brother Tony's shield number and the code number he'd been assigned by the telephone company, which I happened by mere chance to stumble across at his place one day. I forget just where, in some drawer or his wallet or wherever.

I asked the helpful Miss Hanoran, if her computer worked that fast, could she tell me of any long distance calls that had been made after 4:22 that afternoon from the Ginces' number. I was hoping, of course, that wherever William was, it wasn't in a motel just around the corner.

"Just one sec," said Miss Hanoran. After slightly longer than that she was back on the line, saying, "At four twenty-four a call was placed to four-one-six seven-eight-seven-four-one-one-two." I repeated the number to her, writing it down.

"Four-one-six," I said. "Where's that?"

She told me.

"Oh, merde," I said. "I mean, merci for everything."

"Bonjour," said Miss Hanoran.

"Well?" the twerp said eagerly as soon as I'd hung up.

"I'll give you a hint," I said. "It's worse than Timbuktu. I'll tell you if you tell me what 'Sybiline' means."

"Like a oracle or fortune-teller," she said.

"Montreal," I said. "Go get down that cheap atlas you gave me and let's see if it's even on the map."

CHAPTER EIGHT

Now don't get your dander up, all you Eskimos and Frenchies and wheat farmers and canoe paddlers, all you Malamuts, pea soupers, Hans Brinkers, and Newfies north o' the border, I was just having my little joke. Everyone knows Montreal is not only on the map but it's also on a big river, the name of which escapes me at the moment. It could be the Mackenzie. And as all sports lovers know, Montreal also has a huge cement igloo that cost the earth and then some where the ever-hopeful Montreal Expos try and play baseball. And speaking of which manly pursuit, remind me to pass by Fred's and put a goodly sum down on the Dodgers winning the World Series, even Tim'll have to give me at least a hundred to one. And I better do it afore I go, it is hard counting out greenbacks one by one when you've lost half your fingers from frostbite.*

Montreal . . . it has had a decent hockey team from time to time, I admit, not too surprising for a city that has only about three days of summer and an awful lot of ice the rest of the time. And when you've got that much ice, you can't put it all into highball cocktails, you have to skate on it and bowl

Editor's note: The L.A. Dodgers did not win the World Series that year but finished a distant last in their division.

on it and have horses race on it and fish through it and mush over it, it made me shiver just thinking about it. But Montreal in early April, maybe it would be spring up there by now, like it was in sensible places—I started rummaging through the wastepaper basket under the desk.

"Now what'cha doin'?" said Sara.

"Looking up what the temperature was yesterday in Montreal," I said. I dug out yesterday 's *Herald* and found the weather page, on which they always listed temperatures of major cities around the world, primarily to give Californians something to gloat about. "Guess what?"

"What?"

"Yesterday the mercury shot all the way up to thirty-eight in Montreal," I said. "That's almost a heat wave for them. The natives probably stripped down to their last parka."

"What a sissy," she said. "Me, I don't mind the cold, I kinda dig it."

"Who cares about you," I said. "It's me that's going to have to break the ice in the toilet bowl before I pee."

"Me too," she said smugly.

"No way," I said firmly.

"Wanna bet?" she said. "You know so much about Montreal, bet I know something you don't."

"Bet you don't," I said. "Bet you don't know anything about anything I don't, except maybe about things nobody knows about, like oracles."

"What do they speak there?"

"Aside from Eskimo, what do you think they speak, Hindustani? English and a little Français is what they speak."

"No more English," said Miss Smarty with a namby-pamby air. "They passed this law. Everything's in French, all the street signs, all the directions, all store names, and you try speaking English in all but one or two areas and you get lynched."

"Oh, come on," I said. "Where'd you get all this rubbish from? Anyway, even if it was true, what's it got to do with you? You don't speak any more French than I do and all I know is *merci, merde, garçon, La Mayonnaise,* and snails."

"George does," she said. "And he is completely in my thrall, he won't go anywhere without me." The latter part of that statement was so ludicrously unimaginable that I ignored it and concentrated on the first part.

"And how come Willing Boy parlez-vous all of a sudden?"

"His mother was born there," she said. "In Quebec City, actually. She went back after her divorce and still lives there. And guess where George goes to visit every time he's got a few days off?"

"Give me a hint," I said. "Does he pack his hockey stick and puck? But I'll be damned, I didn't know Willing Boy spoke anything but Hell's Angel."

"There's lots about George you don't know," she said. "Guess what else."

"I give up!" I said somewhat testily. "I suppose he speaks Russian, Finnish, Erse, Basque, and Chinese sign language, too."

"He's an actor," the twerp said, with love in her voice, as if that was something to be proud of. "Or at least he's studying to be one."

"So's half L.A.," I said. "The other half's writing screen plays. So what?"

"So if you consider it objectively instead of trying to be funny, don't you think it might be helpful to have someone who speaks the language along and who can also act real good? You're always making me pretend to be someone else and I'm like an amateur."

"You're telling me," I said.

"Oh yeah? You would have been dead that time in Mexico if you didn't have Benny translating for you and him and me playing your stooges."

"I hate to admit it but you might actually have a valid point there for once," I said. I had needed Benny's impeccable Spanish. And as for Willing Boy, he was quick on the uptake and certainly didn't mind breaking the law, or bending it, anyway. In a good cause, of course. OK. I thought I just might take Willing Boy along for the ride. That would mean separating Romeo and Juliet for a few days, though. I stole a glance at her. Could I really get in the way of true love? Need you ask.

"What are you gonna do with this guy when you find him?" she said then.

"Don't know yet," I said. "I'm not supposed to do anything, just let the odious Fats, he's the guy who hired me, know where he's hiding."

"Can't you find out by calling someone, like you did before? Like, call the phone company in Montreal and con them into telling you the address that belongs to that telephone number you got?"

"Sure I could," I said. "No big deal, I might not even have to pretend to be Tony, what do they care? I'm not after secret information. Then I wouldn't have to go shopping for fur-lined Jockety shorts, then fly to Montreal and then this and that, all I'd have to do is call Fats and tell him the address and earn myself a tidy piece of change for two phone calls and one house call by you. But."

"But," she repeated.

"But what if that phone number is just a cutout or simply a number he calls to get messages from? Then he won't be at that address. But there's another but," I said. "But I don't really like it, and I don't like Fats, either. Maybe Willy really did run off with Fats' dinero but there's more to it that that, Curly, Fats handed me over five Cs like it was Monopoly money, without even haggling."

"Oh yeah?" Sara said, glaring. "You said it was a token sum."

"Did I?" I said vaguely. "I don't recall. Anyway, shut up for a minute, will you, and let me think."

I thought.

After a while she meandered over to the bookcase, took down the atlas, and began leafing through it.

I broke the silence by saying, "Don't forget to pack your woollies." She squealed with excitement, then leapt at me and kissed me on the cheek before I could defend myself.

"How come you changed your tune?"

"Sara," I said, "I am not so narrow-minded that I cannot openly and publicly declare that it is possible that you and Willing Boy might conceivably be of some small use to me up there. Also, if we're going to screw Fats, why not do it royally. Maybe I'll put you guys on the payroll, too, maybe. I wonder what they use for money in Canada—probably beads or walrus teeth. Are you sure Willing Boy can get off work?"

"I'm sure," she said, blushing, trying to hide her face by peering down into the atlas that she'd opened up on the desk. "He's already asked for the rest of the week off."

"Aha," I said, waggling my eyebrows suggestively. "Planning a little trip, were we? Not . . ." I put on a deeply shocked look. ". . . not eloping? Sara! Have you introduced him to your folks yet?"

"Are you kidding?" she said. "They only feed him three times a week. Mom thinks he's the most gorgeous thing she's ever seen."

"Who doesn't," I said. "But still, marriage is a big step . . ."

"Grow up, will ya? We were thinking of driving up to Tahoe, if you really must know. There," she said, pointing at the right-hand side of the map of our friendly neighbor to the north. "Montreal. And that river it's on is the St. Lawrence."

"Thought so," I said. "Wonder how often dog sleds leave for there. Sara, if you really want to earn your keep, get on to Rogg Travel. Ask for Ron. Tell him the usual three for two round-trips to Montreal, via New York, return open, leaving tomorrow morning. Ask him to book us the New York–Montreal and Montreal–New York portions in different names, maybe you and Willing Boy as a mister and missus, as in married, and our seats shouldn't be together. Ask him to book us hotel rooms for a couple of nights, too, somewhere central. Then call Fats. The number's in here under 'Fats.' " I got my address book out of the drawer and flipped it to her. "Tell him you're my secretary, I got a lead and I'll be out of town for a couple of days but you don't know where and you don't know when exactly I'll be back. Then you better get on to Willing Boy and tell him the news, likewise your folks. Got it?"

"Consider it done, Prof." She went to work on the phone. I gazed at the map of Canada for a moment. As far as I could recall, I'd only ever met one Canadian, or at least one who would admit it, an artist who lived off Laurel Canyon Boulevard and who painted nothing but highly realistic and greatly detailed female nudes. He also smiled a lot. I often wondered if there was any connection. Canada—Jesus, it even looked cold. Half the towns in it were named Fort something, which was hardly reassuring, and the other half had names you couldn't even pronounce, like Flin Flon, Michipicoten, and Povungnituk. Look it up for yourself if you think I'm kidding.

"Tickets will be waiting for us at the TWA desk at the airport," the twerp reported about then. "And the other ones at Air Canada, in New York. There's the flight number, eight forty-five departure tomorrow morning. Hour and twenty minutes layover at Kennedy. Arrive Montreal about ten-thirty their time that night. He'll try and get us rooms at something called the Windsor Hotel, if he can't, he'll get back to us." I didn't ask her how many rooms she had booked, what business of mine was it anyway, I wasn't their durn chaperone. I did resolve to have a long talk with her before we left about the birds and the bees, I was sure there was a lot she could teach me. "And while we're on the subject," she said, "what's the usual three for two?"

"It's what you do when someone else is paying," I said. "You cash in your first-class ticket, go steerage, and pocket the dif, I thought everybody knew that. In our case, we cash in two first-class tickets and buy three steerage. Even I couldn't justify hitting Fats for traveling expenses for three people, two maybe. I'm going to have enough trouble getting my dough out of him as it is."

Shortly thereafter, Sara, having completed her calls, betook herself home or into the arms of Willing Boy. I too betook myself homeward after making a couple of calls to put off what few appointments I had scheduled for that week. The last thing I did before leaving was to tear up into shreds Sara's cab receipt for $44.50, take out of the back of the second drawer on the right a pad of receipt vouchers from Celebrity Cabs, which I had been fortunate enough to come across in the glove compartment of a Celebrity Cab one soiree when I was minding Lew and when the driver had hopped out briefly to buy some smokes. I write out a new receipt for $57.50, then added "Tip—$5.00." There— that looked better: despite crippling pangs of guilt I managed to drive all the way home without psychiatric help.

Social Notes from the Studio City *Star* (published weekly, circulation two hundred supermarkets)—"V. Daniel and Evonne Louise Shirley were glimpsed by this reporter billing and cooing in Dave's Corner Bar the other eve. . . . Surely this will put paid once and for all the catty rumor that Studio City's most arresting (!) PI had a new enamorata . . . why don'cha come up and take *my* fingerprints sometimes, you hunk, you . . ."

I took Evonne home early, as I had packing to do, and the following morning would have to allow myself enough time to rub crankcase grease all over my body against the cold. I kissed her good night outside her back door; her mouth tastes slightly of rum and slightly of sparerib sauce, with a pleasant aftertaste of Evonne Shirley. I didn't know whether to kiss her, eat her, or drink her. I'd told her of course where I was going and when and more or less why, and that I was taking along Willing Boy and Curly out of the goodness of my heart. She said don't forget to send your mom a card and me too and try the moose stew while I was up there. I said I wouldn't miss it for the world but that I would miss her, like I always did. It's nice to have someone specific to miss, especially someone as specific as Evonne; before I met her I tended to sort of vaguely miss some fantasy female I didn't even know. Functioning brain cells is really what I was missing back then.

I wound up packing that night, as anything is better than having to choose between almost identical pairs of socks at 6:30 A.M. I had an old parka, God knows why, I threw in, also a pair of hiking boots, also a heavy woolen sweater I hadn't worn for decades. Ear muffs I figured I could get up there, likewise a balaclava, thermal underwear, and snow goggles. Then I rubbed a modest amount of vanishing cream Evonne had left behind onto my visage, without noticing anything doing much vanishing except the cream. Then I set the alarm and went to bed.

The kids were already at LAX waiting for me when I arrived the following morning, sharing one of the chairs in a row against the wall facing the TWA counters. Sara's mom had given them a lift out; I'd done what I always did—drive to a certain hotel not so far away, parked for nothing in their lot, then hopped on the hotel's free minibus shuttle. On the way I remembered to make an entry in my memo pad under "Expenses"—"Prkng, 3 dys, $27.00."

"Did you pick up the duckets?" I asked Sara after we'd exchanged our greetings.

"Yep."

"Lost them yet?"

"Nope."

Our flight was announced about then so off we trundled. Willing Boy in his second-best leathers, Sara in some sort of trouser suit, a ratty-looking fur coat of dubious origin, either left over from her highly unlamented punk period or made from what her mother ran over on the way to the airport that morning, slung over one arm. Ah, my merry band of brothers, I thought, we're off to the wars again.

We spent the next five-and-a-half hours doing what grown-ups do in the sophisticated flying machines of today—sit all hunched up in kiddie chairs, drink a lot, and wish we'd stopped at Fred's Deli for a bag lunch. Talk about the Ku Klux Klan's or the Freemasons' oath of allegiance—the one the airline caterers take to adamantly refuse to ever serve once one thing edible must be a killer. However, I will say that in the two most important respects the plane did what it was supposed to—it took off and then it landed again, and in the dark, too. Can you believe a big boy like me used to be terrified of flying? Now I'm just scared stiff.

Now, I was sitting a few (empty) rows behind the kids and we were all busily pretending we didn't know each another, just in case. But I did very much want a few words with Willing Boy. So when the nitwit unglued herself from him long enough to take herself to the john, I fell into casual conversation with him by some simple ruse. It turned out he could parlez-vous Français after all, which was lucky for him. Not that I had been in any way suspicious, mind you. Also, it turned out not only did he have a mother, but an elder sister married and living in Raleigh, North Carolina; he even produced pictures of them. Both were the exact physical opposite of him, being short, dark, dumpish, bespectacled, and unbeautiful. Some guys have all the luck. You know what he told me his sister wanted on her tombstone? "Scratch and sniff." I said I wanted "That's all, folks" on time. Sara, typically, came up with "All are creative, few are artists" for hers, then looked at me challengingly.

"Très poetical," I said. "Who said it?"

"Dunno," she said. "I heard it somewhere."

"Probably at a Sex Pistols' concert," I said. Willing Boy grinned.

After we landed, we passed an hour and twenty minutes doing what grown-ups who are waiting in airports for connectors flights do—listen to babies crying and smile with false sympathy at irate travelers whose outgoing flights are six hours late so far.

Part of that time I spent at an Air Canada check-in counter, where a man with a ferocious cold stopped sneezing long enough to print out our tickets.

Part of that time I spent at an Air-Canada counter, where an man with a ferocious cold stopped sneezing long enough to print our tickets. Mine was in the name of Holmes; most amusing, Sara. Hers and Willing Boy's were in the names of Mr. and Mrs. E. B. Browning; again, highly funny. I asked Willing Boy if we should change some money, he said, no sweat, we could do it tomorrow, most cabbies and hotels and the like in Montreal were delighted to accept U.S. currency as they murdered you with the exchange rate. I said what else was new.

The flight northward, ever northward, to the land of the midnight sun, was exactly the same as the L.A.–New York one, but shorter, of course, and half in French. Georgie Pie didn't have to translate because the broadcaster did it himself immediately after the French version. Gee. . . there I was on my way to yet another foreign country—along with Mexico and Houston, that would make it three in four years. Who was the madcap gadabout all of a sudden? I wondered if my upcoming adventures with the world's most beautiful woman would involve travel to foreign climes. Estonia in April—a catchy phrase, no doubt, but one that does perhaps lack the Gallic charm of the original. Likewise April in Hitler's bunker or April by the Dead Sea.

Merde, Montreal was looking better, every minute.

CHAPTER NINE

La ville de Montréal has an old international airport, Dorval, and a new international airport, Mirabel. As Dorval was conveniently close to Montreal and fairly easy to get to, say a half-hour's drive, the fed's, over the local government's dead bodies, decided to build the new one out in the middle of the prairies in southern Alberta, thus delighting such worthy citizens as cab drivers, bus operators, Admunson of the Pole, and Avis employees, but infuriating everyone else.

Or so I was told by my seatmate, a grizzled, mustachioed, red-faced Canuck, on the Air Canada flight north. His name was Chuck something and he hired out to smaller construction companies those huge cement mixers that creep along highways blocking the whole road in front of you making cement as they go. Then he wanted to know, if I was interested in making a fortune.

"If," I said, "you are suggesting a small game of chance to wile away the time, and you just happen to have a deck of pasteboards with you, can I save us both a lot o time and energy that could be better spent drinking this good beer of yours and just hand over all the money I got in the world right now?"

Chuck roared.

"*Tabernac!*" he said, I think. "Nothing like that, eh? See, with cement, once in a while a whole load seizes up on you, like it goes hard as a rock, no one knows why, and you can imagine what a bitch it is afterward dealing with it, eh?"

"I sure can," I said.

"So all you got to do is invent a cement that doesn't seize up."

"Can I have until Friday?" I said. "I have a couple of simple tasks to perform first, like mush to the Pole and discover oil."

He laughed again and shouted at the stewardess for four more beers, paying for them with, among other assorted currency, a pink two-dollar bill that looked as phoney as hell to me but didn't seem to bother the stewardess any. I wondered if all Canadians were as friendly as Chuck, laughed as much, and drank as much beer. To spare the suspense, it turned out they were, they did, and did they ever. Good beer too, Labatt's and Molson and Carling; not as good as Corona and Dos Equis and Tecate, to my highly developed taste, but a lot better'n Coors and Miller and Bud, eh.

Chuck had a veritable host of amusing anecdotes about the cement business. He'd just finished up one about the time a guy dumped a whole truck into and over a rival suitor's parked convertible, when we landed. And at Dorval, luckily for my bankroll, because, as know-it-all Chuck piped up to say, Dorval was used for all U.S.–Canada flights as well as most charters. I don't know why, but Canadian customs and immigration authorities seem more worried about lettuce entering their country illegally than Yankee wetbacks like me, but that's their business. Anyway we had no problem; my guy even spoke English to me. So did the mademoiselle at Avis who rented me a bright red Ford. Even the free map she gave me of Montreal and its surrounds was in

English. I gave Sara a dirty look in the rearview mirror after we'd climbed in and were about to take off, with Willing Boy beside me to navigate.

"Everything in French, eh?" I said. "I haven't heard a word of French since I got here."

"What's that, Swahili?" she said, pointing to an overhead road sign of which only one word, "exit," was understandable.

"Point taken, chérie," I said. "Boy, some country, where your copilot not only has to navigate but translate, too."

"Want me to drive?" Willing Boy offered. "I think I could manage it if you showed me where the gear stick is. Maybe it's this little doodad here." He flicked; the windscreen wipers started working.

"No, it ain't that," the twerp put in from the backseat. "Try something else."

"Try shutting up and stopping fooling and start navigating and translating," I said.

"Oui, my masterful leader," Willing Boy said. Sara giggled.

I drove. At least the road was fairly decent, it actually had more than one lane and was paved. We got to Montreal somehow, finally, after passing through a lot of terrain once featured in Chaplin's *Gold Rush*. On the way I discovered Montreal was an island, which I did not know. Well, did you? We even managed to find the hotel. From what I could see of it, at night, the gay Paree of North America seemed large, clean, slumless, old, new, and lively, with many a park and many a square, which cannot be said of many cities in the New World. It reminded me somewhat of a colder and more sedate version of San Francisco, with lots of water and lots of hills in close proximity. It seemed to have an awful lot of McDuck's restaurants, but when I pointed out this interesting observation to Willing Boy, he grinned and said the big

M's were all stops for the city's underground system, or *le métro*.

"Just joking," I said. I noticed Curly had been right about the store signs, too, they said things like *boulangerie* and *charcuterie* and *brasserie* instead of plain-old bread, deli, and bar, which should be good enough for anyone, if you ask me.

I checked us in under our phoney traveling names, Holmes and Browning, leaving off the initials "E. B." in case the desk clerk, who spoke English to me, by the way, was moderately literate. I left him two hundred U.S. as a deposit for the rooms as I only had (with me) credit cards in my real name. I'll tell you sometime how to get a wad of legitimate cards in someone else's name when I'm in the mood. I might however mention briefly how you can get all the major credit cards for yourself without having any credit, any employment, and or any money to speak of. True, I should really check over the details with my financial adviser, Benny the Boy, who first told me about it, as it is complicated and I'd hate to steer you wrong, mes amis, but what the hell:

Roughly, you have to form a corporation somewhere it's easy and cheap to do so, reputedly, say, Nevada, and where no proof of assets is required. Then you need a simple contract drawn up that says the corporation agrees to pay you, say, ten grand a month, in cash or stock, so now you have, on paper, one of the requirements for obtaining credit, a well-paying job. Next you have to set up a bank balance at least in the "low threes," ass the banks put it to anyone checking up on your savings balance, meaning roughly a few hundred bucks. There are a couple of ways of doing this, according to Benny the Boy, one requires a hundred-dollar outlay, the other a measly twenty, but both demand four bank accounts and a lot of well-timed shifting of (imaginary) funds from one to the other. Banks, disgracefully, take anywhere from ten to fourteen days to clear a check;' the slower the better, of course, as far as they are concerned, as they have the use of the money during that time and they are the ones who pocket the interest on it. Anyway, Benny once diagrammed for me how to use this delay and by writing checks on the correct account at the right time you can build up a sizable balance in one of them. It would be illegal to draw cash against it, of course, but the balance does exist, and any credit card company checking up would be told so. And voilà, there you are, with a wallet full of plastic at last. A *free* copy of Benny's diagram can be obtained by dropping a postcard to Yours Truly; please enclose $10.00 for postage and handling. However, I have a sneaking feeling this scheme is out of date by now because due to consumer pressure, the banks have greatly reduced the time they take to clear a check, so you might have to fall back on the old-fashioned but tried and true means of obtaining credit cards—mugging.

So: a contemptuous bellhop showed us up to our fourth-floor abodes. I was in a single, with a queen-size bed, the kids sharing a double, with a king-size bed, I noticed when I poked my head in to see if they were comfortable. How tempus fugits, even in Canada. In my day, even if you presented a valid marriage certificate at the front desk, along with color photos taken at your twenty-fifth wedding anniversary, they'd still put you in one room and the lady in another, and probably on different floors as well, if not different wings.

I don't know what the kids did then, although I might have taken a wild guess at it, but I unpacked a few necessities—my nightie, my old teddy, special scalp preparation, and the like—took a quick shower, and then hit the hay. Flying is especially tiring when you know that the only things keeping you up in the ozone layer is your steely will power and continual alertness. I blew Ruth a good-night kiss, then hastily did likewise to Evonne.

The bedside phone buzzed me out of sleep the following morn; it was half of the lovebirds wanting to know if I was awake.

"I am now," I said. "See you downstairs for breakfast in half an hour."

"We already had it," the twerp said. "We've been up for hours. We even went out for a walk, it's gorgeous out."

"If you're a caribou," I said. "Anyway, see you up here in an hour for a council of war, OK?"

She agreed it was OK by them. I got myself together, went down, found the *caféteria* by following signs that said CAFÉTERIA, wound up eating pancakes with maple syrup by ordering something called "*crepes au sirop d'érable*," had the bill put on my room number, left a U.S. dollar as a tip for the mademoiselle, and got back up to my room just as Curly and Willing Boy were emerging from theirs to look for me. They were attired in daring look-alike outfits of jeans, sweaters and boots. I was attired in every bit of clothing I'd brought except the nightie. She said they've been out changing money. I said I'd been eating pancakes. Then we got down to the day's business.

After a moment or two of panic, I managed to find the scrap of paper on which I'd written William Gince's number, or rather the number I hoped was his. Then I inquired of Willing Boy if he knew the name of a big butcher store or a big grocery chain in town.

"Provigo," he said.

"I'll take your word for it," I said.

"Thank you," he said.

"Now here is what you are going to do," I said. I told him. He got up from the chair by the little desk by the window in which he was slouching and began walking around muttering to himself and waving his hands in the air.

"What's the matter with him?" I asked the twerp, who was on the bed beside me. "Was it something I said?"

"You really are stoopid sometimes," she said. "He's only preparing, don't you know anything about acting?"

"Are you kidding?" I said. "I've walked out in the middle of more plays than you can find rhymes for 'snow.' I just didn't know—and there's one to start you off—thespians had to prepare anything, except their wigs. I thought all you did was bring up the footlights and they immediately started emoting.

After a while Willing Boy crossed over to us and muttered tensely, "OK. Ready. Let's get it on. I'm up for it." Sara gazed up at him lovingly. I just gazed up at him.

"There's the phone, Marlon," I said.

He picked it up, dialed, and then unleashed a torrent of French, which, after he'd hung up again, he roughly translated as, "Madame? Congratulations! It's Provigo here, Provigo, your friendly family grocers? You've just won a free, ten-pound, glazed Virginia ham for your Easter dinner! No, madame, you do not have to enter any competition, you do not have to purchase any goods from any of our thirty-two retail outlets in the Province of Quebec all you have to do is make sure someone's home when our delivery van passes your door. Of course you will have to heat it up, heh-heh, and we don't supply the sweet potatoes to go with it. . . . Really? This is the first you've heard of it? Madame, we've been doing it for years, twenty-five glazed Virginia hams at Easter, twenty-five free-range turkeys at Thanksgiving, and then of course the same number of geese, or turkeys, your choice, and there's always plenty of choice at Provigo, for Noël. . . . Well, how we do it is, and I'm not supposed to really tell you this, it's my daughter Debbie, she's almost four already, she does it, she just points to numbers at random on different pages of the phone book, and of course I have to check them after to make sure none of the winners works for Provigo or has any family member who does. . . . You don't? Good!

"Something else I always do, I always give the winners a call to see if they are still at the same address 'cause I'd hate for one of our vans to get out there and find you've moved recently because people often keep the same phone number when they move, but not the same address. . . . heh-heh, that would be tricky, wouldn't it . . ."

Here Marlon had covered up the receiver briefly and whispered frantically, "Pen! Pen!"

"You can sign autographs later, you ham, you," I whispered back. I handed him a pen.

"St. Michel, eight five five, um hum, that's what we have . . . just below Beaubien, the house with the white fence and there's only the one bell, fine. And your name? Mrs. François Leduc. Would tomorrow afternoon suit you? Anytime between two and five, swell, Mrs. Leduc, we'll be there . . . and thank you, Mrs. Leduc. Congratulations again. Bye-bye."

Marlon hung up and fell back on the bed, utterly drained by his labors. Ham is right, I thought. Actors—give them one simple call to make and they not only have to spend twenty minutes preparing but they have to go to a health farm afterward to recover.

"You would've really been in the sit if she was Jewish," the twerp said, stroking Marlon's fevered brow in a motherly fashion.

"I happen to know many Jews do eat ham," I said. "Only they call it Zebra. Anyway, well done, Marlon, although I did think it was a mite niggardly of you not to throw in a few spuds."

"Thanks, thanks," Marlon managed to gasp. "No flowers, please. Telegrams, OK."

"Now what?" Sara asked.

"As soon as Sir Marlon has recovered," I said, "from giving the definitive performance of a Provigo clerk, we might just go take a look at eight five five Rue St. Michel and see what we can see." I opened up the Montreal map I'd retrieved from the car after breakfast and spread it open, then put my glasses on so I could read the damn thing.

"There's Beaubien," Sara said after a minute, jabbing at the map with one finger. "And there's St. Michel."

"Can you get us there, Marlon?" I said.

"Can I act?" he said. "Easy. We'll take like Sherbrooke over, then turn left and then turn right."

"Well, mush, you huskies," I said. They went next door for their coats, I got my parka out of the cupboard and we went downstairs to the underground parking lot, climbed in the Ford, and mushed, Marlon not only navigating and translating but providing a running commentary as we did so. It was cold in downtown Montreal, and snow lay unevenly round about, on lawns, in trees, on roofs, on parked cars and fire hydrants. It might have been April and thus spring for some, but not yet for Montrealites.

"Sherbrooke, where the elite meet to shop, hop, and bop," Willing Boy sang out after a moment. "Up that mount on our left, which is named Mont Réal, by the way—"

"As against Mont False, I suppose," I said.

"Which means royal, not real, man," Marlon said. "Where the city got its name from, get it? Anyway, up that there mountain is Westmount, where all the bread is, or at least what's left of it."

"Where'd the rest go?" I said for something to say.

"West, man, west," Marlon said. "Soon as the natives in these parts started gettin' uppity a while back, wanting their own language spoken and all that, a lot of scared Anglo money hit the road."

"No!" I exclaimed. "How utterly pushy. Next thing these demned Frenchies will be wanting is the vote. And then—who knows? Tumbrils may yet roll again along these cobbled streets." At which time la petite twerp suggested that I put a sock in it as she'd seen the movie, thanks.

After we left the high-rent area we came to a part of the city that looked more like what cities were supposed to look like—tenement buildings, small businesses, sex shops, counter joints, cut-rate drugs, Jewish delis, and carpeterias. We even passed a couple of drunks arguing on a corner.

"That's more like it," I said, stopping carefully for a red light. "How can you have a decent city without winos."

"Mordecai Richler," the tour guide said.

"So what," I said.

"He came from around here, St. Lawrence Main, St. Denis, poor Jewish and poor Catholic fighting it out."

"Never heard of him," I said. "Who did you say he played for?"

Willing Boy tossed his tresses out of his eyes and directed me left onto Beaubien, which we cruised along for a stretch. I turned down into St. Michel and drove slowly past 855, which turned out to be a wooden-shingled, steep-roofed duplex, with a small porch out front and the low white fence Mrs. Leduc had mentioned. In the yard next to it was a large snowman with a carrot nose and coal eyes, an old broom tucked under one of its rather shapeless arms. Someone in an old clunker he just managed to start pulled out from the curb a few door up; I backed deftly into the space he left and then cut the motor.

"Now what?" Sara wanted to know.

"Now we wait awhile," I said. "See what happens. We might get lucky."

"Why don't we just knock on the door and see what happens?"

"Because we might get unlucky," I said patiently. "He could have friends in for tea. Large ones. He could have things called firearms, which make a lot of noise and then kill you. When I do approach him, I'd rather it was somewhere nice and public so if he does have a gun he won't be as likely to use it and maybe he's left it at home anyway."

We waited awhile. I started up the motor from time to time to reheat the car. Sara toyed with the nape of Marlon's neck from time to time; he didn't seem to mind. After another little while he dug out a roach from one of his pockets and they both took a toke on it while I kept an uneasy eye out for guys on horses in red coats and Boy Scout hats.

It wasn't even an hour before someone came out of Mrs. Leduc's half of the duplex who could have been our man William, if Fats' description had been accurate, and why would he lie about that part of it whatever else he might be lying about. The man was small, nondescript, with a receding chin and large glasses. He waved at an upstairs window, took an unsuspicious look around, checked the sky for what I don't know, maybe passing geese, then he headed briskly off toward Beaubien.

"We better split up," I said hastily. "You two take him on foot, you're smaller than me, he's not likely to think you two drugged-out freaks are tailing him but try and look Canadian just in case. See where he goes. If he's headed for a car parked somewhere, I'll take him. See you back at the hotel. Go."

They went, the twerp stopping just long enough to make a snowball and check it at the windscreen. I started up the car and, staying well behind the parade, followed William as far as Beaubien and then along it until he disappeared into one of the big M's for *métros*. The kids tagged along after him. I drove back to the hotel, only losing my way twice and once almost.

I know what they do on a rainy night in Río but what do you do on a cold afternoon in Montreal when the salmon aren't running? I suppose I could have gone sightseeing or read a good book or, even better, some good rubbish. However, when I am in a new town I've always found it fruitful to try and get a feel for the place by mingling with John Q. Public in one of his typical habitats, so I changed some money at the desk and then, although it was undeniably early in the day, I decided a tavern I'd noticed just around the corner from the hotel would be a sensible place to begin my studies. I found a seat at the bar, ordered a Molson Export from the innkeeper and shifted the bowl of free pretzels a soupçon closer to my elbow. I was happy to see that the St. George's tavern looked remarkably similar to a lot of other low-class joints I've had the luck to visit over the years during my investigations of the local populations. It had the usual beer signs on the walls and miscellania behind the bar and a shuffleboard game along one wall; even the drunks looked familiar.

There was a little fellow sitting two stools down from me who was frowning at some words he'd just scribbled in a kid's lined exercise book on the bar in front of him. He had a red, white, and blue woolly hat with a large *C* on it on his dome, horned-rimmed glasses on his roseate nose, and worn over a lumberjack's checked shirt, a T-shirt that said, in English, INSTANT ASSHOLE—JUST ADD ALCOHOL.

"Like the message," I said after a minute, when I'd caught his eye.

"All men should learn to hear truth," he enunciated carefully more or less in my direction. After another peaceful moment or two had passed, I asked him politely what he was writing, was it mayhap a letter to mother? Which reminded me—postcards, to the folks back home. But not one to Lew Lewellen, that . . . that film producer.

"At the risk of evoking your ribald laughter," the guy said, "and it is a considerable risk, one that I would not undertake did I not perceive you to be a visiter to these fair shores, I am endeavoring to scribe the great Canadian novel."

"A worthy labor," I remarked, falling easily into his professional venacular. "I happen, at this very minute, to be traveling with a noted Californian poetess who, unfortunately, has only been privately published so far." Fortunately is more like it, I thought.

"Indeed," the fellow said. "Not unlike myself."

"I wonder if I might contribute to the encouragement of Canadian letters in a modest way by offering you some warming libation?"

"Double C and C, Samuel," the guy said instantly.

"Comin' up," Samuel said.

When Sam had served us both refreshers, I asked the scrivener how long he'd been working on his great epic. He looked at his watch and said, "About twenty minutes."

"And how is it progressing?"

"Brilliantly," he said. "I have the first three chapter titles already. 'Out of the Closet and into the Saddle—A Short History of the Royal Canadian Mounted Police.'

'Birchbark—Fact or Fiction?' 'The Use of the Moose in Saskatchewan Dance Hall Mythology.' "

"A great start!" I enthused. After I'd put away a tasty snack of two pickled jumbo wieners, two pickled eggs, and one giant pepperoni stick, my erstwhile companion furthered, if not increased by several hundred percent, my knowledge of Canadian history by informing me that the ex–prime minister of Canada, one Pierre Trudeau, once had a wife who always wore, next to her skin, a cameo brooch containing a lock of Mick Jagger's hair. He also told me the Canadians had once marched south and burned Washington; I didn't know which statement was the more unlikely.

I got back to the hotel about two-thirty; the kids showed up, bursting with news, about a half-hour later. They also burst into my room, where, postcards bought in the lobby all written, like a good boy, I was stretching out on the bed ruminating, not for the first time, on the slim monograph I planned to scribe one day. It wouldn't be as mammoth an undertaking as the great Canadian novel, of course, I know my limitations only too well, it would merely be a few pithy and cogent reflections about those illusive fragments in the puzzle of existence—why did they seem more attainable after six Canadian beers and assorted pickled goods?

As my favorite nitwit was hopping up and down by the bed, I had no choice but to put my idle cogitations away for another day.

"Guess where we're going tonight!" she said. Her cheeks were rosy from the cold and she was wearing what looked like a new woolly hat, in the same colors as my drinking buddy's.

"Where?"

"Ha-ha! You'll find out. So we follow this guy," she said, "down into the depths of the metro or whatever it's called, man, it's neat down there, and warm, and clean, there's no grafitti anywhere."

"Shu!" I said. "Not so loud, that juvenile delinquent posing as a bellhop might hear you."

"We even get in the same car as him, it's crowded, he doesn't have a clue we're there. So we get out when he does and walk along St. Catherine Street and guess where he goes?"

"Into a bar," I said.

"Into the Forum," Marlon said.

"Aha," I said. "Last time I heard, the score was still lions, six, Christians, nothing."

"Not that Forum, stoopid," Sara said. "The one they play hockey in. So I buy this," referring to the hat, "staying out of the way, and I woulda got you one but they didn't have one big enough, and George lines up behind the guy and gets us tickets too. They're way up top somewhere but George says he was lucky to get even them. So that's where we're goin tonight, if it's public enough for you, to watch the Montreal Canadiens play who?"

"Washington Capitals," Marlon said.

"Did you know those damned Canucks once marched south and burned Washington?" I remarked casually.

"Probably started with his teeth," Willing Boy said. "Everyone knows they were made of wood."

That's all I needed, Brando branching out into comedy.

Chapter Ten

It was the end of the first period. Les Canadiens, also known as Les Habitants, were leading 2–0 on goals by Carbonneau and Naslund, and the seventeen thousand or so fans in the joint were lapping it up and living it up.

I was sitting next to the gent we were hoping was William Gince, with the twerp, in her new cap, which was in the Canadien's team colors, I had figured out by then, on my other side and Willing Boy next to her. The guy who had been sitting on the far side of William had just been chucked out by the Forum fuzz for fighting with the guy behind him after a ten-minute exchange of insults, spilt beer, and the like. Which altercation, however, had been mild compared to the mayhem down on the ice; fortunately the carnage was interrupted from time to time by some fast, furious, and highly skilled ice hockey. I'd never seen a pro game live before although my mom and her best chum, Feeb, who was my apartment landlady and lived below me, used to watch the Los Angeles Kings occasionally when they were in a particularly masochistic mood.

The teams had just skated off to their dressing rooms to suck orange halves and have their wounds cauterized and munch a few uppers and get their tetanus shots. An invisible organ up somewhere in the gods like us was playing a medley of old-time chansons and a guy on a funny little water wagon was driving from end to end of the rink repairing the ice surface. William took himself up the aisle for a leak or a beer or a smoke or maybe *un hot dog;* he had a Canadien's scarf wrapped around his neck and had been enjoying himself thoroughly, shouting, booing, cheering the goals, and screaming at the referee, just like everyone else, including us.

"That water cart is a Zamboni," Willing Boy told me. "Invented by a dude called Zamboni." Sara hugged his arm and looked at him like he was Einstein.

"You ever play, Marlon?" I asked him.

He curled his upper lip at me. "Are you kidding? Everyone in Canada played. I started in like a peewee league when I was six, then played all through high school, and on the scout team. A lean 'n' mean left winger, I was."

"I'm surprised you still got any teeth left at all," I said.

"Oh, I've got the full complement," he said. "And they're all mine, too, I paid for them. Or at least Mom did." He showed me most of them in a dazzling grin.

"I knew they were too good to be true," I said, catching sight of our quarry who was making his way carefully back down the aisle, a large paper cup in each hand. As soon as he'd sat down again and had taken a long swig, I put on my most dazzling grin, leaned toward him, and said, "Mr. William Gince, by any chance?" He jumped a foot in the air, which wasn't bad from a sitting start, spilling some beer on the shoulder of the man in front of him, who luckily didn't notice. I put one outsize mitt reassuringly on his arm and also to make sure he didn't try going anywhere in the immediate future.

"Now, now," I said. "Relaxez-vous, there's nothing to worry about, I just want a quiet word with you and I figured here'd be as good a place as any."

"Who the fuck are you?" he said.

"Well, if he's the ham," I said, pointing to Marlon, "I must be the glaze."

"What does that make me?" the twerp said.

"The sweet patootie," I said.

"Well I don't want a word with you here or anywhere," William said, "whoever the fuck you all are. Beat it or I'll call a cop."

"Spill any more of that suds on the guy in front and you'd probably get all you want without calling," I said.

"Fuck off!" he said.

"William," I said. "Calm down. I've come from your mom and sister, OK? That's show I knew where you were." Which wasn't totally untrue. "And if I was going to do anything unpleasant, like breaking both your legs with a goalie stick, which is the farthest thing from my mind, my associates and I would hardly have chosen the Forum as a meeting place, now would we?"

"How should I know," he muttered. "All I know is your fat fucking friend Fats must have sent you, right?"

"In a way," I admitted. "But he ain't no friend of mine, I can assure you."

"Oh, no?" he said. "So what d'ya want, then?"

"Maybe I can help," I said. "I hear you can use a little help these days."

"I bet," he said. "Help dump me in the river someplace." He stared gloomily into his paper cup, then thrust the second cup he was holding in my direction. "Here, fucker," he said. "I ain't thirty no more. Hope you choke on it."

"I hope it's hot cocoa." I said, taking the cup and peering into its depths. "Oh, darn, beer, but thanks anyway." I took a satisfying swallow. A roar went up as the teams skated back onto the ice. I felt William tense up; he started looking around furtively.

"No chance, William," I said, tightening my grip on his skinny arm. "Anyway, I've got Mrs. Leduc's attractive house over there on St. Michel staked out, too. Loved the snow-man next door." William sighed and slumped in his seat. The organist played a series of ascending chords, the crowd shouted encouragement. The second period got underway; we watched without talking for a minute. A dastardly Capital body-checked a Habitant from behind, sending him crash-ing into the boards. He bounced once, then lay still. William jumped to his feet. So did I, just in case.

"Jeez, did you see that!" he shouted. "Send the bum off!" He subsided into his seat again. I did likewise. The Washington player skated slowly off toward the sin bin to the boos of the crowd. The announcer said something in French. The crowd cheered. A minute later, the Canadiens, playing with the extra man, scored their third goal from a slap shot from just inside the blue line. The announcer said something in French again.

"Look at it this way, William," I said as soon as the cheer-ing had died down. "Worse shit you could not be in. It took me all of ten minutes to find out where you were, and if I could do it, so could someone else, someone a lot more unpleasant than I could ever be even in my wildest dreams." The twerp leaned up against me trying to listen in; I gave her a friendly shove away. "I'll tell you something else. Not only is Fats not a friend of mine, I do not like him overmuch. I don't trust him overmuch, either. I've taken his money for services performed once or twice but that doesn't mean he owns me. Or my brain. He did hire me to find you. When I did, I was supposed to let him know where you were. I found you. I have not yet let him know where you are, which is watching a hockey game from a seat so high up you got shown to it by a stewardess."

"How much?" William said then, finishing off the last of his beer. I did likewise.

"You mean how much not to let him know I found you?"

"Right on, bro'."

"How much you got?"

"I got a few bucks put away," he admitted.

"Saving up for a new car?"

"Saving up to buy off cheap fuckers like you," he said bitterly.

"Cheap is puttin' it mildly," the twerp tossed in. I ignored her uncalled-for and totally untrue interruption.

"As for how much, if you give one good reason why I shouldn't tell Fats where you're holed up, nothing is what it'll cost you, I'm already getting a fair whack out of Fats, or at least I hope I can get it out of his obese hide. It might cost you a bowl of moose stew somewhere, but that's all."

He peered at me suspiciously through his steel-rimmed specs, while I tried to look like the honest, upright, and well-meaning citizen I was. Then he took out a large red handkerchief and wiped both his face and his glasses. Then he crushed his empty paper cup with one foot. Finally he said, "They're with you, right?" indicating Marlon and Curly with a jerk of one thumb.

"Right. Their names are Marlon and Curly. Me, I'm Vic. They're just along for the ride, really, I do all the work." Sara gave me a dig in the ribs I could have done without.

"How many you got staking out the house?"

"Well," I said, "just that snowman, actually."

He gave me a small grin. "I figured," he said. "Give me a minute, will ya?"

"Take two, they're small," I said. Willing Boy leaned over to ask me how it was going. I gave him the thumbs up sign. William furrowed what there was of his brow and thought. Down on the ice the Capitals scored two goals in under a minute. The crowd was not pleased. The game was stopped briefly as a team of slaves with miniature snow plows cleared debris off the ice. The loudspeaker said something in a foreign language again.

Then William turned to me and said, "OK. You like good pastrami or would you rather go for the stew?"

"I'd kill for good pastrami," I said, "but I don't think the Stage Delicatessen in New York City delivers this far north."

"You got a surprise comin', bud," he said. "Now is it OK if we watch the rest of the game?"

"Vic," I said. "Not 'bud.' Or 'Prof.' "

"Will," he said. "Not 'William' or 'Willy.' "

"Sara," the twerp said. "Not 'Curly.' "

"George," Willing Boy chimed in. "Not 'Marlon,' please!"

"Shut up, you two, will you?" I said. "Some of us are trying to watch the game."

We watched.

We all had a beer, on me, but Sara, who had a hot dog and a Pepsi and then some potato chips and then began working her way through a pack of Wrigley's spearmint chewing gum. Les Habitants won it in the end, 6–4, and we all trouped out with the happy and only moderately rowdy fans into the chilly night air. Twenty minutes later we were installed at a table in a crowded eatery known as the New Ben's and ten minutes after that I was eating the best pastrami sandwich of my life, and I'm here to tell you a lot of pastrami has in my life passed under my expensive bridgework. The pickle was only the second best I'd ever eaten, my accountant Harry had a Polish cleaning lady whose dill pickles were beyond the stuff o' dreams.

Willing Boy was working away diligently at a huge plate of boiled beef 'n' cabbage, with a stack of potato pancakes on the side. Curly was daintily attacking a bowl of chicken soup that had little raviolis in it, and Will, like me, was well into the first of his two pastramis on rye.

"Why do they call pastrami smoked meat up here?" I inquired idly between large mouthfuls.

"They don't," Will said.

"Oh."

"They are two different things. Different things usually have different names, which is how you tell them apart."

"Oh. Marlon, don't hog the pickles."

After the cheesecake, when we were finally replete and had put in our order for three coffees and one tea, which came in a glass, for Sara, who always had to be different, I turned to Will and said, "Monsieur, I thank you, that was indescribably sensational. My associates thank you. Thank the monsieur, children." They thanked the monsieur profusely. "Now it's story time, kids, so gather round. Will, take it from the top. Take your time. Remember, we are your friends, and those that have broke rye bread together have broke rye break together."

"That almost makes sense," Will said. "OK. So what did Fats tell you?"

I told him what little Fats had told me, that there was this guy who couldn't come up with five big ones plus the vig who had taken off somewhere, and that the whole thing sounded fishy as hell to me, there had to be something else going on even if that much was true.

"That much is true," Will said, sipping at his coffee. "I couldn't even come up with the vig. I went to ask him to give

me another week. I'm sitting in that posh office of his beg-
ging when some drunken dame bursts into the front office
and starts carrying on with some punk out there. Fats goes
out to see what the fuck's goin' down."

"How come you went to a shark like Fats in the first
place, Will, if that's not too personal a question?"

"Stupidity," he said, "if that's not too personal an answer.
Guy named Benjy, supposed to know all the angles, he worked
at the garage where I did, he had it all worked out. He welded
a second gas tank inside the real one of his beat-up Chevy
he had, took him two whole nights after work, beautiful job.
He's got a solid connection in Tijuana all lined up, he's done
business with him before, this guy is gold, his merchandise
is first-class. We all kicked in what we could come up with, I
should'a got back twelve grand for my five plus the grand vig,
not bad for doing sweet F.A. for a few days,"

"No shit, Geronimo," said the twerp.

"So that's show come I was into Fats," Will said.

"Bet you a buck," I said, "the first place the federales
looked was the gas tank."

"Tell me about it, pal," he said disgustedly.

"Bet you guys," I said to the kids, "a buck Benjy isn't
where you think he is right now."

"He's gotta be in a Mexican jail, doesn't he, George?"
Sara said, sucking the slice of lemon from her tea.

"It would appear so," he said cautiously.

"Tell you what," I said magnamiously. "If I lose, I pay off
in U.S., if you lose, in Canadian." At that time the U.S. dollar was worth roughly a fourth more than a Canadian one.

"Deal," said Sara. "OK, Mr. IQ, where do you think he
is?"

"Elementary, my dear Miss Dunce," I said. "Somewhere
in the good old U.S. of A."

"Pay the man," Will said. "He's back workin' at the garage doin' lube jobs. That mother even told us he had a buy in San Diego lined up."

"Bet you he won't be for long," I said.

"Forget it," Sara said, counting me our four Canadian quarters.

The pretty waitress came by and said something in French to Willing Boy. He said something back to her in French. From the glare she got from Curly, you'd have thought she'd asked him to elope with her. She went away with a backward look over her shoulder at him. Not even my gray-haired mother ever looked at me like that.

"What led you to that brilliant deduction, Holmes?" Willing Boy asked.

"He just guessed," Sara said.

I smiled at the child. Ah, youth—so impetuous, so quick to come to totally false conclusions.

"If you know the angles, like Benjy was supposed to," I said, "what you do not do is anything remotely as stupid as making a big score in Tijuana, or any other border town, for that matter. Nor do you run the border in a beat-up old wreck, it is a mite obvious. And if you are dumb enough to run the border in a beat-up wreck, don't stash your dope in anything as trite as a false gas tank, a false brassiere— pardone me, Sara—would be better even, how old hat can you get? It's like a spy using a hollow heel. But the real, fundamental stupidity lies in making a big score next to the border in the first place. All the connection has to do is tip off the fuzz and he collects a reward from them, and also gets to stay in business. This is the main problem making a large buy anywhere."

"So. No one's that stupid anymore. If you know the angles, it's you who wants to wind up rich. What you do is find some hungry-looking federale, and I'm reliably informed that, although an endangered species these days, one or two still exist."

"Get on with it, why can't you," the twerp muttered, noisily finishing up the last of her tea.

"To cut a long story short, as I was about to, anyway," I continued, "Benjy has to protect his back in case one of his investors like Will, here, gets suspicious and stakes out the border and not with a snowman, either, which is what he needs the federale for, among other things. Either the federale, forewarned, or a pal of his at the border, likewise, stops Benjy on his way through."

"Benjy was smarter than that, even," Will said. "*He* suggested we have someone at the border just in case, so we did."

"Who sees Benjy get stopped, then sees the fuzz poking sticks into the gas tank, then sees Benjy taken away in handcuffs and his wheels driven off, presumably to a police garage to be taken apart in small pieces. A noche or two later when the tumult and the olés have died down, our friendly federale escorts Benjy quietly across the border and Benjy subsequently reports to you masterminds at the garage that he jumped bail or bribed a cop to get out or whatever."

"What happened to the dope?" Sara wanted to know.

"Never was any," I said. "Which is the real reason the cops let him go. True, he's out his wheels, five hundred bucks or so of beat-up Chevy, and whatever he donated to the federale's retirement fund, but I bet there was plenty left."

"We kicked in twenty-two grand altogether," Will said. "Masterminds, right?"

"So he's home free with like twenty thousand dollars," I said, "which is more than even I make for a couple of nights' work."

"You should'a heard him when he got back," Will said, "bitching and moaning because his precious wheels were trashed and describing what Mexican jails were like, would you believe that fucker even tried to get us to kick in some more bread to help cover what he claimed it cost to buy himself out? Anyway. I'm up at Fats'. I am not a happy man. I am dumb and unhappy, I hadn't even figured out that Benjy had scammed us, for Christ sake. There's this commotion. Fats takes his fat ass out and closes the door behind him. He's forgotten to lock the drawer he took my particulars out of, so I have a quick look, don't I, and there's this bowling bali bag pushed in the back so I unzip it and what d'ya think I spy?"

"Bet you a buck it wasn't a heavy, round, plastic ball with holes in it," I offered.

"Diet Coke for his lunch?" Sara said.

"Crack?" Willing Boy said.

"Hundred-dollar bills," Will said with an evil little grin. "Before I thought about it even I zipped it up again, closed the drawer, and chucked it out the window."

"Will," I said, "I've been underestimating you." I shook his hand warmly. "That was a brilliant idea. I presume it was caught by some passing wino who still can't believe his good luck. Pennies from heaven, OK, but century notes?"

"You lose," Will said. "It was caught by my good buddy Paco, who works at the garage with me pumpin' gas, he ain't a mastermind like me but he ain't afraid of nothin', neither, maybe 'cause he's always stoned out of his gourd. I brought him along just in case Fats started gettin' clever, like splashing my blood all over the woodwork. Paco takes off. I close and lock the window. I sit down. Now I am dumb, unhappy, and scared. They get rid of the drunk lady finally. Fats comes back in. I beg some more. He gives me another week but then the vig will be up to two grand. I thank him with tears in my eyes. I depart rapidly, makin' sure it's obvious my hands are empty all the way up to my neck, nor am I walkin' out lookin' like the hunchback of Notre Dame, either, with something large and round tucked under my shirt in the back. Paco and me meet up later at his pad, he lives with his mother down off Alverado. Inside that bowling ball bag there is sixty-two thousand five hundred dollars in used hundreds. I give Paco a little walking around money, not too much, like two-and-a-half bucks, 'cause like I said, Mr. IQ he ain't. If he's got money, he'll spend it won't he, 'cause that's what he thinks it's for, to buy stolen ghetto blasters a block long and maybe another plastic chandelier for his mother and get some more tattoos done on his sister.

"I make it home without once touching the ground. I pack in under a minute. I say good-bye, farewell, and adiós to the family and leave them Fran's number in case something comes up as it is bound to do sooner or later and probably sooner, and when it does, let me the fuck know so I can take off for like Nome, Alaska."

"Phew," I said.

"No wonder Fats is lookin' for you," the twerp said.

"I'm surprised the entire world isn't looking for you," Marlon said. He smiled up at the pretty waitress who had stopped by our table. She smiled back, leaned down, and gave me the bill, despite the fact the whole thing had been Will's idea, you will recall. Oh well; I guess waitresses do get pretty good at picking out who the big tipper is at a table.

I looked at the after-tax total and winced, then I remembered I did have an expense account, after all, and if a late-night snack at Ben's wasn't a legitimate business expense, what was in this troubled world. I relaxed and looked around—the place was still full; many of the patrons had obviously been at the game because they were still talking about it and about the Canadien's chances if they ever got to the Stanley Cup finals.*

"Is Fran in on any of this?" I asked Will.

He blushed and looked away.

"Ah," he said, "nah, she's just an old friend."

"Tell you what to do," I said, "so she'll go on believing in Santa Claus and the Easter Bunny, and Provigo. Get her a ten-pound glazed ham tomorrow and tell her you met the delivery truck up the street looking for her house and you wanted to save the kid a trip."

"Good idea," he said. "Listen, was that you, too, the other call I got from my sister, somethin' about havin' a baby?"

"Not me," I said. "That was the Mother of the Year Sara here."

"That'll be the day," she muttered darkly.

"What was all that about," Will asked.

I tried desperately to summon up a blush but failed.

"It seemed like a good idea at the time," I said weakly. Will looked puzzled, but let the matter drop.

"Got any more good ideas?" he said. "Like what the fuck we do now?"

"Why don't we send the kids home to some nice hot milk and then to bed," I said, counting out a lot of money to cover the bill, "and then perhaps you and I might retire to a friendly tavern and discuss that very subject at our leisure."

"OK by me," Will said. "I better call Fran first so she don't worry about me, like I been mugged or somethin'." He bustled off toward the phone at the back. The waitress departed with my money.

---

*Added by me later: Les Habitants (or familiarly, Les Habs) didn't get to the finals a few months later; they were knocked out in a preliminary round, by Buffalo! Or it might have been Hartford-who cares? Some hick town, anyway.

"I don't wanna go to bed, is there any night life in this town, George, can we go dancing maybe?"

"Stick with me, blue eyes," Marlon said in his Humphry Bogart voice. "And I'll dance your pretty feet off. Say goodbye to Will for us, will you?"

I said I would. They got up, collected their coats, scarves, and hat from the rack near the door, and left to dance their pretty feet off. Will returned, looking pleased about something. The waitress returned, looked around unsuccessfully for Lover Boy, probably to give my change to, then said, "*Attend*." I *attended*. She got out her order pad, scribbled a phone number and a name on it, tore out the page, then gave it to me, then gave me a wink. I winked back.

"*Pour lui*," she said.

"His name's Marlon, actually," I said, tucking both bills away carefully in my wallet. What a forward hussy. If she thought I was about to put any obstacle in the path of my dearest friend Sara's love affair, she could just think again, and besides, I had another use for that second bill. I wonder why she thought he was poor. I left her a sizable tip—two pinkbacks and the four quarters—and we got out of there.

Short minutes later we were comfortably installed in a first-floor *boîte* called the BC Lounge. At the far end of the room from us a black gentleman in a green tuxedo tinkled the ivories of a white upright, delicately improvising his way through that old Oscar Peterson favorite "Autumn Leaves." Someone once told me Mr. Peterson was a Canadian, but you can believe that if you want to. I was sipping a brandy and ginger ale, William nursing a scotch on the rocks and from time to time covertly eyeing two giggly matrons at the table next to ours who were enjoying their night out on the town.

"Sixty-two five," I remarked after a while, "is a considerable sum."

"Tell me about it," Will said.

"Which brings up again the interesting point, why did Fatso rope me in on it? It couldn't have been just my good looks. I take it, Will, that we both agree the money was dirty money because if it was clean, Fats could have called in the cops. Which leaves the question, or begs it, even, why did he not enlist the services of some of his many Italian or Sicilian associates?"

"Search me," said Will.

"I figure it was because he didn't want them to know he'd lost the money because it was theirs," I said. "Which thought came to me a minute ago in the men's room. We know Fats operates as a middleman between fuzz and felon, and versa vice. Say the sixty-two five was just another regular monthly payoff from one to the other. To sever the connection between the two, it makes a brief pit stop up at Fats' on the way. You better believe he won't want either one to hear he's carelessly mislaid their money—at best he's out of a highly lucrative job, at worst he's chucked off the roof of an extremely tall building."

"Without wings," said Will.

"Probably without a parachute, either," I said. "He's got to figure you copped his dough. If not you, who else? Also you took off immediately afterward, which was a bit of a giveaway, my friend."

"Better'n hangin' around and gettin' a few flying lessons myself," he said, "like one solo."

"He's got a chance," I said, "if he can find out where you are quick enough. The handover is likely this weekend because that's the deadline he gave me. What if he says, someone lifted the dough despite it being locked up and guarded. I found out who it was and I found out where the little fucker is, pardon my French. I wonder why they say that—fucker's not French, is it?"

"Probably international by now, like cornflakes," Will said.

" 'So,' " Fats says, 'I got a man watching him right now. Before I did anything, I thought it only correct to ask you, you want in, or you want me to handle it? I thought you might want in because you got your own highly individual means of discouraging such behavior because you like word to get out about exactly what'll happen to anyone who tries to cross you.' "

"Maybe," William said. "Maybe that's what I'd do if I couldn't come up with sixty-two five of my own in a hurry to replace what got took, if I could I'd keep my mouth shut about the whole thing."

"Giving you more time to go looking for the dirty rotten crook," I said. "But you don't want too much time to go by, because the more time that dirty, rotten little crook is out there with the money, the more time he's got to splurge on items like red roses for Fran and small vials of expensive liquids that smell good and crystals of carboniferous matter that sparkle."

"Aw, Jeez," Will said, looking away. The pianist began a dreamy rendition of "Satin Doll." I ordered us another round; Will insisted it was on him. I let him have his way out of politeness. The ladies next door did likewise. One of them smiled in a friendly fashion in our direction and waved a cocktail stirrer at us. I smiled back in a friendly fashion in their direction.

"If the money you chucked out the window so carelessly belonged to an aging widow," I said, "or was destined for a home for unwanted puppy dogs or some other good cause, that'd be one thing. As it is, I figure you've got as much right to it, or most of it, ahem, as anyone else. If you can hang on to it."

"Amen," said Will. "And lotsa luck, too."

"Oh, I dunno," I said. "All we have to do is get you off the hook, get your mother and sister off the hook, keep Fran out of it, and get me the rest of my money from the fat one."

"Is that all," he said, not looking any too happy.

"Don't worry, Will," I said, patting him on the arm, "I figure I can take care of all that, but there is one little thing you have to do for me. It's just a trifle, really, it shouldn't take you long."

"Like what?"

"Disappear from the face of the earth," I said, raising my refill to the ladies.

CHAPTER ELEVEN

Who was it who sang, cowgirls get prettier as the night gets later and the last dance nears? Well, cowboys must get better looking as well, otherwise me and Will wouldn't have had a chance with those two ladies from the adjoining table.

Their names were Valerie and Bonnie; they hailed from Lachute, wherever that was, and their husbands were up at Ste. Adele, wherever that was, for a curling bonspeil, whatever that was. Val, the shorter, latched on to me; Bonnie, a foot taller, to Will; ain't it always the case. Not that anything remotely resembling hanky-panky developed or, indeed, was ever considered, Evonne my little cabbage. All that did develop was two tables sort of merging into one and then a few laughs and a few drinks and even a dance or two. Will was a marvelous dancer and the ladies not far behind. If I've had just enough but not too much to drink, I can managed to make it through a slow fox-trot without stumbling too often if my partner is a good leader.

As for hanky-panky, I doubt I'd either hanky or panky with another woman even if I did have the chance. I have enough trade secrets from Evonne already without having that sort of monstrous secret between us; bad news. Bad manners, too, I've always thought. Evonne asked me once when we were not so idly badinanging back and forth what

I would do if she had a fling with someone else. I'd be very civilized about it, I said. I said, you're an adult and not bound to me by law, and I accepted that there were in the world a handful of males more handsome than me and, yes, even one or two sexier. Also, a little fling, one moment of madness, it could happen to anyone. If it did, I'd have a good cry. Then, if he was smaller than me, and the odds on that were pretty good, I'd beat the living shit out of the guy. And then, I told her, I would pull up every plant in her vegetable garden in alphabetical order, from aubergine to zucchini. And after that, I'd enlist in the Foreign Legion. What I would really do, aside from bleed through every pore, I do not know. I thoroughly hope I never find out.

It was just after two o'clock when the ladies went off in one cab, Will in another, and this dancing fool in a third. I went to sleep thinking about a line one of those long-stemmed, MGM tap-dancin' celluloid dolls once said: "I was just a pretty good hoofer who got a lucky break." My breaks should be so lucky.

The following icy Thursday morn found us in a sort of Dunkin' Donuts place in a huge underground complex of stores, restaurants, supermarkets, and what-have-you at Berri–De Montigny. The previous noche Will had suggested we meet there as it was roughly equidistant between our hotel and Mrs. Leduc's mansion and also he was determined that we got to see some of the sights of the city while we were still around. Frankly, well-traveled gent that I am, I have seen sights more awesome than a shopping mall down a tunnel, but I held my counsel for once. I had to admit it wasn't that stupid an idea; who wants to go sneering at summer squashes in an open-air market, no matter how picturesque it might be, during a Montreal winter, i.e., when it's so cold outside even polar bears fly down to Sarasota for the season.

Some kind soul had left behind a copy of the local English-language newspaper, the *Gazette*, on a nearby table. I glanced through it while fueling up for the day on blueberry muffins. By a coincidence, I'd telephoned the paper's main offices downtown earlier to pose a simply query or two and talked to a most helpful and amusing chap: I do believe Canada was starting to grow on me. Among other items of world import, the *Gazette* informed me that the pretender to the French throne, the would-be King Charles XII, had three children and was selling real estate in Stouffville, Ontario.

When I put the paper away, I said to Will, "I have a present for you." I took out a scrap of paper from my wallet and read out, "Ministère des Affaires Sociales. Hotel du Government—Population Register—Québec." I handed it over.

"*Merci beaucoup*," he said, taking it. "And what am I supposed to do with it now I got it?"

"I can think of something," the twerp said.

"Don't be vulgar, Sara," I said. "Birth certificate, Will. That's where you write to get one, the guy at the *Gazette* told me."

"I already got one," Will said.

"That's where you get your new one," I said. "Your new name, too."

"I'm not with ya," he said.

"Will, what did we decided last night, aside from deciding to offer the ladies one last drink?"

"What ladies?" said the twerp immediately.

"None of your business," I said. "I didn't pry into what you two got up to last night, did I?"

"Me and the little lady went dancing," Marlon said. "On Crescent Street, man, has that changed, it's jumping these days."

"Yeah, if you like shitty discos playing crappy songs that were already out of date when I was still wearing rubber underwear," Sara muttered. "And chicks with more makeup than brains, wearing plastic miniskirts and phony-looking hairpieces and phonier falsies trying to butt in all the time." She shot Marlon a hurt look. He looked innocently gorgeous.

"Disappear, Will, remember?" I said hastily. "How do you think you do that?"

"Jeez, I dunno," he said. "I ain't no magician."

"He is," Sara said. "When it comes to getting out of picking up the tab." All right, she was upset about something, was that any reason to lash out at me with her petulant slanders?

"Let me ask you another question," I said calmly. "When Fats comes looking for you again, as he well might do whatever I tell him, maybe in a year or two, how will he go about it?"

Will thought for a minute, then shrugged.

"He's not going to post men at every train station, airport, and bus station in the western world, is he. How could he, where would he get the manpower from. The cops just might be able to, but even if he could get them to look, you're not going to look like you anymore, are you, you're going to have contact lenses, maybe a sportly little mustache, and your hair another color. What Fats'll do is think like this: sooner or later you'll show up back in the States, if you aren't still there, because your money won't last forever and you'll get tired of Rio or wherever you are and want to go home. So he'll hire some bright kid in a year or two and pay him a couple of grand and that kid will plug his computer into every credit card system, every airline booking system, maybe every bank, looking for traces of one William Something Gince, which isn't that common a name, by the way."

"William V. Gince," Will said. "*V* for Vincent."

"Perfect," I said. "So that's why you need a new name, mon ami. And a new name starts with a new birth certificate. A name alone's no good, you can't get a driver's license, open a bank account, sign up for Blue Cross, get Social Security, fly abroad, and a million others, without ID. I happen to know this guy, a friend of a friend, who could provide you with all the ID you'd ever want or need, including a valid passport. The whole package, including credit cards and army discharge papers, would set you back something like two or three grand, depending. My way costs you five Canadian bucks."

"Settled," said Will, giving my hand a fervent shake.

"Go up to the *Gazette* office," I said. "They got a back issues room that's open to the public, I checked. Go through the recent obituaries. And the 'In Memoriam' announcements—the problem with those is they don't usually give you a place of birth, which is what you're going to need, along with the names of both parents, to apply for a new certificate. Find someone roughly your own age who died recently. You might even be lucky enough to find someone with the same first or middle name as yours, to make it easier for you and close friends like Fran. You write the funeral home that's mentioned in the obit. You say you think the deceased might be an old army buddy or school pal of yours and would like to send the family your condolences, but as you don't want to impose by making a mistake, would the funeral home please send you in the enclosed stamped envelope the date and place of the deceased's birth. Once you have that, you drop a line to the address I gave you ear-lier, enclosing the necessary pittance, and there you are, in business, with your very own, legitimate birth certificate. Canadian, but legitimate."

"I like it," Will said, leaning forward eagerly.

"I don't," the twerp, who had been listening carefully, said.

"Me neither," I said. "Why don't you?"

"So he tried to get a credit card in his new name," she said, "and they see he's already got one with a big *D* for dead under where it says 'withdrawn for what reason?' How does he apply for a driver's license if he doesn't know whether or not he's already got one? Likewise a passport? Likewise God knows what else?"

"Good girl!" I said warmly, patting her curls. She scowled at me. Willing Boy grinned, took out his foot-long comb, and began running it lovingly through his blond locks. In the following half-minute or so I told Will how to obtain a birth certificate without the build-in defects of the other. What you do is apply in the name of some child who unfor-tunately died before the age of five, say, the theory here being that although the old obituary will not mention, or may not mention, where the child was born, just when, it is surely odds on that, at such a young age, the birth occurred in the same county where the child died. Anyway, Will now had a choice—he could nip south of the border and deal with the appropriate county or state officialdom, after hav-ing perused back issues of a local rag there, or he could go fast, Canadian, cheap, and no traveling required, but end up with a limited product. I love choices, as long as it's oth-ers who have to make them.

"Either way," I said. "Don't wait too long. I'll try to put Fats off for a while but for all I know he's got someone else on your trail right now, we could even have been followed here. We weren't," I said quickly, before Will started panicking. "While these two were taking in the sights I was keeping my eyes wide open on our backs the whole time, except for when the pastrami came."

"And when you were buying ladies drinks they probably had too many of already," said Guess Who, and it wasn't me, Marlon, Will, the voice of Christmas past, or the waiter, who chanced by then to see if we wanted more of anything. Just the bill, please, I told him. And if the above quiz proved too difficult for you, try figuring out who he presented the bill to when he returned; I was afraid to look at the back of it in case he'd scribbled his phone number down for me. The damn thing was useless for expense purposes as it had both the name and the address of the donut joint on it, unlike the one from Ben's; I'd gone to considerable pains to hide from any potential prying eyes the fact that we three had made a side trip out of New York and I wasn't about to blow Will's whereabouts that stupidly. Besides, I had a drawerful of old restaurant bills at home I could have a look through for a suitable replacement.

After I'd settled up, we all hoped *le métro* back to Mrs. Leduc's. Will wanted us to meet her, for one thing, and I had a little business left to finish up with Will. The snowman was still there, but someone had knocked his head off. The entryway to Mrs. Leduc's was littered with boots, overshoes, rubber boots, shoes, even a snow shovel, for the path, I guessed; we all added our footware to the clutter before Will led us into the front room. On the way he shouted out back, "Fran! I'm home!"

After a minute Fran, in plaid trousers, a hand-knitted-looking heavy red sweater, and woolly slippers fashioned to look like pink bunny rabbits, came in to join us. Despite her name, her ancestry was Scottish and Irish, she informed us as she bustled around making us comfortable. Ignoring my protests that we could only stay a minute, she insisted we all take our coats off, which we did, then she whisked them off to the coatrack by the front door, then went out to the kitchen to heat up the pea soup, I guessed. The kids parked themselves in a huge old sofa, me beside them in an old, high-backed armchair with an antimacassar even. Then Will said, "Back in a minute," and he took himself off, leaving us to twiddle our thumbs and feast on the visuals, of which I will only mention six porcelain cats in descending sizes sitting in the fireplace, a draft excluder in the form of a snake stretched along the bottom of the front bay window, and a great deal of contemporary jig-saw puzzles that had been glued on to a backing and then framed, the other half paint-by-number landscapes of Canada in autumn. The kids started giggling and pointing out various high spots of decor to each other; I told them to can it.

Will came back then, beckoned me into the hall, looked nervously over his shoulder, and handed me a well-stuffed envelope. I tucked it in a back pocket without looking inside.

"For you, pal," he whispered. "Least I can do."

"*Merci beaucoup*," I whispered back, giving him a pat on the head as he led the way into the living room again. The kids were still giggling.

"What's so funny?" Will wanted to know.

"Aw, just something he said," the twerp lied. "What were you two doin', helping Fran bake a cake?"

"Will had a little surprise for me, more a souvenir, really," I lied. "A program from the game last night, I forgot to get one." If the envelope did turn out to contain a folded up Les Canadiens program from the game last night, or any

night, I thought, Nome, Alaska, would not be far enough
for Will; Mars would not be far enough.

Mrs. Leduc, flushed and a little excited to have unexpected guests, I suppose, returned then, carefully pushing
a well-laden serving cart in front of her. Will immediately
offered to help but was waved off. She poured us all tea in
fluted blue teacups with gilt handles, then insisted we all try
a slice of her Cinderella cake, whatever that was. Then she
handed us all dainty embroidered napkins for us to dab our
lips with. The kids looked at each other again.

"It is a pleasure, Mrs. Leduc, to be offered tea that is
not only served correctly, but in such a lovely old service,"
I said. "Out in the jungle where we come from, if someone
dropped in without warning, like we did, they'd be lucky to
get warm instant coffee in a used paper cup."

Fran accepted the pretty compliment gracefully, checking with one hand the back of her recently permed coiffure.
If the younger generation felt suitably abashed, they hid
it well. I remembered that I needed to know if Will had a
passport; I asked him casually and he said he did. I couldn't
think of anything else I wanted to know that might be useful in the future, so I then asked him if, from his side of it,
there were any details we hadn't covered. Again, I did so in
a casual fashion as Mrs. Leduc was supposed to be ignorant
of her sweetheart's latest escapade, and we three had been
introduced to her as acquaintances from out west who had
amazingly run into each other at the game. If she had any
suspicions, she kept them to herself.

Will thought we'd pretty much covered everything. In
that case, I said, could Sara kindly use their phone to make
us airline reservations as unfortunately business was calling
and we would have to tear ourselves away from the joys of
Canada in April and their hospitality almost immediately.

"Help yourself," said Will. "It's in the hall."

"I'll do it," Marlon said quickly, untangling his long legs and getting to his feet. "As soon as possible, right?"

"Right," I said. He left. I wondered vaguely why Willing Boy had volunteered as I had noticed he was deeply inclined to let girls do the chores for him, and did they ever. Whether this is a character trait of the very handsome, or the actor, or both, I am not in a position to state from personal experience.

We made small talk until he returned—about Canada, about Canadian weather, about California, about Californian weather. Mrs. Leduc said she'd met Will (who she called William, by the way) in Cleveland when she was in her final year of nursing college, it was so many years ago she shuddered to think about it. William was an ambulance driver then, she said, and the cutest little thing you ever saw in that cap he had that was too big for him. The whereabouts of a Mr. Leduc was not mentioned.

"Aw, Jeez, Fran," Will said happily.

Marlon returned just after Fran told us about winning the ham. Really! we said. Imagine that!

"It's all set," he reported. "The flight leaves at two-fifteen, plenty of time to go back to the hotel and make it to Dorval. With the time change in our favor, that means L.A. by eight-thirty this very night." He made a small bow.

Soon after, we made our reluctant good-byes, offered our profuse thanks, got invited back anytime, then began donning our snow gear again in the front hall. Will wrapped his Canadiens scarf around my neck as a farewell present. I still have it, I ran across it the other day on the top shelf of the clothes' cupboard, wrapped around a shoe box hidden from Mom in which I keep my junior G-man disguise kit, such as it was. I know she wasn't living with me anymore but so what, you don't stop hiding things from people just because they aren't around any longer. They both waved us good-bye from the porch. I detoured into the next yard, jammed the head back on the snowman, sneakily made a snowball, and let it fly at the back of Sara's toque, missing it by a whisker. By the time she had whirled around I was looking innocently up into the clouds, whistling aimlessly.

The fight began in *le metro*, continued in the lobby of the hotel, in the elevator and down the hall to our rooms, and was still going on twenty minutes later when we met up again downstairs, luggage all packed and ready to go. Now, as in the envelope given me by Will there resided the tidy sum of $2,500 in used U.S. hundreds, and I was not about to inform the kids of this, some may think the fight just referred to was one between me and my ever-watchful conscience. This was not the case. Some others might surmise that the spat in question was the one that occurred while checking out, between me and le desk clerk over a "trifling error" in the bill, a thousand regrets, monsieur. This was not the case, either, this was but a sideshow, a minor engagement, while the real battle raged on between George and Sara.

George started it all by putting on his most boyish and guileless look and then saying how sorry he was he couldn't take the same plane as us but he'd promised his mom he'd visit her while he was in Canada.

"Why can't Mom see both of us at the same time?" Sara responded. "She losing her vision all of a sudden?"

"Aw, come on, Sara," Marlon said. "Don't be like that. I told you she wasn't well."

"Did you?" she said. "You could have fooled me. When was that, anyway, last night when you spent so much time dancing with Tits McGurk, whatever her name was?"

"Who knows what her name was," he said. "So I danced with her once, look, I'll never see her again, will I?"

"You sure saw enough of her last night," the poor twerp said out of the side of her mouth. "All the way down to her curlies. I'm surprised your eyeballs didn't fall in. 'Oooh, I just love your hair!' " she mimicked. "I've seen better-looking hair in my soup."

And so it went. Of course I felt sorry for Sara but what was I supposed to say—"It was bound to happen sooner or later anyway, kid," or "Suffering is the food and drink of the poetic soul"? I did lower the temperature slightly by telling them they each had five hundred bucks bonus coming as soon as we got back to L.A., but otherwise I shut up and kept shut up. She simmered down enough to let him peck her cheek in the lobby before we headed out the back way to the car and he out the front supposedly to catch a train to Quebec City. But I did not have the gayest of companions during the drive back to Dorval, in fact she uttered nary one word to me the whole time although she did swear a lot under her breath when she wasn't grinding and gnashing her molars in ire. Occasionally she scribbled fiercely in a notebook or diary or whatever it was.

Even without a copilot to navigate and translate, I managed to find the airport in plenty of time. I returned the car to Avis, paid the bill in used. American hundred-dollar bills, which did not particularly please Avis, for some reason, then got us seat reservations at the check-in counter. As the guy at Canadian customs was waving us through, he asked in a friendly fashion, "Enjoy your stay, folks?"

"It was the pits," the twerp mumbled, but luckily not loud enough for anyone but me to hear. I pushed her on ahead.

"Very much so, eh, Inspector," I said, and I wasn't only thinking of capital gains. "The people were great, Montreal was great, your beer was great, the smoked pastrami meat unbelievable, and Les Habitants won the night I was there. I've made my last moose joke, I can tell you that."

He laughed. I wrapped my scarf tighter around my neck and hurried after the unhappy little nerd. I meant what I said about Canada, too, but I did have my fingers crossed behind my back when I made that promise about le moose.

Chapter Twelve

"Take away the moose," I declaimed theatrically, "and what is left?"

Sara opened one eye, glared at me out of it, then shut it again. We were in an airplane somewhere over Kentucky. High over Kentucky. I went back to what I was doing and had been doing for the last two hours and when Sara found out what it was, she'd spring a gusset. I, V. (for Victor) Daniel, was writing a poem for a change, in the hope it might cheer her up a bit. I'd already tried losing to her on purpose at cards, not an easy task for this competitive big fella, and that hadn't worked, but at least she'd said something occasionally, even if it was only "Gin, dummy," or "Read 'em and weep, stoopid." The rest was pretty much silence, except for the time she suddenly blurted out, "I *saw* that conniving bowlegged moose-faced dog flirting with him. I may be dumb but I ain't blind yet."

For a moment my heart stopped.

"What dog was that, dear?" I asked cautiously.

"The dog at the dance, where else," she muttered. "And I saw his flirting right back with knobs on it."

"Oh, that dog," I said with relief. "Miss McGurk, I believe you said her name was. Hell, she was probably only giving him the name of some new herbal shampoo. Anyway, actors flirt all the time just to keep in practice, they don't mean anything by it. So do girls, come on."

"Oh yeah?" she said. "Well, this girl doesn't. And how would you know, anyway?"

"How would I know? I know more about girls than you ever will, that's how."

She gave a little smirk.

I smirked back. "All right, Miss Clever Boots," I said, "who's dated more girls, me or you? Who's danced with more girls, necked with more girls, been stood up by more girls, dreamed about more girls? Not you, I bet." She sighed deeply and turned her back pointedly on me. Poor old twerp. Poor old Marlon, too; what a fate, having women throwing themselves at you every time you go out of the house; no, thank you.

That had been well over an hour ago and since then, out of her—zilch. Hence my new line of approach to attempt to rouse her even briefly from her bed of woe. How hard could it be to write a poem, anyway? Noodlehead did it all the time. Now let's see . . . what rhymes with moose?

We were somewhere over Nevada when I handed her the finished product. Perhaps it could have used a touch more polish, maybe the meter was slightly flawed here and there, mayhap there was the occasional loose rhyme and a couple of words still to be filled in, but it was still better than her junk, and it had only taken me five-and-a-half hours to write.

"What's this shit?" she wanted to know when I handed it over.

"Naught but a little poetical pick-me-up," I said carelessly. "But please do not think I am trying to butt in to your professional territory, I'm strictly an amateur."

"You can say that again," she said. Actually, I had composed one other poem in my life, for a Valentine's card, when I was about ten. I can't remember all of it but I remember rhyming *pink* with *stink*. Here follows my second (and

last) endeavor in verse form. Please note the use of capital
letters and proper punctuation:

There was a day
There were no rules on what to say.
The whole world was a comic's oyster.
From his something something cloister
A gagster could let rip at Frogs,
Yids, and mooses, Litvaks, Wogs,
Chevies containing just one Mex
And them of indeterminate sex.

And when the last laff had been sought
From Limey, Paddy, and the Scot,
When the final giggle got
From Polish Pope and Hottentot,
There was always ah, the ladies,
The one who had so many babies . . .
The one who liked her mustard hot . . .
Who made it with the astronaut . . . .

No more male jokes re Adam's rib,
Not since the rise of Woman's Lib.
To the subject of the fairer sex we've put paid
As male chauvinism today can (a) get you in
    serious trouble
And (b) seriously unlaid.

What's left for the fool to make fun of:
Mooses, and himself, except that's already
    been done
By the King o' Comedy up above.

Hey, take a look at me.
I'm a scream. Kiddies wee
Their panties when I amble by.
"Where's your hoop and net?" they cry.
"Do noses like that really run
In your family?" The fun's been done;
There is no more to make.
So I think I'll take
Up tragedy, like Zeus.
Long live the moose!

Sara read it all the way through in total silence and without once changing her expression. Then she handed it back to me, then she burst into tears.

"That bad, eh," I said. "I know I'm no Dorothy Parker, but still."

"It's not that," she said. 'It's just, oh, like everything." I put my arm around her and she had a good cry into my shoulder. The stewardess came by and arched her eyebrows at me as if to ask, is she all right? I nodded back reassuringly and tried to look like it wasn't my fault. I remember thinking the last time anyone had cried on that shoulder it had been her too, after she found out that her real mother was dead; the people who'd raised her, the Silvetti's, were her adoptive parents. Lucky she had me around from time to time is all I can say.

The plane landed, finally. I ungritted my teeth and we alit, me and weepy Sara, into hazy warmth. I retrieved my car from the hotel parking lot without problem and without handing over any money and northward we went. A quiet drive later I dropped the poetess off at her apartment building and drove east to Windsor Castle Terrace, where I lived and Mom used to until last year. It was a little late to call her at the retirement home she was in, so I put it off until tomorrow. I did call Evonne, but she was out. I unpacked, puttered around for a bit, turned the TV on and then switched it off again, then said to myself, oh, the deuce with it! and popped around the corner to Jim's bar, the Two-Two-Two, for a couple of large brandies and ginger ale. I needed something to rinse the taste of the airline's Bloody Marys out of my mouth and unfortunately I was fresh out of mouthwash at home.

I had a quiet think, too, in Jim's, about what to say to Fatty the next day. If he was still in circulation, that is, and not already encased in solid cement twenty feet under some new freeway extension. Maybe tomorrow, Friday, I wouldn't even open up the office, just do whatever errands I had to do first, then see Fats, then take the rest of the day off. That way a certain lilac-eyed stunner wouldn't be able to get hold of me and send me off to slay dragons for her in the wilds north of Oakland. The last thing I needed was to become foolishly involved with her; one love-bitten, long-suffering wreck in the family was more than enough. So stay on your guard, Daniel, the heart is a wayward child, obeying mysterious rules of its own. Right. Now you're thinking.

Hell, if I collected from Fats, what with Will's contribution, I wouldn't even need another job right away. So: Man/Tana sleep in late. Do expense sheet. Errand(s). Fats. Leisurely lunch at Fred's. Get bet down on Les Habitants winning the cup. Siesta. Evonne. Candle-lit supper. Evonne. Late snack. Evonne.

I got to the office Friday just on opening time, which, as the sign on my door said, was ten o'clock weekdays and weekends by appt. I might even have been a bit early, who knows, but it's me who pays the rent, I can open when I want to. And if that lying petticoat did call, boy was she going to get a piece of my mind.

The phone rang once that morning. I answered it by saying coolly, "Victor Daniel here," but it was only some hustler—an out-of-work thespian, he sounded like—trying to peddle me ball-point pens or key chains with my name or company logo on them; I suggested he stick his rubbish up a narrow, dark passageway. There was nothing in the accumulated mail to occupy me for longer than it took to chuck it all in the wastepaper basket under the desk, so I got to work on the expense sheet for Fats. Who said art is dead? I even scribbled out a receipt, in pencil, from a mythical cab driver called Ramón, dated yesterday, for $7.45. And I did manage to find an old bill I could use to replace the unusable one from Dunkin' Donuts. When I was done, the total came to a tidy $1,244.50. Most, if not all of the entries were backed up with stubs and receipts and the like, which I neatly stapled to the expense sheet after I had neatly retyped it. Well, it soon adds up, what with the plane fares, the cabs, including the one Sara took in L.A., various bribes, all those long-distance phone calls, airport parking fees, meals and so on. I had to swallow our plane fares back and forth to Montreal, unfortunately, as that leg of the journey was our little secret. Added to the expenses of course was the five hundred dollars remaining of my fee—all right.

The phone didn't ring.

I phoned the home about eleven but Mom was not available, I was told; why, I was not told. I called Evonne at her school and she was available. She was also available that evening, she informed me, but it meant breaking her date with Clint Eastwood. I laughed heartily. She said she had a "welcome home" present for me. "Was it bigger than a breadbox?" I asked her. I had a present for her, too, I'd bought at the last minute at Dorval—no, not moose paté—some real maple syrup to put on the waffles she made once in a while if I promised to wash the waffler afterward. I'd promise almost anything for her waffles. I had a present for Sara, too, that I bought when she wasn't looking, a book of ballads by that terrific Scottish versifier Robert Service, who writes those great poems about the Canadian northwest like "The Cremation of Sam McGee" and the one about the lady who was known as Lou. I hoped she'd learn something from it about real poetry.

I rang Fats, told him I had news and made a date to pass by his office after lunch. I called John D. at the Valley Bowl just to shoot the breeze; we shot it until he had to go back to work. I tried the Lewellens and got the runaround again.

The morning dragged on. The phone didn't ring. I stuck it out till twelve-thirty or so, then closed up shop and strolled down to Fred's Deli for some brain food, i.e., cream cheese on toasted raisin twice, a slab of peach pie, and a large glass of buttermilk. Two-to-One Tim was propped up in his customary booth just inside the front door; I joined him for a minute. He remarked he hadn't seen me around for a few days. I said that was because I hadn't been around for a few days, I'd been closeted with back issues of the *Sporting News* but now I was ready to plunge. He wanted to know what kind of plunge I was interested in taking. Fifty on the Dodgers, fifty on Les Canadians, I said, both to go all the way.

Tim whistled through his teeth, of which he had just enough left to whistle through.

"Dunno if I can handle that much action, Vic," he said. "I might have to lay part of it off."

I grinned. We haggled good-naturedly about the odds; you could always haggle over the odds with Tim, but it was odds on it would get you where it got me—nowhere.

After lunch I walked the two blocks to the travel agency my pal Ron owned half of and caught him just as he was going out for his lunch. Ron Rogg was an obliging, mild-mannered, corpulent gent of some forty summers, who had a fondness, or is it weakness, for embroidered waistcoats and tartan caps; he'd been Evonne's travel agent before becoming mine as well. On the wall behind his desk was a glass-fronted cabinet containing a tiny portion of his collection of hand-painted, lead toy soldiers, all from the Napoleonic era, about which he'd bore you stiff given the slightest opening.

Ron had half my requirements already waiting—first-class round-trip L.A.–New York TWA ticket stubs. It took him but a minute or two to provide the other item I needed, and then photo copy it; he wouldn't take a dime for it, either, sterling chap that he was. I paid for the tickets with plastic, winked at Evie, the lucious signorina at the next desk who'd been with him at least as long as I had, then Ron went for his belated lunch and I drove downtown to Fats'.

I was prepared for Fats. I was even prepared for Fats if he was prepared for me in some sneaky way. I was wearing a lightweight white cotton jacket over my Hawaiian shirt, with my wallet in the inside breast pocket. I had my story together, with documents to prove it, I hoped, and I had that more-than-together expense sheet.

After ten minutes of circling the block his office was on, plus a few adjoining ones, I finally left the car in an official parking lot; what the hell, this was no time to quibble over a few bucks. Five, actually; those bandits.

Fats buzzed me in and I went up. The front office was empty except for the water cooler, which was also empty. I continued on to the inner office, where Fats was relaxing in his favorite armchair.

"Where's Legs Diamond, Jr.?" I said. "Out playing marbles with the other kids?"

"Dunno," Fats said. "I think he went back to Chi. He kept complaining there wasn't enough weather out here."

"Better no weather than what Chicago gets," I said, sinking into the chair opposite him and laying the folder with my paperwork on the glass table in between us.

"Fats," I said. "here it is. I got some good news and some bad news."

"I hate conversations that start like that," he said. "Dom DeLouise, you know him? Comic right? Heard him once say in Vegas his wife once started a conversation with him like that. The good news was she was leaving, the bad news not till next week."

I smiled, although you well know by now that I am not particularly fond of any humor based on antifeminism.

"The good news is," I said, "I found William Gince."

"No shit," Fats said. "How?"

"By spending two days with my assistant in a small room at Kennedy Airport in New York, New York."

"So where is William Gince?"

"Ah," I said. "Thought I'd hold that little detail till I laid the bad news on you."

I opened up the card folder and tossed him the expense sheet, and receipts appertaining, to which I'd added the ticket stubs from Ron.

"Voilà," I said. "That's French for something."

Fats examined the sheet, occasionally checking an entry against one of the bills. He looked at the scribbled cab receipt from "Ramón" with particular distaste.

"I know, I know," I said. "Guy could hardly speak English, let alone write it." Fats passed to the next item. "Airport bus into town," I said. "For two of us, twice, a lot cheaper than a cab. And please note there's no hotel receipt for the night we spent in New York, we stayed with friends of mine, what the hell, why run up your bill needlessly?"

"Thanks a million," he said. Too bad it's so hard to fake hotel bills these days as they are all computer printouts. I wondered if my PC couldn't produce a passable imitation of one if I knew how to do it and had the appropriate stock. Certainly something to look into on a rainy day.

Fats had a few additional queries but his heart wasn't really in it; with surprisingly little reluctance he took out his wad and peeled me off $1,244, plus the $500.

"And fifty cents, please," I said, tucking the bills away in my wallet and replacing it in the jacket pocket.

"Excuse me," he said, digging out the change and dropping it on the table. "Now, if there's nothing else—maybe you hired a helicopter and forgot to tell me—where is that little welsher Gince?"

I took out the one slip of paper remaining in the folder and flicked it across the table. "That's what took two days to get," I said untruthfully; it had taken five minutes at Ron's. It was a photocopy of an airline ticket he'd made out for me on a proper Air France ticket form, and it revealed that one William Gince had taken Air France flight 229 to Paris three days ago and from there had gone on to Rome, or at least he had been ticketed to, the following day. Fats looked it over, then looked me over; there was not a lot of warmth in his regard.

"Two days," I said bitterly. "You know how many flights leave Kennedy? About one a minute, I almost went blind. And I had to call in outside help. I might've been able to persuade one airline to give me access to their recent passenger lists by telling them some yarn about trying to check on a friend I missed contact with at the airport, but not them all. A New York cop I know helped me out; it cost, check the expenses; he and a security type at Kennedy split four hundred, but it got us into a small room, it got us two computers to use, and it got us all the access codes. Did you know passenger lists aren't alphabeticized? I do, now." (Whether they really are or not, who does know, or care.) "What we were checking on was every flight out of the country since Tuesday; there was only about a million. If we came up empty, then we planned to cover all interior flights we had time for, although as Willy could have used any name for one of those, good luck."

"How did you know he was in New York?" Fats said.

"From his sister," I said. "I went to see her. She heard him phoning for a reservation L.A.—New York. She told me he had a passport that he took; the whole family got them at the same time to go to England one vacation. London was so quaint, she said. And so old!"

"So I heard," Fats said. "Maybe she knows where he is now."

"No way," I said firmly. "Know what she said when her mom was in the kitchen making us all a nice cup of tea? See, I didn't know how much Willy might have told them about the fix he was in, but they sure knew something was rotten in Denmark, he took off so quickly, he didn't even tell his boss where he worked he was going. I convinced them I was a friend, like his only hope, and there could be serious consequences for him if I couldn't get in touch with him before some far-less-friendly types got to him. Sis was practically crying by then. What she said was she only wished she could help but Willy had deliberately not told them where he was going so no one would come bothering them, there'd be no reason – least he could do was try and keep them out of it." I hoped Fats believed me because that was my plan, too. "Oh, yeah, he did say that if anyone did hassle them he had a way of finding out about it and he'd drop the fuzz a line, naming names. But hell, Fats, you wouldn't go bothering a widow lady and her only daughter, now would you?"

"Perish the thought," Fats said.

"But I'm a mite confused, Fats," I said. "What's he running all the way to Roma and, who knows, Singapore and points east, over a few measly grand? It must have cost him half that for his plane fare, for God's sakes."

"With small-time crooks like that, who can figure," he said.

"Who indeed?" I said.

"So that's it, eh?" he said.

"That's about all she wrote," I said. "But I do have an idea. He's not going to stay away forever, what's he going to do, and on what? He'll probably be back in six months with a dose of yellow fever or something. He's also probably too dumb to change his name even if he knows how, so what you do is wait awhile, then get some hotshot kid to run a computer trace on him. If you don't know anyone, I can put you in touch with a guy I know, Phil the Freak, who is frankly unbelievable, he taught me what little I know about computers when I got mine. Ever tell you I call it Betsy? That's the same name Davy Crockett, king o' the wild frontier, gave his favorite rifle."

"Live and learn," Fats said. He got to his feet and wandered over to the window. He didn't seem particularly upset by my news, but then that was one of Fats' few, if not only, redeeming characteristics, you never saw him get upset about anything.

"Right on!" I said brightly, getting up as well. "Sorry you're out the five grand, Fats, but I did my best and, like the man said, win some, lose some." I patted my breast pocket reassuringly, then departed. He didn't bother to wave me good-bye.

I paused briefly on the stairs outside, readjusted my personal belongings slightly, and descended, whistling.

It was only a few minutes' stroll to the car park; I waved at the guy in the booth and headed toward the back of the lot where I'd left my Nash. Just as I was unlocking the door, I got jumped by the punk kid from Fats' office—who had a new pig-sticker, I couldn't help noticing—and a tough-looking black kid in some flashy gang jacket who was brandishing a tire iron; they poured out of a black Ford that had been following me ever since I'd left Fats'. Which is why, I suppose, he hadn't waved at me, he was too busy waving at them. There's one I owe you, Fats.

Well, there are times to get tough and times to get moving. I got moving. "No! Please!" I screamed at the top of my voice as I was rolling over the hood to the far side of my car. 'Here! Take my money!" I threw my wallet at them and took off, sprinting for the entrance and people and crowded streets. They followed a few steps, then went back and collared the wallet, then jumped into the Ford and screeched after me. I ducked down a line of cars trying to figure out what to do if they followed; they didn't, which was lucky for someone, probably me. The front gate was up; they flew through it, hung a right, and disappeared into the traffic. I got up from my crouch, dusted my hands, and made my way briskly back to my car. I took off immediately, not thinking it would be all that smart to linger. When I was well away from the area, I pulled over to calm down and count my losses.

Which were: one two-dollar wallet, bought at a yard sale. One American Express credit card, in my name, reported lost or stolen by me a while back when I had merely misplaced it and had found it again the next week. Hopefully, the punk would try to use it, maybe to buy a sword this time. Also included: nine fake twenty-dollar bills, but good fakes, good enough so maybe the dynamic duo would try passing a few of them; a photo of Sandra Dee, which was in the wallet when I bought it: one used, slightly greasy, comb; and a perfectly genuine U.S. one-dollar bill. Too bad the boys were in such a hurry; they could have been the new owners of my elegant Rolex Oyster timepiece as well. Evonne bought it for me on a street corner that time we visited Mexico together. I recall we had been slightly suspicious as to whether or not it was the real thing as *oyster* was spelt "oister", and even I knew that was wrong. Also the price, forty-five thousand pesos, translated into American dollars, comes to two of them, plus fifteen cents. Roughly. So children, your nature lesson for today is—in the jungle, watch your ass.

I drove home without hitting anyone, or anyone hitting me, and without seeing any trace of the black Ford. I'd just retrieved Fats' contribution to the family exchequer from my back pocket, where I'd so wisely transferred it outside Fats' office, when the phone rang. I picked it up.

"Hi," a husky voice breathed. "It's me."

"Hi, you," I breathed back. I might even have breathed something more inane, like, "Hi, me." As Curly would put it:

> That poets are fools, 'tis well known,
> When Helen of Troy is on the phone.

"So you're back," she said. "I've been trying to get you."

"No, I'm not back," I said. "You're lucky to catch me at all, actually, I just dropped by the office to pick up the mail and I'm off again." There; that was better, that was telling her.

"Oh," she said.

"Yeah," I said. "Something's come up. Awfully sorry and all that. Where would you like me to send the retainer you gave me, the Fairfax Hotel, where you're not, or maybe the United Jewish Appeal?"

"Oh," she said.

"And how's Mummy, by the way?" I said. "Would you believe Kaiser has no record of her being a patient there? I'd sue them if I was you."

"Stay there," she said.

"No way," I said, firmly.

"Please," she said. "It's important."

"Forget it," I said. "I'm gone. I am history. Be right there, dear!" I called out to some imaginary female. "Sorry, I've got a lady waiting in the car."

"No, you don't," she said.

"Oh, yes, I do," I said. "And she's taller than you, and prettier, and is completely within my thrall."

"Funny," she said. "I can see your car, if yours is the one that looks like a bumper car, and I don't see anyone in it. Maybe she's hiding in the trunk."

"Where the hell are you, anyway?"

"Somebody's Taco-Burger," she said.

"Mrs. Morales' Taco-Burger," I said to a dead line. 'Don't have the combination plate, whatever you do."

I had just time to scatter a few papers around on my desk so I could appear to be deeply engrossed when in waltzed Miss Ruth Braukis. She was wearing a white linen suit, a red ruffled blouse, red high heels, and she had a red ribbon in her ebon hair. Her shoulder bag was red, also, as were the frames of the sunglasses she was negligently twirling in one hand.

"Hi," she said. "Sorry to be such a nuisance."

"Who've you got a letter from this time?" I said. "Golda Meir?"

She smiled. Her lipstick was exactly the same red as all her accessories.

"May I sit down for a minute, please, Mr. Daniel? Just for a minute?"

"What's mine is yours, Miss Braukis," I said, gesturing toward the chair opposite mine. "Especially as I don't see how I can stop you without doing something ungentlemanly like giving you the bum's rush."

She sat herself down demurely.

"Back in a sec," I said. I went to the small washroom in the back, got her six hundred dollars' worth of travelers checks from the safe, ran a comb hurriedly through my hair, then rejoined her in the office. I aligned the checks neatly and placed them on the desktop between us. "Excuse the mess," I said, indicating the paperwork, "but it's all go these days."

She didn't even glance at the money. She made a non-committal noise, then took a long look at me, as if she was trying to make up her mind about something. I trusted her long looks as much as I did her Estonian fables. Then she said, finally:

"I did lie to you."

"That, Miss Braukis, is yesterday's news," I said. "But do continue."

"There were reasons, good reasons."

"Such as?"

She hesitated.

"Here we go again," I said.

"Mr. Daniel," she said with some asperity in her tone. "It is possible there are things it's better you don't know."

"Better for who?"

"You," she said, pointing one finger at me. "And for 'better' read 'safer'."

"Oh," I said. "I didn't know you cared."

"I can tell you this much," she said. "We've had a possible sighting."

"A UFO?" I exclaimed. "Really! How thrilling. Where? Up near Lafayette?"

"A sighting," she repeated patiently, "of one person in a long list of people we've been looking for on and off for over forty-seven years."

"You must have started young," I said. "But I can't say I'm overwhelmed with surprise, I knew it already, I knew right away you were after one of those old shits."

"We need confirmation," she said, "of the possible sighting."

"From Uncle Theo?"

"We hope so," she said. "That's why we brought him here."

"All the way from sunny Estonia," I said.

"Well," she said, "he did stop off somewhere else on the way, for about thirty years."

"Bet I can guess where," I said. 'Bet it's got a lot of sand and a hell of a lot of navel oranges."

She smiled again briefly. I don't believe I ever did see her laugh, but you could pry a smile out of the serious Miss Braukis from time to time. It was worth the effort.

"Why me?" I said. "Why not use your boyfriend what's-his-name, Lethal Lou, who was in the car with you last time and is probably waiting around the corner right now?"

She arched her eyebrows in mild surprise.

"I have my little methods," I said smugly.

"The blond boy on the motorcycle," she said, nodding. "We thought so. First, the man you refer to is my colleague, not my boyfriend. Second, his name is Shlomo, which is short for Solomon. Thirdly, he is comparatively new out here and does not know the terrain as intimately as you do.

Nor is he as experienced a babysitter, to use Mr. Lewellen's term."

"Call me what you will," I said. "Baby-sitter, watchdog, bodyguard, stooge . . ."

"Lastly," she said, "you, Mr. Daniel, are a licensed investigator and a U.S. citizen, he is an alien here on a temporary work permit, with no official status in the United States."

"Implying he's got official status somewhere else," I said. "I don't even want to know what it is."

She shrugged.

'One other little thing you neglected to mention," I said. "I can legally possess firearms and carry them in certain situations, unlike Solomon."

"Why, Mr. Daniel," she said, widening her amazing eyes innocently. "That never even occurred to me."

"Perish the thought, " I said. She uncrossed her legs and then got to her feet.

"Wait a minute, wait a minute," I said. "Hold on. Where does Uncle Teddy come in?"

"He doesn't," she said, smoothing down the front of her jacket, which looked smooth enough already to my untrained eyes.

"He doesn't. But Uncle Theo *is* due in tomorrow afternoon from New York?"

She nodded.

"Then what do I do with him?"

"You take him to the same place as before, to a hotel in a town called Locke, which is somewhere east of Lafayette."

"Right near where Uncle Teddy used to live," I said. "That letter from him in Russian, which is in my safe out back, where did it come from if it didn't come from Uncle Teddy?"

"A friend of Shlomo's," she said.

"Why invent an Uncle Teddy in the first place?" I said. "To say nothing of poor Mummy."

She put her sunglasses on carefully. "It was decided the less you knew the better, as I said. We didn't know how you felt about us or where your sympathies might lie." She came around the desk and put a hand on my shoulder. "And there are people who might be frightened of running into one of those 'old shits,' even after all this time."

"Maybe sissy types," I said. She laid one cool palm briefly against my cheek. I looked up at her. "So I take him to the hotel, then what?"

"Then nothing, Mr. Daniel," she said, moving away. "You book in for one night. The following morning Theo will be gone."

"He will, eh? Well, well." I got up and followed her to the door. Before I opened it for her, I said, "And the rest of my modest fee plus my even more modest expenses?"

"Will be sent to you," she said. "Or, who knows, delivered to you personally."

"You personally or Solomon personally?"

'We'll see," she said. "We will see." I opened the door for her.

"If it's not a silly question," I said, "why didn't Solomon personally approach me in the first place and put it to me man to man, so to speak?"

She turned her fabulous face up to mine, smiled and said, "He's not called Solomon for nothing." And then she was gone.

CHAPTER THIRTEEN

And so it came to pass that at 3:44 the following afternoon, there I was back at dear old LAX, waiting outside the appropriate exit and holding aloft a large cardboard sign, just one more tour guide awaiting his flock. And it is totally unfair to suggest that I was in that ludicrous position merely because of certain physical attractions Miss Ruth Venus Braukis might have had for me, there are such things as the call of the wild and the lure of the unknown; danger is my business, after all.

Uncle Theo's flight was on time; so was Uncle Theo. I recognized him immediately from the photo Ruth had given me of him, so I probably hadn't needed that silly sign with his name on it after all. He was a small, elderly, worried-looking man in a rumpled brown suit and brown fedora, toting one small, cheap suitcase. He saw my sign at about the same time as I spotted him and raised one hand straight up in the air like he was asking teacher if he could please leave the room.

We approached each other and shook hands. From under his hat he had curly white wisps of hair sticking out, something like Ben-Gurion.

"*Zdrastvouiti, Tovarich,*" I said as best I could.

He looked surprised.

"*Vy guevariti parouski?*" he said, doffing his lid to reveal a heavily tanned and well-creased forehead.

I figured that meant "You speak Russian?" so I hastened to tell him, "Nyet, nyet." ("Forget it, babe.") I handed over "Uncle Teddy's" letter; he opened it and began reading it eagerly. When he was done, he tucked it away and said something else to me in Russian. I shook my head and gave him one of the two Russian–English phrase books I'd bought the day before from a specialty bookstore down on Western. It wasn't going to be much help knowing how to say 'Where is the Stade Dynamo, please" to each other, but it was better than nothing. I'd spent some time in bed last night (my own) after leaving Evonne's looking up potentially useful phrases, and I tried out one of them then:

"*Ia vach novei ekskoursevot,*" I read. He looked blank, so I pointed out the phrase in my book: "I am your new guide/escort," at which he nodded several times.

He went searching through his copy and finally came up with "Where do we go next?"

"Airplane," I said. Actually, I didn't say "airplane," I pointed to a picture of one in the book, but to save time, from now on I'll report our conversations, such as they were, as if we said them to each other instead of pointing them out.

"Airplane." He nodded resignedly and picked up his case. I took it from him, dumped my sign in a nearby bin, and led him off toward the Air Cal desks. While we were in line waiting our turn, I asked him if he was hungry.

"Not hungry," he said. "Not thirsty. Yes tired."

"Me too," I said, nodding sympathetically.

"You baby, big," he said. "Me old, small." Well, maybe I was baby, big, but there was nothing in the works of Karl Marx as far as I knew that said I couldn't be tired, too. I'd had a busy time after Ruth's visit the day before. First, I'd talked at some length with my friend Benjamin. Then I'd talked at some length with Sara of the Sorrows. I had a brief word with Mom, at Hilldale, then one with Dr. Don Fishbein, the bearded bundle of compassionate energy who ran the place; the news wasn't good. I went book hunting. I checked the L.A.–San Francisco flight times with Air Cal. I begged an empty carton from Mr. Nu two doors down and, with a magic marker, made up a sign with Uncle Theo's name on it, copied from the envelope containing the letter for him. I purchased a map of central California. Then I had to rendezvous with Benny back at my apartment. He was in good shape, he told me, and keeping busy with this and that. After he left me, he was off to the office of a real estate broker he knew to get a temporary license, which cost peanuts. He wanted to sell one of the half-dozen properties he owned, all of them in the Anaheim-Fullerton area, and if he listed the property with a broker, he got to share the commission on the sale without doing any of the work.

Then it was time to meet Evonne Louise Shirley at her place to wine and dine the eve away. She thanked me for the maple syrup and promised that waffles would soon be in the offing. I thanked her for her present, which was an extremely rare necktie from the forties; it had "I Luv U" written on it, which, she claimed, you could read only when all the lights were out. I decided to test out this unlikely assertion, so after supper at Mario's, back at her place, I put the tie on, mixed up two tall, fruity 'n' frosty nightcaps, then switched off all the lights. Darned if the little minx wasn't right.

"I've heard of guys doing it with their boots on," she said at one stage, "but a tie?"

"Class will tell, snookums," I said into the back of her neck, which is where my mouth happened to be right then. Later, when we were holding hands and sipping our drinks, I told her I had to go away again for a couple of days. She said an unladylike word and wanted to know where I was off to this another-unladylike-word time, and for how long, and why.

"Guy I know called Solomon," I said vaguely. "Wants me to deliver something for him near San Francisco, shouldn't take more than a day or two. Montreal," I said, changing the subject as quickly as possible. "You haven't asked me one word about Montreal."

"How was Montreal?" she said sleepily.

"Very French," I said. "Had a great time. Saw a hockey game, made some money, wrote this poem that's probably Pulitzer Prize material. Sara didn't enjoy it much, though, Willing Boy is giving her a hard time, poor old twerp."

"Well, what d'you expect from men, anyway," she said. "Especially here-today – gone-tomorrow types like you."

"Yes, dear," I said.

When I finally did manage to escape back to the safety of my own bed, I had *The Little Russian Phrase Book*, by one N. Pogarieloff, to leaf through, and it was after two by then, so there were good reasons why I was tired the next day, Uncle Theo—baby, big, tired, and still jet-lagged, don't forget, and about to become even more so.

Air Cal was delighted to sell me two tickets to San Francisco. I bought one-way tickets as Uncle Theo wasn't supposed to be coming back with me. We had a half-hour to wait until boarding, which I spent slouched in a chair thinking of nothing much in particular, and Uncle Theo spent feeding quarters into one of those one- person TVs you find in a lot of airports these days; maybe if I was from Estonia and couldn't understand English, I might be able to take afternoon TV, too. When our flight was finally announced, he didn't react; I made gestures to him indicating it was time to go.

He dozed through most of the flight north to San Francisco; I would have too if I could have found some position to squirm into where my head made contact with the headrest. I wonder why airlines don't have a demountable version of those gadgets you attach to the top of car seats to avoid whiplash? I wonder why they don't have a lot of things. One of the stewardesses had words with a tobacco addict behind us who tried to sneak a quick hit; the smoking ban was OK by me. I'd puffed away as a smart-ass kid, like all smart-ass kids, but after spending three weeks cold turkey in a private hospital in Fresno having some holes plugged one time, I luckily never got the yen again.

You know those notice boards they have in airport terminals that say "Messages for passengers," and that never have a message for you? I checked the one we passed in the corridor after disembarking at San Francisco and lo and behold, tucked into the Ds was one for V. Daniel, from Curly. It contained no good news. It contained bad news, which, although not unexpected, still wasn't the same as good news.

"Could be. Love, S." is what it said. I crumpled it up and put it away in a pocket. Uncle Theo looked at me inquiringly.

I looked up the word for *mother* in the vocabulary at the back of my phrase book and pointed it out to him. He looked slightly baffled, so I added, "Telephone. Telephone mother."

"Da," he said, nodding.

Curly had been at LAX from three o'clock onwards that afternoon, watching my meeting with Uncle Theo. She had not been pleased when I'd informed her she'd have to take the airport bus out, but I didn't want to drive her out in case anyone was watching and I sure wasn't about to cover taxis for her there and back because you are talking eighty bucks easy, amigos. I couldn't use Willing Boy as a backup as (1) he was either in Montreal with Miss McGurk or Quebec City with Mama and (2) he'd already been spotted. Benny was otherwise occupied, so that left Sara, girl sleuth. What she was looking for, of course, was anyone who showed untoward interest in me or Uncle Theo, such as, to name but one, Solomon, whom I'd described to her as best I could. And it seemed she'd spotted someone , all right—"could be." I'd spotted her without getting out my magnifying glass, she was decked out in her old Born Again Mother Hubbard outfit and was handing out petunias or whatever they were. She even handed me one, the twerp, and tried to sell me a fish-shaped Christian symbol on a cheap chain.

Goodie goodie, I thought. That's all I needed, Lethal Lou circling around just out of sight. Bring back the moose, I thought. Where were those halcyon days of yore when all I had to worry about was Fats, the Mob, the fuzz, snow blindness, and too much Cinderella cake?

After Uncle Theo came back from the washroom, Avis came up with yet another bright red Ford. Why so many of their vehicles are bight crimson, I do not know. Maybe the color is supposed to appeal to us sporty types, us daredevils of the macadam.

I settled my companion into the seat beside me, helped him to buckle up, and off we went. San Francisco's airport is located south of the city and we the famed Golden Gate Bridge, which Uncle Theo had excitedly pointed out to me from the plane as we circled out over the Pacific before making our approach in to land. The town of Lafayette lies

east-northeast and you get to it, as we did, after bypassing
most of the city, by joining tens of thousands of commuters
heading homeward over the never-ending San Francisco–
Oakland Bay Bridge. The bridge debouches onto a freeway that takes you north of Oakland through the Coastal
Mountains to towns like Orinda, Lafayette, and Walnut
Creek. If you headed eastward, inland, for a couple of
hours you'd wind up, if you weren't careful, in Stockton or
Sacramento. If you hit a left, you could enroll in civic disor-
der at the University of California, Berkeley, if you should so
desire. North lay deltas and oysters; Jack London country.
Did you know Jack started as an oyster pirate, then later got
a job catching oyster pirates? Anyway, so claimed this pint-
sized fount of information I ran into later that evening in
the Round-up Saloon in Lafayette. We'd decided to spend
the night there as it was getting on for eight o'clock when
we hit town and we were both flagging somewhat.

I booked us separated rooms in the shingle-fronted
Ponderosa Pine Inn, a hostelry just off Lafayette's main
drag, Mt. Diablo Boulevard. A leaflet in my room, kindly
supplied by the local Rotary Club, informed me that the
Ponderosa, and the Monterey pine, unlike the coast red-
wood, or *sequoia*, were only introduced in the nearby reservoir park in the 1930s. Well! Maybe me and Uncle Theo
could go for a row around the reservoir mañana before leaving, that'd be oodles of fun. We might even be able to catch
a glimpse of the rare Chinese pistachio (*pistace chinensis*).

After I'd cleaned up a bit, I collected a newly bathed and
freshly attired Uncle Theo from his room and we crossed Mt.
Diablo Boulevard to Freddie's Pizza, which had been recommended to us by a helpful lady at the check-in desk. I didn't
think the odds were too good on finding an Estonian eatery
in town. We had to wait awhile for service, as Freddie's was

jumping with high school kids, whole families, pops waiting for takeout orders, and so on, all of which was a good sign. Theo went through his half of the large, extra cheese, anchovies, olives, and garlic pizza almost as quickly as I devoured mine. Delicious, Freddie, and I told a pleased Freddie so on the way out. He gave me a gift of a green whistle with the name of his emporium on it, and presented Uncle Theo with a red lollipop, I guess he figured they had enough whistles already in Estonia.

I escorted Theo back to his room, pointed to ten o'clock on my watch, and said, "Tomorrow."

"OK," he said, in English. I grinned.

"*Dobreivie tchir,*" I said, which means goodnight.

"Good night," he said, which means *dobreivie tchir.* We shook hands formally. He went into his room. I waited till I heard him lock his door, the dropped in the aforementioned Round-Up Saloon after a short stroll around town to stretch my legs and my lungs a bit. Bill's Drugs, across the road from Freddie's, was just closing up. The post office, like our hotel, was disguised behind old-fashioned wooden shingles. The streets were clean, the drivers sedate, the cars and station wagons large, new, and expensive. The color of the citizenry was white.

To be truthful, I have hung around a lot of bars in my time. Occasionally they've hung around me, but I put that down to the thoughtless follies of laming youth. The Round-Up was just my kind of bar—large, rambling, with lots of wood, a couple of pool tables, a pretty girl in short cutoffs behind the bar, chilled steins for the beer, and hanging all over the walls, an assortment of bridles, types of bits, reins, and other leather and metalware associated with the horsey life, of which there was plenty in the hills and dales around Lafayette.

Deer, too, according to the geezer on the next bar stool, the expert on Jack London and shellfish who'd started talking to me the moment I'd sat down beside him and so far hadn't stopped except to take the occasional swig of beer. Like I said, he was a little shaver, dressed in brown jeans tucked into cowboy boots, a checked wool shirt, and a cap that said "I've been to San Diego Sea world."

"Deer, eh?" I said politely. "No kidding . . ."

"Jenny!" he called out. "How about a couple more down here for me and Slim."

"Sure, Mike," she called back. "Be right over."

"That's right decent of you, Mike," I said.

"What the hell, it's only money," he said.

He lowered his voice and leaned closer. "Thing is, I'm leaving town tomorrow, OK? I've had enough. I've been working for this fat-assed dude owns a car lot, he dumped his load on me once too often so I am off on the morning train."

"I hear Canada is nice this time of year," I said.

"Canada, shmanada," Mike said. "I can get a job anywhere, anytime, like that." He snapped his fingers. "There's only one thing I'd like to do before I leave, and what d'ya think that is, friend?"

"Say good bye?" I ventured. I swung around on the stool and took a casual look again at the assemblage without seeing anyone who looked like what I thought Lethal Lou looked like.

Mike laughed and slapped my arm in a comradely fashion. I had a good idea of what he was about to claim he wanted to do before leaving town, but what the hell, I always like watching hustlers in action, there is always a chance to learn something new without it costing more than a leg. Thus I let him run his string out.

"See, it's like this," he confided. "The boss won't be on the lot tomorrow, he's going to a funeral or something over to Orinda, so what I'm going to do is put the shaft in him, twist it a couple of times, then break it off. You want an Impala, under five thou on the clock, air-conditioning, radials, tape deck, you name it, Blue Book says thirty-two five, give me a grand, drive it away, fuck him. I got a gun-metal Porsche, make your mouth water, but she's already promised to Jerry over there, that big guy shooting pool? Fifteen hundred, fuck him."

"Gee, I sure wish I could stop by, Mike," I said, shaking my head regretfully, "but me and the little woman got to get the camper on the road by seven-thirty latest, we got a goddamned shower of one of her cousins to go to in Sac."

"No sweat, Slim," Mike said. "Just trying to do you a favor." Sure he was, he was trying to do me the great favor of selling me some overpriced clunker that might make it up the hill out of town if there was a following wind. While his fat-assed boss, if he even had one, watched the transaction out of the back window and laughed till his sides split. A slightly more sophisticated version of the same scam is for the hapless salesman to get shat on or otherwise deeply insulted by the boss right in front of the sucker. The boss takes off immediately for lunch or some make-believe errand, leaving the salesman a clear field to take his "revenge".

Then Mike wanted to try me out on dollar-bill liar's poker, where you each take a dollar bill supposedly at random from your pocket and, using the serial numbers, proceed as you do with poker dice, alternately announcing higher hands until one calls the other, who either has the hand he claimed, and wins, or is caught bluffing, and loses.

Of course your opponent is inclined to get suspicious if you play with a carefully preserved dollar bill you take out of your wallet's secret compartment, so Mike's version was to offer to use any one of the bills Jenny had given him in change when he'd bought the last round of drinks. Would pretty Jenny slip him a bill with, say, five of a kind in its serial number and sporting, say a slightly crinkled corner for easy recognition if Mike gave her the wink? What an idea. Oh—I forgot to mention that Jenny's T-shirt said NO LAYTEX? NO LAY, TEX.

Anyway, when I declined, on the grounds that I was a terrible liar and couldn't even fool the little woman one time out of ten, he immediately suggested a new version of marienbad, that match game where the guy who has to take the last match loses, only in Mike's version he wins. Again, I declined politely. Then he offered to take me on wrong-handed on the shuffleboard game; no luck there. Then he tried to snag me with a couple of sucker bets, in one of which he offered to bet me a buck that Joan of Arc wasn't French. I must admit he almost had me with that one, what else could she be?

Finally, when he'd done everything but try and sell me a map of a lost gold mine, and he was probably warming up to that, I said to him, "Mike, give up. Cease. Desist awhile. Whoa. I wouldn't even bet you Joan of Arc was woman. I'm just country folks, I know when I'm out of my league."

"No sweat, Slim," he said again, looking around for some livelier action. He didn't find any. I ordered up the next round. Mike shifted from actively trying to skin me to merely amusing me with coins, wooden matches, swizzle sticks, and various tidbits of local lore. He laid out five coins alternately heads and tails on the bar and wanted to know if I could reverse their faces turning over any two at a time three times. I couldn't. He could.* He arranged six coins in a pyramid and wanted to know if I could shape them into

*See appendix for the solutions: Ed.

a circle in three moves, each coin moved being required to touch two others. I couldn't. He could. He said there was town wit who snuck out late at night and rearranged the letters on the movie marquee into something dirty: his latest effort was to change PARIS, TEXAS into SEX IS A TRAP. He said the local branch of the D.A.R. hung a banner across Mt. Diablo Boulevard, reading, "Lafayette says no to drugs." Underneath, some wit, perhaps the same one, had added, "Lafayette says no to everything."

Mike wanted to know if I could discover the one lightweight bag of nine bags of coke, in only two weighings. That one I figured out finally. He said, "Two traveling salesmen were born on the same day of the same month in the same year and both died at the same time in their fiftieth year. So how come one lived a hundred days longer than the other?"

He said, "When the same two guys were drafted, they gave their names as Jim Riley and John Riley, the only children of the same parents, and as we know, they were born on the same day of the same month in the same year. So why weren't they twins."

"You got me, Mike," I said.

Then he laid out five matches like this, I I I I I, and wanted me to move any two to make an all-day sucker. I couldn't. Then he asked me if I knew how to pour a whole pint of beer into a half- pint mug. I didn't.

I strolled back to the hotel trying to figure out the last stinker he laid on me just before I left. It seems there were these three guys in a cathouse. In came five ladies, three with bright red lipstick on, two with pale pink. The lights go out. Each guy who figures out what color lipstick is on his dome gets a freebie. After a while, one guy says, "I know" and he does. Given that there is no trickery with mirrors or some of the ladies having kissed all their lipstick off, how does he know?

The outside door of the hotel was locked but I had a key and let myself in. I went upstairs and paused in front of Uncle Theo's door for a minute; all seemed tranquil. I wondered if Uncle Theo was dreaming, and if so, of what. I'd enjoyed the brief respite offered by the Round-Up Saloon, but I couldn't help thinking it was but the calm before the storm, these last few minutes in the trenches before going over the top. And, amigos, I am not noted for my ability to foretell the future; I have trouble sometimes foretelling the past.

I hit the hay after doing what a lot of us keep-fit fanatics do—drink a lot of water as an antihangover precaution. I wondered why there were so many languages in my life I couldn't speak all of a sudden, my ignorance was getting to be a nuisance even to me. I had just about figured out the solution to those lipstick traces when I fell asleep.

CHAPTER FOURTEEN

Came the dawning of the new day.
Several hours later, I arose.

A while after that, after having partaken of breakfast at a
counter joint up the road from us, Uncle Theo and I hit the
road. I turned the wrong way out of the hotel's parking lot
and had to take a small, winding lane to get back to the freeway entrance. On the way I spied a Red Indian up in a tree
menacing us with a bow and arrow! I refused to panic; however as the fearless hunter's mother was standing at the foot
of the tree telling him to climb down immediately before
he fell and hurt himself, or else. Then I spied a horse being
silly in a field, and after that a fencepost-hole digger at work.
A hawk that had been following us to see, I surmised, if we
spooked any field mice or whatever that it could snag for
its breakfast swooped down one more time and then disappeared. I even thought I glimpsed a *Symphoricarpos albus,* or
snowberry, but I could have been mistaken.

We did see a goat farm just after picking up the east-
bound freeway and I wondered vaguely what anyone wanted
with so many of the hairy critters, turn them into goat-hair
throw rugs? Who knew.

After another while we passed through Alamo, then
Danville. About then I pulled over to check the map I'd purchased from Mrs. Martel, Stationer, the previous day, then

on we continued toward San Ramón, finally leaving the hills behind us. Uncle Theo sat quietly beside me. From time to time he pointed out some feature of particular interest, like a gang of naked to the waist asphalt layers who were resurfacing a stretch of the highway. It was Benny, I think, who once told me that what those guys did, first thing in the morning, was to wrap up a couple of chickens and unpeeled potatoes and an onion or two in foil and then tuck them in a corner of the hot asphalt so they'd be good and juicy by lunchtime. Where does he pick up stuff like that? I bet he'd even know what they did with all those billy goats.

Onward, ever onward . . . passing miles and passing thoughts . . . and then there was Fats, was one of the passing thoughts. Fats, to whom I owed one, you may recall. I could rat to the Mob about him. I could ditto to the cops. I could sic Used Car Mike on him. I could devise some appropriate trickery of my own. Or maybe I should just let sleeping curs lie, as long as he left Will's family alone. I didn't want him really mad at me, after all, he might start thinking, he might even conceivably get someone to gain access for him to Air France passenger lists, and then where would I be. How long did they keep those things in the computer, anyway? I knew passenger lists were entered daily, covering such subjects as name, sex, destination in seven different categories, starting point, fare paid, and method of payment and so on, but probably not even Benjamin knew how regularly they were expunged from the system. What I thought I would do was to merely drop Fats a polite note in which I would suggest that (a) it was Zit-Face who made off with the sixty-two five, not Will, and (b) Zit-Face had also held out on Fats when he reported on the almost penniless state of my wallet.

Onward. Finally we turned off the main road, cruised past a trailer park, then into the town of our destination,

Locke. Locke is not your average small Californian town, kids, replete with gas stations, fast-food joints, dogs, and teenagers. Locke is made of wood, firstly, and Chinese, secondly. All Chinese, with one or two exceptions. We parked behind the town's one hotel, the one we had been directed to, a semiderelict-looking all-wooden monstrosity; even the fire escapes were wood. We alit, then strolled along a (wooden) sidewalk past a short row of (wooden) homes and storefronts. A sign along the way informed us that the town had been built in 1912 to house levee workers and that it had once had a population of 1,500 plus a real live theater. We peeked in the windows of Yuen Chong's General Store; one or two of the items of foodstuffs looked almost edible. An old Chinese gent half dozing in the sun on a stairway gazed at us briefly as we passed, then went back to stroking his long gray goatee. We turned a corner and passed a shop called Locke Ness—get it? We noticed the Dai Loy Museum was closed. The whole town, with its false wooden frontages and Asian extras, was so cinematic I kept expecting Bruce Lee to suddenly leap out and scream bizarre noises. Which was not the reason I was nervous, by the way. I was nervous because I was already nervous. Was there such a thing as a Nazi Chinaman? Benny, where are you?

We walked back to the hotel via Locke's number two street; two was about all there were. There were two people in the cavernous lobby when we entered—a youngish Asian fellow in a spotless white T-shirt at the reception desk, and some nature lover, complete with hiking boots, sun hat, knee-length mosquito-proof shorts, and long woolen socks, who was sprawled in a bamboo chair in the corner looking at a map through a magnifying glass, a well-stuffed orange knapsack at his feet out of which unidentifiable rods of metal jutted, much like those chopsticks from Momma's bun. His face was bright red with sunburn, or maybe embarrassment, and his windbreaker sleeves were almost covered with sewn-on badges saying "Greenpeace," "Sierra Club," "Save the Whales," "Bike for Health," "The Audubon Society," "No to Nukes," "Dolphins Are People Too," and God knows what else. Repressing a shudder, I turned back to the desk clerk, who neatly folded up and then put away his Chinese-language newspaper before attending to our needs. Which he did, it is perhaps unnecessary to add, in perfect American, and with extreme politeness. I booked us two single rooms, for one night, in my name; he refused either a deposit or a look at my plastic. He insisted on carrying Uncle Theo's small bag up to the first floor, where our rooms were, opened them up for us, and then refused a tip. My room was small but clean and moderately comfortable. Once me and Uncle Theo were downstairs again, our host informed us that, in case we were hungry, there were two restaurants in town but only one, Dago Don's, served lunch. Then he snapped his fingers, made an apologetic gesture, and produced from under the counter a package that he said had come for me. "Perishable!" it said on the outside. I thanked him kindly, directed Uncle Theo to a chair, in which he sat, then made haste back up to my room to open my parcel. And I felt a lot better, hombres, when I saw the comforting sight of one of my own, my very own, .38-caliber Police Positive nestling inside on a bed of confetti, and beside it, a substantial supply of ammunition. I checked it out, tucked it in the shoulder holster I'd brought with me in my airline carry-all, slipped on a lightweight windbreaker to hide it from prying eyes, and then rejoined Uncle once again downstairs. Uncle was making "no spika da English" gestures to the nature freak, who had bits of a fishing rod spread out on the worn carpet. Evidently one of the couplings had come loose in the recent past and he was showing Uncle how he'd cleverly fixed it by himself, alone, out in the wilderness, with naught but a tendon from a tree frog's leg and a dash of Superglue. Close up the guy smelled of a combination of rubber and bug repellent.

I got Uncle out of there and we headed for Dago Don's famed bar and eatery, which we'd passed earlier on our stroll. I may not spot every *Symphoricarpos albus* when I'm strolling, or driving, but you can bet I don't miss all that many bars.

Dago Don's—what a place. There was so much dusty bric-a-brac on the walls and hanging from the ceiling it was ten minutes before I noticed the stuffed ostrich. I was too busy putting away a couple of brews and admiring the lobster with the decals on it, the blowfish with the corncob pipe in its mouth, the ratty old deer head—or was it a small moose?—and the old photos of the old days and the hundreds of dollar bills stuck mysteriously to the ceiling.

"Ok ,I'll bite," I said to the bearded geezer tending bar, who might even have been Dago Don himself, for all I knew, "how do they get up there?"

"Got a buck?" he said.

"Yeah, I got a buck," I said, handing him over one. "But I get the feeling I won't have it for long."

He grinned through his nicotine-stained whiskers, took a silver dollar out of his watch pocket, folded the, or rather, my, dollar bill around it somehow, dipped it all in beer, then lofted the ensemble ceilingward, where it stuck, what else? After a minute or so my dollar bill, traitor that it was, unfolded itself just enough to go on sticking up there but to let the silver dollar slip out and fall down into the bartender's awaiting palm. Bet Mike never saw that one, I thought. But who knows—maybe it was Mike behind all that beard. Or even Lethal Lou. Which reminded me—I took a quick look around—at the clientele this time instead of the artifacts—no Solomon. There was a husband and wife, obviously sightseers, drinking soda pops at one table, and three deaf folks, drinking booze, signing away busily at one another. I wondered if they ever said to each other the equivalent of, "What a chatterbox that woman is! Doesn't she ever stop signing?"

About then an old-timer wearing a chefs hat and a long white apron appeared in the doorway to the dining room. He was holding a large brass bell, which he proceeded to ring violently.

"Come 'n' get it," He said, "if you want it. Special's pot roast." He surveyed the room briefly, then scuttled back into the dining area. Uncle Theo looked at me inquiringly. I pointed to my mouth and made chewing sounds. He nodded eagerly.

We had the pot roast. So did the husband and wife, the three deaf people, and a table of four locals next to us. I divided my attention between the food, (terrific), our fellow diners (harmless, as far as I could tell), and an intriguing business card which was propped up against the mustard pot on our table "Charlie Chan's Tattooing," it said. "No drunks. Free Hand. Ladies in private. 100s of designs. Wide choice of colors. Noon to midnight." Hum, thought I. A tattoo, thought I. Something tasteful, of course, nothing ribald. Perhaps merely a heart entwined with flowers, and underneath, "Evonne." That'd show her I was willing to endure grievous pain over her, that I wasn't just some fly-by-night incapable of suffering over a woman. I changed my mind when I perused the back of the card. "Remove bandage in 24 hours," it said. Bandage?? "Use medication on tattoo for first 3 days. Spray with alcohol frequently." That bit was easy, just breathe heavily. "Light amounts of neosporin or der-massage is recommended. Your tattoo should form a light dry scab that will fall off in about 7 to 10 days. Do not pick it off." No way, José, I thought. Maybe I'd try a little mental suffering instead.

Uncle Theo and I finished up with store-bought apple pie, the kind with too much cinnamon in it, à la mode, then I settled up, asked for and was given a receipt by the matronly waitress, then we departed without seeing any more of the feisty little cook. My dollar bill was still stuck to the ceiling, I couldn't help noticing on the way out. What a racket.

I stuck pretty close to Uncle Theo the rest of the day. If I'd stuck any closer we'd have been sharing the same BVDs. If he sighted whoever it was he was purportedly there to sight, he didn't bother letting me in on it. We didn't do much, we took another stroll around town after lunch, then read for a while in the hotel lobby, me a top-notch Len Deighton called *Yesterday's Spy*, him a who-knows-what and in what language. The hotel business in Locke wasn't exactly booming. I snuck a look at the register when no one else was around and noted that apart from me, Theo, and a Henry C. Clam, alias Nature Boy, there was only one other guest, a lady doctor, and she remained invisible, as did, thankfully, Nature Boy. Then, as I recall, we both took naps, then went for a spin out of town, along one of the levees. Then we returned to the hotel to sit around some more and attempt to communicate by means of our phrase books, not all that easy a task as most of the phrases therein were thing like, "*Tavarich predaviets! Chto koupit dlia malien keve mal tchike?*"

Which means, roughly, "Comrade salesperson, what would you recommend for a little boy?"

"A little girl," Uncle Theo pointed out, which wasn't bad for an uncle. Or any one else, either, come to think of it. Then I betook myself back to Yuen Chong's General Store, where I made a couple of purchases. Once back at the hotel I dropped my purchases off in my room, trying to see if I could walk down the hall without making the floor creak. I found I could if I kept to the edges. I checked out the second floor briefly; the stairwell to the floors above was firmly blocked by a screwed-in sheet of heavy plywood. I checked out the fire escape, too, briefly; it looked solid enough to take a person's weight. It had a barrier as well separating the second story from those above but it was only waist high.

We had supper in the town's other restaurant, Sam Li's, which was down behind the museum, hot egg rolls, Chinese spareribs, noodles, wonton soup, the usual stuff. Uncle Theo made no attempt to hide the admiration he felt at my dexterous use of the chopsticks. I noticed he blew on the soup in his spoon to cool it, a habit my mom particularly disliked. Which reminded me.

I called her up after supper, using the old-fashioned wall pay phone in the hotel lobby. Uncle Theo planted himself in front of the TV.

"Is Mrs. Daniel available, please? It's her little boy."

"Hang on, I'll check," a woman's voice said.

I hung on. While I was hanging on, Nature Boy came bustling in, holding a large bunch of what looked like weeds to me. He disappeared up the stairs; maybe he was going to mash them up for his supper.

After a lengthy while, the voice said she was sorry but my mother didn't seem to know who I was. I said I was sorry, too, and hung up. Then, what the hell, it was marginally more than watching "Dallas" with Uncle, I shoveled some more change in and dialed the twerp's number. Her mom answered.

"Is your charming daughter available to come to the phone, Mrs. Silvetti? V. Daniel here, calling from the wilds of upstate California."

"I think she's in her room, mooning. Hang on, I'll see." I hung on. After a minute or so, the twerp said, "Yeah? What do *you* want?

"I don't want anything but the pleasure of hearing your sweet and soothing tones," I said. "So how are you doing, anyway?"

"Shitty," she said.

"Willing Boy back?" I said.

"No," she said. "Not that it's any of your business."

"Thanks for your message at the airport, by the way," I said.

"You owe me for the phone call," she said.

"In the mail," I said.

"Also for my time," she said. "Do you know how long it takes to get to that airport by bus?"

"Also in the mail," I said.

"Sure, sure, " she said. "Now if there's nothing else, so long."

"Wait a minute, grumpy," I said. "There is something else. If I don't call you by, say, ten o'clock tomorrow morning, give me a call up here in the sticks, or chopsticks is more like it." I read her off the phone number from the dial.

"Why?"

"Oh, I dunno," I said vaguely. "Just in case. Who knows what dangers lurk in the back room of Charlie Chan's tattoo parlor."

"OK," she muttered. She hung up, or slammed down is more like it. Ah, young love, I thought. I remember it well.

"Sleep tight, don't let the bedbugs bite," I said to the empty line.

I went back to the man at the front desk for another handful of silver. He was scribbling away in an exercise book.

"Studying?" I asked him.

"Studying."

"What, may I ask, just to pass the time?"

"For a belated Ph.D. in Paleontology."

"Oh," I said. "I never was much good with languages myself." He unlocked the cash drawer and converted a five-dollar bill into change for me.

"I thought you might be taking a course in hotel management or something like that."

"I'm just helping out Pop," he said. 'He owns this mausoleum. I keep telling him it would be cheaper to close it up, but not my pop. He's kept the old registers that go back to when his father bought it in 1917, he remembers when it was full, all four floors, I've closed up two of them already and I'm shutting down another someday when he's out fishing."

"Ah well," I said. "Tempis does fugit."

"Not for my pop," he said, returning to his studies. I returned to the phone and called up Precious. Precious was out. I could leave a message after the pip. I left a rude noise after the pip and went to rejoin Theo on the battered old sofa in front of the TV. I couldn't swear to it, but I suspected Theo had already developed a crush on Victoria Principal. Hell, join the club.

So we sat through the "Dallas" rerun, then watched Columbo get his man again, only this time it was a woman, then we switched the TV off and went upstairs to our rooms. Uncle Theo started leafing through his phrase book outside his door to find some suitable words of parting. I sighed, and said "Come on, Uncle, give over, you probably speak English as well as I do. Maybe even better."

"When did you find out?" he said finally in accented but otherwise correct American.

"Shit, I've known it for years," I said.

CHAPTER FIFTEEN

Now that we had a language in common, wouldn't you know Uncle Theo clammed up; we communicated more with those useless phrase books. And what he did tell me was more likely another pack of fibs, misrepresentations, and evasions, to say naught of the complete and utter falsehoods.

It was a few minutes later. We were sitting on the bed in my room and I was trying to get a few answers out of the polylingual ex-Estonian, if he was even that. I'd answered his questions frankly, openly, and with almost complete candor. I told him that what gave him away wasn't so much what he did but what he hadn't done, aside from the basic fact that whatever Miss Ruth Aphrodite Braukis told me I had learnt the hard way to disbelieve. Therefore, as she told me that Uncle Theo could only speak Estonian and Russian, I immediately assumed he was not only fluent in every major tongue but most of the minor dialects as well. Why the pretense in the first place, Uncle Theo refused to say.

"I don't speak languages, like some I could name," I said with an admirable lack of jealousy, "so I know what it's like. But I can always pick up a word here and there if I try, lots of words are the same or almost the same in Spanish or French or Canadian even; you couldn't pick up one word, not even easy ones like San Francisco, over the loudspeaker.

Hell, even I know a few words of Russian, I go to the movies, I read a lot of spy books; who hasn't picked up a few words of English? You protestedeth too much, Tovarich. Also, it's hard, what you were trying to do, like pretending to be deaf, or blind. Next time leave it to us experts."

"There won't be a next time, I hope," he said, looking slightly crestfallen.

"Me too," I said. "But if there is, may I suggest once in a while try to go through a door that is marked, 'Do Not Enter' instead of not trying to go through it. You picked the right washroom, too, and it wasn't one of those with the figure of a little man above it, 'Men' is all it said. You also downed that pizza as if it wasn't the first one you'd ever seen in your sheltered life. However. Onward. Tell me this, Uncle—what's going on? Don't you think it's about time you filled me in?"

He shrugged.

"You know all I know."

"That'll be the day," I said. "How about your sighting, how's that coming along?

He shrugged again.

"Still planning on leaving tomorrow?"

This time he nodded.

"Solly going to pick you up, or What's-her-name, maybe?"

"Maybe."

"Why don't you leave tonight, if you've seen what you wanted to see?'

"I was told to stay here."

"Could you get in touch with Solly or What's-her-name if you wanted to?"

"Nyet," he said.

"Which doesn't mean yes," I said. "Bet'cha they're in one of those campers at the trailer park we passed on the way in. That's where I'd be."

Theo looked innocent.

"So how do you like living in Israel?"

"It's a living," he said.

"What do you do there, Theo?"

"Retired teacher. I live on a kibbutz in the Negev with my daughter. Still teach a bit. Run the library. Help out in the machine shop. Garden. Usually go on a dig in the summer. Make wine in a modest way."

"Some retirement." I said. "Especially when you chuck in and go to war every few months. Do me a favor?"

"Maybe."

"What's your real name, anyway?"

"The kids call me Abba," he said.

"What's that mean?"

"Pop."

"That's a big help," I said. " OK, how about this, I want you to switch rooms with me for the night. I am being paid to baby-sit you, after all. I figure it couldn't hoit, whoever you sighted or didn't sight or are going to meet or not going to meet or get a phone call from or a smoke signal or a grapefruit with a secret message inside."

He thought it over for a minute, then said, "Why not?" He got up, went out, and returned in a minute with his pajamas and toilet articles.

"Uh-uh," I said. "You can keep the bottoms, I need the other stuff." I took them from him, collected the necessities from my room, pulled down the window blind, asked him to hand over his false teeth, which he did reluctantly, told him to lock the door behind me and keep it locked, then tiptoed to his room without being detected as far as I could tell. I pulled the blind down, turned on the light, then made my simple preparations for the long night to come. I used the extra blanket on the bed and one of the pillows to make up a dummy Theo, then dressed it in his pajama top, shaping it to appear that Theo was laying on one side, facing the wall and away from the door, one pajama-clad arm curling up and around his head to hide the fact he didn't have a real one. I added a few tufts of cotton batting I'd bought at the store for that final touch that means so much.

On the small bedside table I laid out a box of his pills and then his upper plate, in a plastic glass of water. I hung his pants over a chair. I lined his shoes up neatly by the bed. I put the book he'd been reading on the table as well, then a small pocket mirror I chanced to have in my toiletries. Ah, vanity. Then I switched off the overhead light, remembering to unscrew the bulb so I wouldn't be dazzled if someone turned it on suddenly and also to prevent anyone throwing too much light on the subject. Who looked pretty good, all things considered, as I found out when I checked the dummy Theo by the light of the miniature flash I'd also picked up at Mr. Chong's. In the darkness, I tested the window to see how easily it opened—very, unfortunately. And its only lock was a simple hook and eye anyone could open from the outside with a penknife. And the door's lock wasn't much better.

Into the bathroom I went. It was roughly the size of one you'd find on a Pygmy Airlines flight. The door opened the wrong way, too, for me to be able to watch the window and the door directly. I sat on the uncomfortable do-it-yourself plastic toilet seat, closed the bathroom door all but a crack, and peeked out. The mirror I'd left on the bedside table to give me a reflected view of the window was at the wrong angle. I snuck out, rearranged it, then went back to my perch. OK. I'd changed earlier into my basic black outfit (all but the pearls, dear) plus a comfortable old pair of sneakers, so as soon as I'd strapped my shoulder holster on and assured myself that the gun was loaded and the safety on, there was nothing to do but wait.

So I waited.

And waited.

Then waited some more.

All was quiet in the hotel, except for the occasional creak as I cautiously stretched a leg and as wood contracted in the cooling night air. All was quiet in Locke, too, except for the occasional pooch barking in the distance and once a car starting up. And once I heard brief high-pitched snatch of a conversation in Chinese coming from the parking lot out back. Otherwise it was quiet as a giraffes' tea party. Oh—my stomach made the occasional noise as well—probably those damn greasy spareribs. Good, though.

Did I really expect some ancient storm trooper to come sneaking in, Luger blasting, as soon as the witching hour struck?

Part of me did, part of me didn't. The back of my neck did and the palms of my hands did. The logical part of my brain did not, it mocked the very idea. But who do *you* trust these days, amigos? Right. I hear ya talking.

I waited some more. I sucked my way through a package of butterscotch I'd had the foresight to stock up with. There was a day I could have chewed my way through it. I had a sudden moment of panic and reached for my Police Positive. It was still there. Under my breath I intoned a litany from the past I'd forgotten I'd ever learned: action, barrel, chambers, cylinder, cylinder latch, ejector rod, firing pin, forcing cone, frame, front sight, grip-stock, hammer, hammer block–transfer bar. Muzzle, rear sight, spur, star, trigger, trigger guard, yoke. Amen. In the trade, they like you to call cartridges rounds; anything but bullets. You charge a magazine, too, you do not load it, landlubbers.

More creaks. Florida is weird. There anyone can take a course that lasts a few hours and then if you answer a bunch of questions correctly and hand over your fifty bucks ($50.00) you can apply for a permit that allows you to carry a concealed weapon. Even I can't carry a concealed weapon in California, crime-busting fool that I am. I was in Florida once and I went through a course at a place outside Miami called the Open Fence Range. Some of the questions in the exam were pretty tough, though, as I remember. See how you do with a few I can recall, and I am talking memory here, not make-believe. 'When unloading a revolver, keep your finger off the ——." (Fill in the blank.) "The rounds should always —— the gun." "Keep firearms out of the reach of ——." If you have any trouble with the answers, ask any five-year-old kid.

I never did use the permit after all, the lead I was on turned out to be a red herring, but I did run into a high school teacher from Missouri called Debbi, and oh my God I hadn't thought about her for a donkey's years. She ate banana sandwiches for breakfast.

I thought about old Nazis.

I conjectured about the difficulty of bringing some old Nazi to trial for atrocities he was alleged to have perpetrated almost fifty years ago—it is hard enough rounding up witnesses and evidence these days relating to crimes committed a year ago let alone a half-century. And that's not even bringing up details like the statute of limitations.

And who gains anyway by incarcerating some half-dead old geezer, no matter what he's done. Yes, Victor, all this is fine, but what some of those old geezers did was so unspeakably evil they deserve to be pursued by some avenging nemesis for hundreds of years let alone a mere two score and ten. Longer, even. We all know Who said, "Vengeance is mine," but who said, "Let justice be done though the world perish?" I happen to know, for once, who said something. It was Emperor Ferdinand the One. Whoever he was.

More creaks. A snuffling sound from outside, coming from a dog or maybe a raccoon, that American nocturnal carnivore related to bears who is a specialist at opening unopenable garbage tins. I shifted my weight uncomfortably on the narrow toilet seat; no chance of falling asleep on it, which is why I was on it instead of the floor. I flexed my arm and leg muscles regularly just in case I needed them.

The beam of light that swept over the bed was so tiny I didn't realize what it was for a moment; it flickered like a firefly over the supposed sleeping form. Then there followed a muted coughing sound, twice, in rapid succession. Two small indentations appeared in the dummy. Off went the light. Swearing under my breath, I pulled out my firearm and stuck my head gingerly out the bathroom door, almost at floor level. I snapped my light on and gave the room a quick sweep. The slight swaying of the window blind told me the would-be assassin had retreated the same way he'd come—along the fire escape, which had always been the logical choice. The window was partly open; I eased it up the rest of the way, took a cautious peek out, say nothing, then slid through it like a greased eel and crawled toward the stairs. I'd just got to the top of them when I heard the muffled footsteps of someone ahead of me heading down to terra firma and not wasting any time about it, either. I followed, in a crouch, both afterburners ignited.

I was on the fourth or fifth step down when one of my size twelves broke through the rotted timbers, closely followed by the rest of me. I landed on a rain barrel, back first, then bounced off that onto a pile of wooden boxes and discarded flowerpots. I thought at first I'd broken my back; when I tried to move, I was sure of it.

A dark shadow hurtled down the stairs above me. More coughs. I'd only heard that sound once before in my life, not counting upstairs; it was the sound a silenced handgun makes when it is loaded and someone pulls the trigger, as is no doubt highly obvious by this time. And, like the sound of a revolver being cocked by someone else an inch away from your ear, it is one of the truly chilling listening experiences. Moreover, like a Brooklyn accent, once heard, never forgotten.

Ka-pew! is what I heard next, *ka-pew!* twice, if that is the way to describe the noise an unsilenced, high-caliber sidearm makes when it is fired. Then a third *ka-pew!* Then, mercifully, silence, except for someone moaning. I thought it was me for a bit, then I belatedly realized it was coming from a shape lying on the ground almost right beside me. I turned my head and almost passed out from the pain. When the dizziness subsided somewhat, I saw, in the half-moon light, that the shape was Henry C. Clam, alias Nature Boy, also alias my best friend Benny, and he was bleeding to death from a gaping hole right in the middle of his back.

I shouted something, or tried to shout something, I don't remember what. I tried to crawl the few feet to him; it was a nightmare, I couldn't move. Blood was pouring out of him, I had to do something. I unbuckled my holster strap trying to stay calm, trying not to fumble. I got it off and chucked it and the revolver in the rain barrel I'd landed on; they made a satisfying splash. I was going to be in enough trouble without getting done for illegal possession. Anyway, I needed what was under the holster, my favorite wool shirt. I managed to fumble it off, wadded it up, got my courage together, and made a kind of lunge toward Benny, the hand with the shirt in it outstretched. I half fell, half collapsed on top of him but I had the goddamned shirt over the hole and that's all I cared about. Lights came on around us. I shouted some more and lay there until help came. Benny. Benny the Boy.

CHAPTER SIXTEEN

When I woke up, I was wearing a corset.

No, I had not died and gonw to some sort of trans-vestite paradise. It wasn't that kind of corset, there wasn't a bit of lace to be seen, and no peek-a-boo top, darn it. It was made of white, elasticized material, held together by a strip of Velcro down one side, and covered the area from the small of my back to the upper middle of the chest. Oh—my hands were tied by bandages to the sides of the bed, like-wise my feet to the bottom. My head I could move; I moved it, carefully. I was alone in a four-bed hospital ward. There were no tubes coming out of me or IVs dripping into me, always a good sign. I was pretty groggy from whatever it was they'd given me to put me to sleep, but I've had a lot grog-gier awakenings in my life and ones that weren't the result of medication, either. Lubrication, maybe.

Benny. Silly fucker! What was he doing getting all shot up? Watching my back is what he was doing, instead of watching his own. My left hand touched something—it was one of those call things dangling from a cord that you press and then in rushes a pretty nurse to plump your pillow.

I pressed it. A minute later in walked a highly unpretty state cop, a tall, lanky type with a bushy mustache, one hand on his holster. He gave me an unfriendly look.

"I heard there was a nurse shortage," I said "but I didn't know things were this bad."

"She's comin'," he said.

"How're the others? I said, my heart pounding away anxiously. I couldn't bear to hear his answer; I shut my eyes.

"Two dead," he said. "One in intensive care."

"Oh Jesus Christ," I said.

"Yeah," he said, sucking at his teeth. I didn't know how to ask him who the survivor was. I couldn't ask him about Benny, because he wasn't Benny, he was Henry C. Clam. I couldn't ask him about Henry C. Clam because I wasn't supposed to know Henry C. Clam's name. I couldn't ask him about Solly because in the story I'd decided to tell there was no Solly, and anyway I only suspected the guy who came down the stairs after me was Solly. And I couldn't ask him about Cookie, because I wasn't supposed to know it was the feisty little cook from Dago Dan's who had come gunning for Theo. And anyone else who got in his way. Well, it had to be Cookie, he was the only man in town the right age and the right color that Theo had come into visual contact with, and I was with him every second. It might, also, be conjectured that Cookie did overdo the small-town American local character a trifle, although there may be honest citizens that still say things like "Come 'n' get it, if you want it' "—however, that may be hindsight on my part. But the cop unknowingly put me out of my misery.

"It was the guy you tried to help who made it," he said. "So far, anyway."

I turned away. "Thank you," I said silently. After a minute I said to the cop, "You must have been out there."

"Yeah," he said. He leaned against the wall. "First on the scene. Me and the sarge." He shook his head. "Bodies everywhere, never seen nothin' like it in these parts." A harassed-looking nurse bustled in right then.

"Out," she said to the cop.

"Don't go 'way," he said to me. "The lieutenant wants a word or two with you, he'll be by later."

"Tell him no grapes," I said.

The cop left. I opened my mouth to ask the nurse how I was; she immediately popped a thermometer in it. I closed it again. She took my pulse and wrote down the result. When she'd entered whatever my temperature was on my case sheet, I did manage to pop the question.

"You'll live," she said. She produced some scissors that were bent at the end out of her pocket and began cutting away the restraining bandages.

"What were those for?" I asked her.

"To keep you immobile while you slept. You are not supposed to move."

"And this darling corset?"

"To prevent a recurrence," she said.

"Of what?"

"Dr. Imre will tell you all the details," she said. "Now, do you want to go?"

"Love to," I said. "But I'm not supposed to move."

"Very funny, Mr. Daniel," she said. "Do you have to go to the toilet?"

I checked, then said, "No, thanks."

"Are you in any pain?"

I checked, then said, "Only when I laugh, and it doesn't look like there's going to be many of those around here for a while."

"This is a hospital," she said. "Not a circus. Water by your right hand. Lunch in an hour. Dr. Imre will be by before then. Your bell-push is only to be used in emergencies. I understand that policeman will remain outside the ward to prevent any other visitors until his superior arrives." She gave me a disapproving look and took herself out.

"It was a *crime passionel*," I said to her starched back. "I caught her in the act. With two acrobats and Rex, the wonder horse."

The door swished shut. Like babies, all doors should have rubber surrounds and thus be unslammable, is my new and revolutionary theory of a peaceful life. It didn't look like being peaceful for long. Thank God Benny was alive, at least. What a mess.

Last night. The first person on the scene, except for the combatants, was the hotel owner's son. He took one look and ran off to a telephone. The second was the lady doctor staying at the hotel; unfortunately she turned out to be a doctor of Islamic studies, not all that much help in the circumstances. Then other locals began appearing, jabbering away excitedly. I hung on. I could feel that Benny was still breathing. The receptionist came running back. There was no local doctor but ambulances were on their way, likewise the police.

The cops got there first, it wasn't that long; then two ambulances, sirens wailing, screeched into the parking lot and pulled up. Out jumped the paramedics.

"Him first," I said when the first one reached me and Benny. He took one look, ran back to the ambulance, and returned with a pile of absorbent pads of some kind. He said I could take my hand away now. I did. He slapped the pads on, over the shirt, held them with one hand, opened one of Benny's eyes with the other, had a look, then called his pal over, who took over the job of holding the pads in place while the medic got a shot of something into Benny. I couldn't see what the guys from the second ambulance were doing during all this, but a minute later they showed up wheeling a stretcher, lowered it, got Benny onto it with one practiced movement, and off they went. The medic turned his attentions to me.

"Gun shot?" he said, loudly and clearly, his head down next to mine. He looked about sixteen.

"Unh-uh," I said. "Back. Fell on it. Can't move. Hurts like fuck."

"Right," he said. Out came another needle. He slapped it into me. Almost immediately the stuff hit. I was suffused with warmth and love and truth and beauty, I knew the secret at last!

"Mighty good dope, Doc," I said sleepily, grinning foolishly at him. "Don't forget to write me out a repeat prescription later."

"Sure, tough guy," he said. Then it was my turn to get hoisted onto the stretcher and wheeled to the ambulance and then up and in.

"Whee!" I said happily. "Whee whee!"

Off we went, a cop car following us. They took us to the nearest hospital that was both open at that hour and had emergency facilities, which turned out to be St. Helen's in Sac, I remember the medic telling me just before I smilingly went down to visit the sandman. The sandman was home, he was thrilled to see me again. He tucked me into his coziest bed, brought me a glass of wa-wa, made sure I had my teddy, and then kissed me good night.

Then came morning, corset, cop, and nurse, as described. Then came me not moving, waiting for God in the form of Dr. Imre, and God-knew-what in the form of some nameless lieutenant.

The doctor was the first to show, the humorless nurse at his heels. He was skinny and bespectacled, with gleaming black hair, and lots of it. Indian, obviously. Or Pakistani. Maybe Persian. Possibly Ethiopian. He looked surprisingly alert and energetic for someone who'd been up half the night.

"A good good morning to you," he said breezily, scanning my case sheet that was hanging as per usual at the foot of the bed.

"Likewise, I'm sure," I said. "So what's up, Doc?"

"Not us," he said. "For a good few days anyway."

"What did I break?"

"We are not breaking anything at all, amazingly." He grinned widely down at me. "We are merely dislocating one of our lumbar vertebrae. Ouchy ouch! Screams of agony! Shoots of pain!"

"Tell me about it," I said. "So what did you do?"

"Wiggle, wiggle," he said, demonstrating with his hands. "Until it slipped back like a good little vertebra. Some weeny fraction of an inch is all we're talking about. 'Get back in there, you naughty boy!' I was saying. Tell me this, young sir, did we ever have a shoulder dislocate?"

"Probably."

"We are talking exactly the same principle here," he said gleefully. "We want to coax it back into its little socket where it belongs before the muscles stretch. Otherwise we might engender a permanent weakness which we do not desire, no no no, do we, Nurse?"

"No, Doctor," Nurse said.

"Permanent weaknesses we have enough of already," the patient said.

"We are expecting a certain amount of soreness," the doctor said. "Sadly, sadly, this is so. Mistreat any muscle in the body, and what results, Nurse?"

"Soreness, Doctor," Nurse said.

He beamed at her. "We'll ask my favorite osteopath in the whole wide world to drop by later and check you out, but we don't think there is much he can do for you right now except give you a lovely rub all over and . . . what do you think, Nurse, some deep heat? Oh, yes, please!" He squirmed at the thought of it. Nurse looked away. The doctor then looked down at me archly.

"This is far, far from being the first time we are being in a hospital we could not help noticing last night," he said, wagging one brown finger at me. "When you were lying naked as a baby child before our very eyes. Goodness me, no."

"You're right, Doc," I said, looking shamefaced. "I was in once before. For piles."

Dr. Imre laughed merrily. Nurse frowned.

"Thirty-two–caliber piles, you bad boy," he said.

"The worst kind," I said. "Talk about ouchy ouch."

"While you were going beddy-byes," he said, rubbing his hands briskly, "I took the great personal liberty of going through your pockets, you know, with the assistance of a gigantic policeman. We were thrilled to find an up-to-date health card, or at least I was. Goodness knows what would thrill that brute. So we do not have to worry about that part of it anyway, do we, Nurse, such a relief."

Nurse nodded. I could thank my mom for that; she always insisted on me belonging to some health scheme. And I have to admit that despite the lunatic premiums someone in my disreputable line of work, possessing my age and state of health, has to cough up every few weeks, the price is worth the paying. Mighty like a hangover.

"And this charming garment," the doc said, running his fingers coyly up and down the latest addition to my wardrobe, "is to prevent any slippage, you might say, until that muscle heals enough to take over. We are talking a week, ten days. We are taking sleeping on our back. We are talking being extremely careful getting in and out of vehicles and picking items off the floor. We get into a vehicle the same way a matronly lady does—rear end first. We pick fallen tissues off the floor by bending at the knees, not by stooping from our hips. Anything we've forgotten, Nurse?"

"We sit down putting on and taking off our trousers," she said primly. "We do not indulge in any athletic activities but swimming."

"Ten days, eh?" I said. "It'll be terribly frustrating for the little woman but she can always double up on her dance classes. Tell me, Doc, that other guy they brought in with me, whoever he was, how's he doing?"

"Ten minutes ago we were sound asleep," he said. "All systems going. Heart beating normal. Blood pressure way back up. We have three pints of fresh red blood circulating away. Our drainage is in place. If we avoid those nasty secondary infections such as pleurisy, we shouldn't have a thing to worry our poor heads about. Oh, golly, silly me, I almost forgot the best part! Our lung has been completely repaired and is now reinflating in a totally normal fashion."

"Lucky old Benny, I thought, lying there with hardly nothing at all to worry his poor head about. Nurse looked at her watch, then gave her frown lines another workout.

"I am making the assumption from his overall condition that Mr. Clam was not being a professional hockey player or a runner of the marathon, because in that case it is certainly possible that his future performance might be affected negatively."

That's a good one, I am thinking. Whatever Benny was, and he was many things to many people, it is safe to say he was not a long- distance runner. The only time in my life I ever saw him move even briskly was when he had diarrhea that time down in quaint old Mexico, and then his gait was no more than a slow trot.

"Doc, before you go," I said, "thanks for everything, first. Also, I'm curious, just how serious is Mr. Clam's condition? When would he, say, be able to move to another hospital if he wanted to, one closer to his home?"

The doc waved one hand negligently. "A week? If there's no complications. Three weeks, he should be out of hospital completely."

"And me?"

He shrugged cheerfully and gave me a playful little tickle down where my corset ended. I gave him a little slap on the wrist, not quite as playfully.

"How long, how long?" he wondered aloud. "What, three days? Oh! I am forgetting!" He leaped onto one of the other beds in the ward and stretched out stiffly. "Here is how we are getting up. Be watching closely." He maneuvered himself onto his side at the edge of the bed, then in one smooth movement pushed up with one arm while swinging his legs down to the floor.

"And upsadaisy," he said, beaming from ear to ear. "Now you try it."

"Eh, maybe later," I said. "How about dope for the excruciating pain?"

"If we are not foolish, we should not be excruciating," he said sternly. "However, as far as we are being concerned, you can munch Paracetemols all day long." He waved the tips of his fingers at me, then departed, nurse right behind him. Swish went the door—if not the door and the doctor—but what cared I, as long as nurse was around to chaperon me. All systems going . . . he made it sound like he'd stuck a patch on a bicycle inner tube, hell, anyone with an old tube of Elmer's glue could have done it. I was pondering over just why someone would ever bother being a doctor in the first place, especially a proctologist, plus other weighty matters, such as what particular tissue of lies I'd regale the cop outside the door's superior with, when—lo and behold—the cop in question poked his head in the door.

"Still there?" he said affably.

"Just till the cab gets here," I said.

"Well, make yourself decent," he said. "You've got a visitor." He held the door open. In walked a man holding my wallet in one hand and my old wool shirt in the other. He was tall, aged about fifty, his gray hair in a crewcut, and was wearing a brown suit, brown shoes, brown socks, white shirt, and a brown tie.

"Kalagan," he said, sitting on the edge of the bed nearest me. 'Lieutenant, Homicide, Sacramento Police Department. This upstanding young man assisting me is patrolman C. D. Fisher, know to his friends in the department, I believe, as 'Kingfisher,' to the amusement of all concerned. He is here to keep me continually supplied with coffee and to keep a record of the salient points of our discussion, of which I hope there will be many. Patrolman, you may be seated."

Kingfisher sat himself on the bed on the other side of me, took out a pad and pen, and arranged his features into an attentive expression.

"You," the lieutenant said, 'I am reliably informed by the contents of your wallet, are Victor Daniel." He told me where I lived and where my office was located. He told me I was a private investigator licensed by the State of California, and that my license was up to date. So was my driving license. So was my gun permit. So was my MasterCard.

"I used to have a library card, too," I said from my bed of pain, "but I think it expired."

"Your library card was not all that expired," he said calmly.

"So a little bird told me," I said. The lieutenant shot Kingfisher a black look.

"Perhaps you wouldn't mind running over the events of last night for me," he said. "Take your time. Go into any detail you like. Patrolman, when I go like this to you"—he pointed his hand, like a gun, at him—"you inscribe, word for word. Ready when you are, Mr. Daniel."

"Monday," I said. "That would be what?"

"April fourth," Kingfisher said.

"April fourth," I said. "Right. At approximately eleven A.M. I received a visitor in my office."

"Inscribe," said the lieutenant. Kingfisher started inscribing.

"She gave her name as a Miss Ruth Braukis. She gave an address which later turned out to be false. It struck me her name might well have been false as well." Did it ever. If I did think it was really her name, would I have offered it up to the lieutenant? Some question, like "What in heaven's name did you ever see in that cheap, flashy, dyed blond, anyway?" are best left unanswered.

"Describe," he said, cocking his thumb and forefinger again at his minion.

I sighed. "Five foot seven and an iota. Hair, ebon, falling gracefully to her suntanned shoulders. Eyes, heliotrope, flecked with fool's gold. One dimple, left side. Eyelashes, long and well trained. Mouth—words fail me for once. Figure, slim. Chest, forty-two B. Legs, two. Dainty feet, ditto. Perfume, Miss Dior."

"Too bad you didn't get a close look at her," the lieutenant observed. Kingfisher put one hand over his mouth to hide his grin.

"Age."

"Twenty-eight and three months?" I hazarded.

"Vehicle? License plate?"

"Never saw one," I said truthfully.

"Patrolman," the lieutenant said. "Coffee. Lots of. Hot. Milk. No sugar. You?" He arched his eyebrows at me.

"Coffee," I said. "Lots of. Hot. Milk and sugar. Cheese Danish on the side."

"You'll be lucky," said Kingfisher. He departed.

"Onward," said the lieutenant, rubbing a hand over his hair in a weary fashion.

"You look tired, Lieutenant," I said sympathetically. "Been on the go all night?"

"Thank you for your concern," he said. "Yes, I am tired. Yes, I have been on the go all night, or most of it, anyway. I got back from Locke about five. I was at the mortuary till seven. I slept for an hour in my office. I was back out in Locke by nine. I was at the pathologist's back here at ten-thirty. Yes, it is safe to say I am tired, Mr. Daniel, which is why I would like to press onward."

I complied instanter. "Miss Braukis hired me to accompany a man she claimed was her Uncle Theo from LAX to the Star Hotel in Locke, giving me a deposit of six hundred dollars," *In traveler's checks, I recalled bitterly; what were the chances of those being any good?* "She claimed Uncle Theo needed an escort as he spoke no English and she was otherwise engaged."

This time the lieutenant rubbed his eyes.

"Did she say why?"

"Why what? Why she was otherwise engaged or why she wanted him delivered to the Star Hotel?"

"Either, Mr. Daniel," he said. "Or both. I have the feeling it's hardly going to matter."

"The why she was otherwise engaged was she couldn't leave her mother who had recently suffered a stroke. The why she wanted him delivered to the Star Hotel was to rendezvous with his brother."

"Did you investigate either of these claims?"

"I certainly did," I said virtuously. "I established within minutes both claims were highly dubious."

"However, you proceeded to meet 'Uncle Theo' in quotation marks and escort him northward, otherwise you would not have been at the Star Hotel."

"That is correct, Lieutenant," I said meekly.

Kingfisher returned, balancing three paper cups of coffee awkwardly in one large hand. He gave two of them to his boss, the third to me, then returned to his bed.

"Thank you, Patrolman," the lieutenant said. "I cannot say you missed anything of great import. Why?" he then asked me. "Why, why, and again, why?"

"Why not?" I responded, in the best Talmudic tradition. "What could hurt? There's no law against using a false name unless a fraud results. What did I care if he was really her uncle or her fairy godfather? I had half my money down, the other half to come, and all expenses covered, for a few hour's work. I should get that kind of job offered me every day." Well, not every day, maybe about once every millennium, or roughly as often as the Giants stand to win the World Series.

"Let us move on to your arrival in the picturesque town of Locke," said the lieutenant, "unless significant events transpired en route, which I somehow doubt."

I thought about asking him if he knew what they did with all those goats, but desisted.

"What can I say?" I said. "We arrived. We walked around town. Had lunch. Took a nap. Had supper. Watched TV Went to bed."

"Inscribe," said the lieutenant to his stooge. "We are now getting to the gory details."

"Despite a touch of indigestion brought on by a certain fondness I have for pork grease, I fell asleep almost immediately on retiring," I said. 'I was awoken by a noise outside my window. I peeked out cautiously. I saw a man sneaking down the fire escape. Being a detective, and having taken an oath to uphold the law, as have others in this room, I snuck out after him to try and apprehend him, with no thought of my personal safety, armed only by my wits and years of experience."

The lieutenant didn't even bother trying to cover up his yawn.

"I went right through one of the steps on that rotten fire escape," I went on, bitterly. "That guy had better be insured, is all I can say. Look at me! Look at this thing they got me wearing. I may never bowl again. I might have to have someone come in every morning to tie my shoelaces."

"Buy some loafers," suggested the lieutenant. "Then what?"

"Then I landed on the goddamned rain barrel and broke my sacroiliac, is what," I said. "Then I saw Nature Boy lying next to me bleeding to death and only tried to save his life, that's all, while World War Three was going on around me." I took a long swig of the coffee and wished I hadn't. The lieutenant did likewise. Kingfisher took out a stick of gum and began chomping on it. The lieutenant sighed deeply. I sighed even deeper.

"Patrolman," the lieutenant said mildly after a moment, "do you ever get the impression that someone is not telling you the truth, the whole truth, and nothing but?"

"Sure," he said promptly. "I got two kids, remember."

"And let me ask you this. What do you wear when you go to bed?"

"What do I wear? Pajama bottoms, mostly. Or nothing."
Kingfisher looked baffled.

"How about you, Mr. Daniel?"

I pretended to look baffled.

"Me? Oh, you mean if I went to bed early and fell asleep
right away, how come when they found me I was wearing
clothes?"

"That's exactly what I mean," said the lieutenant.

"Those darn sleeping pills," I exclaimed. "They always
do it. I took one for my upset tummy and must have zonked
right out before I had a chance to slip into my nightie."

"Of course," he said absently. "Of course." He took a tattered notebook out of his inside breast pocket and flipped
it open. "Desist," he said to Kingfisher. "Male Caucasian," he
read out to me. "Height, five foot nine. Weight, one hundred
and seventy-four pounds. Hair, blond. Eyes, blue. Heavily
suntanned. Hands show evidence of considerable manual
work. Identifying marks—on lower back and buttocks, scar-
ring probably due to shrapnel wounds, or similar. Scar upper
right deltoid, similar. Scars on upper torso—likely cause, cigarette burns. Unlikely to have been self-inflicted. Et cetera.
Et cetera. Dental work consistent with European techniques,
not U.S. Identification on body—none. Possibility of identification through clothes, et cetera—none. Contents of
wallet—nine hundred forty-two dollars. One pack soft
toothpicks used for massaging gums. Contents of pockets:
one pair cheap sunglasses. One plastic comb. Twelve rounds
thirty-eight–caliber ammunition, suitable for S and W mod
six forty-nine SS Special, found lying beside subject. Paraffin
tests confirm subject had recently fired a handgun.

"Cause of death—to put it simply, he was shot twice in
the heart, at close range, by twenty-two–caliber bullets delivered almost certainly—Ballistics confirmations await—from

a Beretta mod m seventy-one, color blue, length of gun barrel 3 inches. And where was said handgun discovered, patrolman?"

"In the old guy's hand," he said.

"Correct," the lieutenant said. "The old guy—you don't particularly care how tall he is, do you, Mr. Daniel? Or what his exact weight was?"

"No," I said.

"His name was Charles Rivers. Legal immigrant into this country from Mexico in nineteen forty-eight. Name anglicized from Carlos Delrio. Became U.S. citizen in fifty-three. Became owner of establishment known as Dago Don's, sixty-eight. Spotless bill of health from us, state, federal, Internal Revenue, state licensing board, and so on. And so on. What do you think the chances Interpol want him are when we hear from them?"

"Not too good," I said.

"I agree," he said. "Add to the deepening mystery one Henry C. Clam, whose physical characteristics you are no doubt uninterested in as well. Line of work, accountant. Home address, Chippewa Falls, Wisconsin."

Chippewa Falls. If Benny had ever been to Chippewa Falls in his life I was King Zog of all the Slovaks.

"Married."

And if he was married, I was Queen Zog.

"No children. I called his home. A telephone answering machine said he and his wife were on holiday. He could be reached care of the Star Hotel, Locke, and she at a phone number in Los Angeles. I called Mrs. Clam. She was greatly distressed to hear of her husband's condition and is flying up this afternoon. Although I don't think she or her husband have any direct relevance to what happened, I'm looking forward to meeting her."

Mr Lawman, you ain't the only one, I thought.

CHAPTER SEVENTEEN

M rs. Henry C. Clam.
Mrs. Benny the Boy.

The mind boggles, although I don't quite know why. He did like girls, and sometimes they liked him. I started scheming how I might get a look at her, despite my achin' back.

"Of the aforementioned trio," said the lieutenant then, pressing onward, ever onward, "had you encountered any of them prior to last night?"

"Yes," I said. "If Charles Rivers, owner of Dago Don's is also, as I suspect, the cook at Dago Don's, I met him at lunch. He cooked it. Pot roast. I think he put bits of lemon and orange peel in the sauce. And if Henry C. Clam is the name, as I suspect also, of that nature freak I ran into in the lobby of the hotel, then it must be said I've encountered him as well. Once. In the lobby. He was showing Uncle Theo what to do with split ends. Speaking of Uncle Theo, how is he, by the way?"

"Where is he is more like it," the lieutenant said, starting on his second cup of coffee. He actually seemed to like the stuff.

"He's gone?"

"As far as I'm concerned, he never was. By the time I got to checking out his room, it was empty. Cleaned out."

"Oh, he was, all right," I said. "We spent hours together not talking to each other."

"How did you get from San Francisco to here?"

"I drove," I said. "A rental."

"Which is still in the parking lot," he said. "And as there is not an abundance of public transportation out in those parts at three A.M., i.e., none, he either walked out, hitched a ride, or someone picked him up. Which would mean there was someone else on the scene for me to try and fit into the grand scheme of things. Like you."

"Me?" I said indignantly. "My story is not only simple but verifiable. There's the entry in my diary listing the appointment with R. Braukis. There's the down payment she gave me. I've got a copy of the receipt I gave her." I didn't, but could always come up with one if needs be. "There are our airline tickets, plus the airline's records that we actually flew. The car rental. Our checking in here. My case rests."

"Mine does not," said the lieutenant.

"Don't see why not," I said, shifting my weight with extreme caution. "It looks open and shut to me. Unidentified male Caucasian kills cook. Cook kills unidentified male Caucasian."

'Why?" the lieutenant asked mildly. "Don't you like to know why things happen, Mr. Daniel?"

"Sometimes," I admitted. "OK, often, even. Not as much after a few drinks. Not at all when I'm legless. I don't suppose there's any connection."

He smiled briefly.

"Let us examine some of the possible 'whys,' Mr. Daniel, if you can spare a few moments."

I smiled briefly.

"Be my guest. With any luck you'll make me miss lunch."

"Gangs," he said. "It doesn't smell like gangs, does it, Patrolman?"

"No, Chief," he said.

"What does it smell like to you, Patrolman?"

The Kingfisher thought deeply.

"Money?"

"Elucidate," said the lieutenant, doodling in his pad.

"Women, drugs, money, what else do people kill over? The percentage says it's money."

"Flaws," said the lieutenant, "in your reasoning, Patrolman. There are many other causes of aggressive behavior. Drink. Anger. Frustration. Religious mania. Racial hatred. Nonracial hatred. Feelings of inadequacy. Feelings of moral superiority."

"In the line of duty," I chimed in. "For one's country, to protect one's self, one's possession, a loved one. Then there's always kicks.

"Some kick," muttered Kingfisher, to his credit. I've heard it said some cops, and not only cops, actually like shooting at living things.

"To avenge," murmured the lieutenant. "There's one we forgot. Ah well, I don't suppose we'll ever know for sure. As you mentioned earlier, Mr. Daniel, our humble task is to solve, not to reason why, which is probably lucky for some." Here he glanced as Guess Who and it wasn't Kingfisher.

"You never know, Chief," I said encouragingly. "Something may break. Some well-meaning informer, an anonymous letter from a good citizen, perhaps from a woman scorned . . ."

"Sure, sure," said the lieutenant, getting slowly to his feet. "Come on, Patrolman, let us leave Mr. Daniel to his dreams. And his hospital food. To say nothing of his disappearing clients." He strode out.

"See ya," Kingfisher said over his shoulder. The door swished. It swished again. The lieutenant tossed my shirt in the general direction of my bed, missing by a mile.

"Here," he said. "Someone even washed it for you. Hop it didn't shrink."

"Pure virgin wool shrink when it's put through a commercial laundry along with blood stained sheets, surgeon's robes and God knows what from Delivery? Don't make me laugh." He left. Swish. What was left of my shirt lay on the floor. I lay on the bed. I thought. Things could have gone worse with the lieutenant, I thought. Lucky I dumped the gun. Lucky too I had my story together such as it was. Benny's story would be together, too, I had no doubt of that, it always was. If the lieutenant persisted, he could eventually find the link between us, which might lead him to rethink the whole affair, but why should he? Like he said, his task was to solve and solve he had. But a fool he wasn't. "To avenge"—that was a nice touch, that was one way to link up a European, i.e., Israeli, former soldier, and, from the cigarette burns, former what? Intelligence officer? Spy? And why former? Anyway, link him to an elderly immigrant of dubious background who stayed strictly on the right side of the law, never once straying, never once provoking any questions into his past. And, for all I knew, maybe Cookie had a bad burn scar as well, like on his arm, where he had his SS number removed. If SS members did have their numbers tattooed on, I wasn't sure. In any case, careful is what I would have to be for the next few days. Benny likewise, but he didn't need reminding. I hoped his mystery bride would keep her trap shut, whoever she was.

It was Benny, of course, who had delivered me the gun, for all the use it was. You can fly with a gun but there are formalities to go through and the gun and the ammunition for same have to travel in different sections of the plane, which makes for a hassle at the other end, all of which makes it highly obvious to any interested party that you are loaded for bear.

Lunch. Yummy yummy. I was so hungry I ate it, Salisbury steak and all, including the green Jell-o with the fake whipped cream on it. I asked the porter who came to take away the empty tray if he could rustle me up something, anything, to read. He obligingly came back a few minutes later with a copy of that day's local paper, the *Sacramento Bee*, and a well-thumbed Louis L'Amour western. Guess which one I appeared in.

"Blood-Bath in Chinatown!" proclaimed the headline. Then some small-town Hemingway had penned:

> Gunfire echoed through the peaceful, historic town of Locke early this morning, and when the smoke had cleared, two men lay dead in the parking lot behind the Star Hotel, two others, gravely injured.
>
> According to Lt. Keith Kalagan, Homicide, who is in charge of the case, one of the dead men was immediately identified as Charles Rivers, 76, owner of Dago Don's, a popular local bar and restaurant. The identification of the second victim remains a mystery. Also wounded in the fierce gun battle was Henry C. Clay, of Chippewa Falls, Missouri, as well *as please turn to page four.*

I turned to the comics. Then I turned to the sports pages. Then I turned to page four. I was relieved to read that my part in the night's events remained unclear. I was also relieved to read that my condition was described as satisfactory. That wasn't the way I'd describe it, but it was still a lot better than "No flowers. Instead, please send your donations to the Sacramento Tall Club for a plaque to be erected in his loving memory."

A telephone, that's what I needed. I summoned up my nerve and pressed the bell-push thing. After a respectable interval, Old Ironsides poked her head in the door and snapped, "Yes?"

I explained humbly that my poor old mother was unwell and that I greatly desired to call her, if that was all right with all concerned—the hospital, the cops, and her. She disappeared. After another decent interval the same orderly as before brought me in a canary yellow phone, which he kindly plugged into a jack by the head of my cot.

"Automatic," he said. "Call Japan if you want, it'll all go on your bill."

"Sayonara," I said, with just the hint of a bow. How did people with bad backs survive in Japan? They'd never be able to leave the house. I called the car rental, which wasn't the one that tries harder, mine hardly tried at all. I told them I'd need the heap for a few more days, so they needn't bother putting out an all-points alert. I called that polite chap who ran the Star Hotel, who not only asked about my health but brought up the subject of insurance even before I did. He was pleased to inform me that the hotel was fully covered for mishaps such as the one I had suffered, and I was pleased to hear it. He said he would be delighted to keep an eye on my car until I or someone else came to pick it up. Then I took a deep breath and called up Precious.

Precious was out, I was relieved to discover, which meant I could legitimately put off telling her where her ardent

swain had put his big feet this time. I thought about calling either the Israeli Trade Center or the backup number
Miss Ruth Fibber-of-the-World Braukis had given me, but
remembering those words of warning I had given myself
not so long ago—be careful, dope—I was careful, and did
not. Then I tried my mom again, this time successfully. She
didn't remember my last attempt because she wanted to
know how come I hadn't called her when I got back from
Canada and did I have a good time up there?

"Swell, eh, Mom," I said. "Saw a hockey game and
thought about you and Feeb, when you used to go. How are
you, anyway?"

She said she was fine, she was taking a little rest after
lunch was all. I said so was I. I didn't bother telling her where
I was taking it. Or why. If she didn't have enough problems
already, tell me who did. We made the same small talk we
always did when she was lucid, what a word, then rang off.

Then I had a visitor. A reporter visitor, a pert young
thing in a pink jogging outfit and with a pink headband
around her curls.

"Knock-knock," she said, breezing right in. "Anyone
alive in here? Betty Morrison, *Bee*." She waved the hand that
didn't have her camera in it at me.

"Daniel," I said. "V. Other than that, no comment. No
photos, either."

"So what were you doing creeping around the Star Hotel
at dead of night, Daniel? The lieutenant said he was satisfied
your being there was incidental to what happened, and I
quote. You expect me to believe that?"

"At my age, one expects from life roughly what one expects
from hospital cooking—very little, my dear, also lukewarm."

She grinned and hopped up on one of the beds.

"And you may quote me, just this once," I added magnanimously. I wondered if the lieutenant had divulged to her what my line of work was; that I could do without, I'd never get rid of her.

"Well, what were you doing at the Star Hotel aside from being incidental?"

"It was to have been a sentimental pilgrimage," I said. "My wife and I spent the first night of our honeymoon at the Star Hotel. I hoped like a fool, that if we revisited it together after all these years, we might regain some of the happiness we frittered away."

"So what happened?"

"She wouldn't come with me," I said. "She went to visit her mother in Sarasota instead."

Miss Morrison looked at me suspiciously, then sighed.

"OK, OK," she said. "I get it. No comment. How do you like living in L.A.?"

"Been at the hospital records again, have we," I said. "Naughty, naughty. Los Angeles has many attractive qualities. The Dodgers are one, the Lakers are one, and I forget the third one."

"What kind of work did you say you did?"

"I don't believe I did mention it," I said, "but actually I travel in ladies' undergarments."

"Yeah, yeah, tell me another," she said, hopping down off the bed.

"With pleasure," I said. "This here was my father's favorite. It's the tsar of all the Russias' birthday."

"See ya," she said. Swish went the door.

"The tsar," I continued unabated, "was greatly impressed by a trained-bear act. So much so that he asked the trainer and his bear back for his next birthday party, when he wanted the bear to have learned one more trick—to be able to talk in Russian.

"A pleasure!" cried the trainer. "See you next year, oh mighty tsar."

On the way out of the castle, the trainer's apprentice says to him, "Master, not even you can teach a bear to talk in a year, so how come you agreed?"

"Listen, schmuck," the trainer says. "A year's a long time. In a year I could be dead. In a year, God forbid, the tsar could be dead. And believe me, next year at this time if I'm not dead and tsar's not dead, you can bet your last kopek that fucking flea bag's a goner."

And, talking about betting, comrades, I'll bet you 10 zillion kopeks to one you can't guess who my next visitor was, and I'll give you an enormous hint—she was someone's imaginary wife. Not Benny's—mine.

It was couple of hours later. I'd napped awhile, on my back like I was supposed to, and once I even moved, all the way to the bathroom. I pushed myself erect on the edge of the bed as instructed. Ouch. I stood up, expecting the worst. Mild ouch only. I shuffled. Mild ouches, strong swear words. Some genius had fastened metal hand grips on both sides of the toilet, which helped greatly. It didn't hurt that much, actually, a dull ache was all it was, the problem was trying to forget how much it had hurt the night before and overcoming the fear that the slightest movement would make it hurt that much again. Constipation—like living in the land of the rising sun, that's another complication a guy with a bad back does not need, I realized as I sat there trying to make a little hat out of a piece of toilet paper. Pop used to make us kids hats out of a sheet of newspaper. He taught Tony how to do it but I don't remember him teaching me. Who cares, anyway?

I was attempting to do the crossword in the *Bee* in my head because I didn't have a pen when my new buddy the orderly popped his head in the door.

"Make yourself pretty," he said. "Your wife's on the way up." He whistled appreciatively, then withdrew.

Well, at least my wife wasn't the twerp. She turned out to be Precious. Precious entered, lips pursed. She glared at me, then nodded her head several times, then managed to get out, through clenched teeth, "Uh-huh. Just about what I expected, you flat on your back again in another bloody hospital. I don't see any holes, where are they, hidden by that stupid thing you're wearing?"

"That's not a stupid thing," I said, hastily pulling up the sheet to my neck. "That's my corselet, it's the latest thing. Anyway, that's no way to talk to your new bridegroom, snookums."

"Well, I didn't know, did I," she said angrily. "I didn't know what kind of mess you were in, so I thought if I said I was your wife, at least they'd let me see you."

"I'm fine, I'm fine, I got a sore back is all and I'm not in any mess, so calm down and straighten my sheets or something. Better still, give us a kiss."

"I'll think about it," she said.

"What are you doing her, anyway? How did you get here?"

"It was called an airplane, I think," she said. "I got on it in Burbank and got off right here in dear old Sac."

"Sara," I said. "She must've called the hotel like I asked her. Then of course she had to call you up."

"What else?" declared my beloved. "She was scared out of her wits by some idiot clerk who was rambling on about bodies and guns and ambulances and cops and God knows what else."

'He's not an idiot," I said. "I happen to know he's a devoted student of advanced paleontology."

"Who gives a flying fuck what he's studying," Evonne said. She crossed over to my bedside, then stooped and gave me a peck on one cheek. "There," she said. "You're lucky to get that much. You sure you're all right?" she asked in softer tones.

I assured her I was right as rain, almost, and in no time at all we'd be highland-flinging together again just like in the good old days.

"And Benny?"

"Shhh," I said, one finger to my lips. I beckoned her closer; she sat on the bed and lowered her pretty head to mine. "How do you know Benny's here?"

"Sara told me," she whispered back.

"Who else?" I said. "How did she know?"

Evonne shrugged.

"He's here, but he's not Benny," I whispered. "He's Henry C. Clam, and he's a total stranger, got it?"

She nodded. "I got it. I don't understand it, but I got it."

"The bad thing is," I said, "he got shot. I don't know the details, because the cops have cleverly kept us apart till now so we couldn't collude on a story, but I'm afraid he's only using one lung right now."

"Oh, Jesus, no," she said, laying her cheek against mine. "Poor Benny."

"Don't worry," I said hastily. "They're blowing the other one up again, the doc said. But yeah," I said into her blond hair. "Poor Benny. And don't bother piling the blame on me, it's already piled."

I convinced Evonne Louise Shirley that there was no point in her hanging around Sacramento; I'd be up and about in a couple of days and she couldn't even legitimately visit Benny's bedside as long as he was being someone else. I told her a version of the events of the night before that was skillfully edited to prevent her getting any madder at me. The name of a certain Miss Ruth Rotten-Liar Braukis did not, repeat, not, come up even once.

Before she flew home that evening, my angel of mercy did the following—bussed out to Locke. Packed up my things from my room. Paid the bill. Tried unsuccessfully to retrieve my gun and holster, but there were too many sight-seers around. No great problem—its serial number did not correspond to the one on my license and so could never be traced back to me. Then she returned to Sacramento with car and luggage. Then she went shopping for books, maga-zines, including that month's *Pro Basketball*, fruit, candy, and assorted nuts.

And, last but by no means least, she brought me a large brown paper bag, in which was my supper—one pas-trami on rye, one salami on white, heavy on the mustard, a tub of pickles and one of cole slaw, two wedges of plain cheesecake, and a quart bottle of cream soda. Plus a paper napkin. Oh—plus a styrofoam cup of chicken soup. After she hugged me gingerly one last time and left, I devoured everything but the napkin and the plastic fork. The car she dropped off at Sacramento's airport, paying the tab for it as well. Whoever it was who said that love is, after all, the gift of oneself, might have added that a good pickle on the side doesn't hurt, either.

CHAPTER EIGHTEEN

The following early afternoon, just after a lunch of maca-
roni and Velveeta, they moved me to another ward, in
a wheelchair, my overnight bag on my lap and my pal the
orderly pushing. This was both good news and bad news.

The good news was that the law must have passed the
word that it was no longer necessary to keep me in solitary,
otherwise they couldn't have shifted me even though I was
taking up four beds. Maybe I'd get a different nurse, too, I
thought on the journey, one that looked Annette Funicello
instead of Sir Charles Barkley. Down the hall we trundled,
past a dead person being pushed in the other direction.
Into the elevator. The orderly said his name was Fred. I said
mine was Vic. Up one floor. Down the hall. Into a ward containing the bad news—Henry C. Clam. Now, Henry C. Clam
was a sick man—he was in an intensive care ward. V. (for
Victor Daniel was not a sick-enough man to need to be in
an intensive care ward. Therefore if he was in one, especially one containing Henry C. Clam by chance, there had
to be a good reason. And what better reason than Lt. Keith
Kalagan, Homicide. I had no doubt at all that the whole
room was not only littered with bugs but infested with them.

My pal Benny was hooked up, tubed up, roped up, ban-
daged up, and propped up in the second bed down. The
third bed down was invisible behind drawn white curtains.

Fred helped me up onto the first bed down, then put my overnight bag under the metal-topped table beside it. Out he went. Swish. I winked at Benny. He winked back. I held one cupped hand to my ear to indicate I thought we were being eavesdropped on. He pretended to yawn, meaning, What else is new? and pointed one thumb at the invisible bed. I nodded, and pointed one thumb at various light fixtures and the telephones. He nodded.

I eased myself into the bed. I stretched out my left hand as far as it would go. Benny did likewise with his right one. They met, just, and we gave each other's fingers a sort of squeeze. In case someone was watching through a gap in the drawn curtains around bed number three, I said, "Hi, pal. Victor Daniel, we met briefly in the hotel lobby, remember?"

He nodded. "Henry Clam," he said indistinctly around the tube coming out of his mouth. I couldn't see where the other end went; he was lying on his side, facing me, and it disappeared over his shoulder. He was strapped up from his waist almost to his shoulders, with more tubes—perhaps parts of the drainage—snaking out front and back. He was hooked up to an IV as well and the connection for the heart monitor was still there just in case. He had to be hooked up to a bedpan, too, although his bottom half was covered by a sheet. I noticed one of the tubes went through a bottle of water that was gurgling slightly.

"How're you doing, then?" I said.

"I've been better, I must admit," he said in his throaty whisper. "What about you?"

"Aw, nothing," I said. "A sore back, fell through the fire escape. Too bad I didn't land on my head instead. Don't talk if it tires you out, pal, but they told me you were shot, right?"

"Twice," he whispered. "From behind. I never heard anything. I went out to get some flies from my car. I woke up here."

"Yeah," I said. "I heard. Jeez, I'm sorry, Henry."

"I'm lucky to be alive," he said. "That's the way I think of it, Mr. Daniel. Also, thank goodness for Blue Cross. And you, they tell me."

Which made me feel a little better, but not much. Benny fell asleep about five seconds later; he had to be fairly heavily sedated, the shape he was in and all the damage his system had taken. Sleep on, amigo. And sweet dreams. "I went out to get some flies from my car"—dry flies, to fish with, obviously, not tse-tses—right in character, only he wasn't out getting flies, he was covering the foot of the fire escape. Cookie must have been pretty good to surprise him so completely. "Blue Cross"—that was good news; not only because of the astronomical hospital expenses he was running up, but if he had a legitimate Henry C. Clam Blue Cross card, it was odds on he had several other legitimate Henry C. Clam IDs, driving licenses, plastics, and so on. Thus he was well covered from the prying eyes of suspicious lieutenants who wanted to know why. And wherefore.

About an hour later a different orderly this time, accompanied by a marginally less Gorgon of a nurse, came into our ward and vanished behind the curtains around bed number three. Various noises ensued. The curtains opened. Orderly and nurse wheeled out the bed and whoever was in it most smartly. Swish and he was gone. Nice try, Lieutenant, I thought. Now we're supposed to think it's all clear, now we'll spill all the beans about what really happened. Childish, really.

Actually, when Benny woke up later, we hardly talked at all. He opened his mouth once to let the nurse take his temperature, once to take the pills she gave him, and once to ask me to please avoid mentioning any gory medical details when his wife came back as she was not very strong and he didn't want her any more upset than she already was. I told him, naturally, of course, not to worry, go back to sleep.

And when his wife did show up, it would have been about five-thirty, I had to agree with him, she didn't look strong, poor wee mite. She was thin, and only about five feet tall. Her cheeks were reddened, as if she'd been crying. She had a floppy sun hat on her head, a baggy print dress, and on her lower limbs white socks that sagged and tennis shoes that bulged. Mrs. Chippewa Falls to the teeth, also known as Sara Silvetti, champion nerd.

"Did my baby miss me?" she said in some sort of cloying accent as she passed my bed without even looking at me. I gritted my teeth and pulled the sheet up right over my head.

"Let me give my poor baby a big kiss. There! That'll make it well in no time." Please avoid mentioning any gory details, eh, Benny? Not strong, your little wifie, eh?

"And who's your new roomie, honey?" she said after a while. "You haven't introduced us, you bad boy."

He introduced us, in his croak.

"Martha, Mr. Victor Daniel. Mr. Daniel, Mrs. Martha C. Clam."

"Charmed, I'm sure," she said, coming over to my bed and pulling one corner of the sheet down. She tucked something under my pillow while I muttered some sort of greeting. Then, mercifully, she went back to pester her poor baby. She held his hand. She wiped his face with a tissue. She held up the glass of water with the bent glass straw in it so he could take a sip. She wanted to know if he wanted her to read to him. Did he want a telly yet, or how about a radio? Everything was fine back home, she'd telephoned

Daddy and he'd driven past their house to see that everything was all right. Bobby was fine and behaving himself, he
only made a mess once and that was in the kitchen. On and
on she went. Did he need anything. Did he want anything,
any little thing. Then she made her one mistake, she asked
me if I needed anything from the great outdoors. Did I ever.

"One pastrami on rye," I said. "One chicken liver on
white."

"Wait till I get a pencil," she squealed. "OK."

"One order potato salad. One tub pickles. One plain
cheesecake. Two honey donuts. Two ginger ales."

"That all?" she said sarcastically.

"Maybe a butterscotch sundae, two scoops." I said. I gave
her the name and address of the deli that was printed on the
cup of chicken soup Evonne had brought me. "If you don't
mind getting my wallet for me, it's in my bag under the table
there, I don't know if I can bend over that far. It's my back,
you see. Sort of fell on it."

"Oh you poor thing," she said. "Henry put his back out
once, didn't you, dear. He was taking things out of the dryer
and it went, just like that."

"Tsk, tsk," I said.

"Back in a jiffy, dear," she said. "Sure you don't need
anything? Maybe a little surprise from your honey?"

He shook his head weakly.

She said, "Toodle-oo, then," and flitted to the door and
out. Swish. I retrieved what she had hidden under my pillow. It was a large envelope. Inside was the following poetical masterpiece:

April 13, 1988.
Confidential Report No. 18.
From: Special Agent SS.

To: V.D. (Ha-ha)
i feel like a punctured condom
laying on a shopping mall floor
used once discarded with a greasy plop
trampled on by adenoidal valley girls
i see stars
it is only my neighbor a milky way candy
    bar wrapper
cuddled up for comfort gainst a lipsticked
    kleenex

CANTATA THE FIRST	EXPENDITURES
To have to	
Catch a bus	.75
To	
Catch a bus	.75
To	
Catch a bus	6.50
Is bad enough	
When loving arms await at t'other	
end,	
But when 'tis user hostile LAX,	
I tell ya, Tex,	
It's tough on this delicate bit o'	
Fluff.	
But when needs must,	
Watch my dust.	
So: Born Again lives again—	
In Ma's old dress 'n' Granny shoes,	
Dewy cheeks scrubbed and shining,	
Eyes a-burning with that Inner Light	

So annoying to others of lower wattage—
I wonder Y?
Is it fear of X,
The unknown? Or fear of what could B
For me, could also B
For thee?
Did my job. Smiled and smiled
    and distributed posies,   5.00
Skulked and spyed out this boyo
    who looked suss.

                              TOTAL
                           $13.00

"Excuse me, Mr. Clam," I said, "but how do you spell *spied?*
But Mr. Clam was asleep again.

                        EXPENDITURE TOTAL

Telephoned V.D. (chuckle)
In S.F $13.00
Went home   .75
You know how.   8.00
Soup 'n' steak sandies for
    supper.
The phone rang once. It
    was the Speaking Clock,
Wanting to know what time
    it was.

CANTATA THE SECOND

O
Canada,

EXPENDITURE TOTAL

See what you done to me.
It's Tits McGurk   1 toque $9.95 Can.
& George the Jerk
Under a spreading maple tree.

CANTATA THE THIRD

So Benny sez to me sez he,
In the highly unlikely event
That anyone calls your numero
And asks for a certain Mrs. Clam,
You are she. You are married to me.
We dwell in Chippewa Falls,
And our doggy's name is Bob.
Other revolting details followed.
Alerted parents. Yestermorn
When I was yet abed, to my surprise
A call did come. It was de Law.
My hubby shot! Not once but twice!!
What could I do, plead the vapors,
Say I had a more important engagement,
I just had to get my nails done, I
        couldn't possibly
Be seen in public the way they were?
I had to show up in Sac prontissimo
        like a good
Little loyal wifie-poo
Is what I had to do . . .
                    Ticket   84.00
                    New outfits   145.00

"	perfume	20.00
"	makeup	18.00
"	hairdo	25.00
	Motel per night	28.00
	Food per day	30.00
	Carmen rollers	9.95

. . . and what I done.
And what I will have to go on
    doing
Until we get Benny outa here!
Stuck in Sac! I'd rather be
    stuck in
Shit right up to my (newly)
    plucked eyebrows.
By the by the by, flew up here
    with Evonne,
Case she never mentioned it, ha-
    ha-ha-ha.
Yesterday before she left we
    rendezvoused
As per arranged, which is how I knew
You and Henry C. Clam were but
    strangers
In the night,
Exchanging meaningful glances.

TOTAL AND MORE TO COME

$391.65

i feel like a bruised peach
in a skid row supermarket
the kind with barred windows

and saggin tin door
fingered too often by unwashed hands
the deadly softness spreads
wasps gather

"Wasps gather"—spare me! Nurse! I'm sinking fast! I'm making medical history, I'm going to be the first person in the world ever to die of acute doggerelitis, except maybe Rod McKuen's editor. And she flew up with Precious, did she, in case Precious never mentioned it. She knew perfectly well Precious never mentioned it, but rest assured I was going to mention it to Precious the next time I saw her. Very funny, girls. I'm practically dying and they're preparing amusing surprises for me. And that so-called expense account. First of all, she probably made money with those posies, she never mentioned that; people in airports who hand you posies ask for donations, don't they. And I noticed she included that $9.95 Canadian in the ludicrous total without converting it into U.S. currency; what a piker. You'd have thought that love might have mellowed her attitude toward money just a trifle but no such luck. Speaking of love, I wondered briefly how her big affair with Willing Boy was going . . . I reminded myself to ask her discreetly when she got back with my repast, if she ever did.

She did, finally. I devoured the chopped chicken liver on white while Benny was out of the room being X-rayed; the orderly who wheeled him out told me he had to be X-rayed daily to make sure no fluids were accumulating in the damaged lung. The twerp exited with them and did not reappear until the following morning, to my intense relief. I spent what was left of that miserable day not moving and reading the basketball magazine Precious had brought me. There was an article in it comparing the relative merits of Larry Bird, Michael Jordon, and Magic Johnson and what they meant to their team, which were, respectively, the Boston somethings, the Chicago nothing, and the World Champion Los Angeles Lakers. I laughed despite the pain.

Two days later I was discharged, and betook myself, corset and all, palely loitering, out into the real world again. It didn't look like it had changed all that much while I was away. It was late in the afternoon and I didn't feel like flying home that night so I hailed a cab and asked the driver to take me to some not-too-expensive motel preferably on the way out to Sacramento's airport, which he proceeded to do instantly and without a lot of chatter, either. I knew the name of the birdbrain's motel, as she had mentioned it to her "hubby"; you can believe I made sure the cabby did not by some fluke drop me off at the same one. This was not solely from a desire to avoid the twerp's company, there was an outside chance Lt. Potato Eater had someone keeping an eye on me although I hadn't spotted anyone along the way. All we needed was for some busybody to overhear me call Mrs. Clam Sara or nerd or whatever, then, bingo, she's not Mrs. Martha C. Clam, maybe Mr. Henry C. Clam isn't Henry C. Clam, either.

Anyway. The Take-Off Motel had a room for me. After checking in I made a reservation for a flight back to L.A. at two the following afternoon, then went on the prowl for a friendly estaminet, i.e., a bar that would let me in. The motel didn't have one but they directed me to something called the Bunkhouse, a mere fifty yards or so up the road heading west toward the airport.

Toward the Bunkhouse I strolled, along the verge. On the verge, too, of slaking a three-day thirst. On the way I wondered in passing if my putting off my return trip was in any way connected with a reluctance to face up to the immediate future. F-u-t-u-r-e—spelled Miss Ruth Snake-in-the-grass Braukis, for one. And the death of Solomon, for another. And Cookie's history, for another. And my own ineptness, if you want yet another.

The only thing remotely special about the Bunkhouse was that it contained two dart boards, and both were in use when I entered. The jukebox was playing, "Only two thangs money can't buy, that's true love 'n' home-grown tomatoes." I slid onto a vacant stool at the long wooden bar, leaving a one stool gap between me and an angry-looking middle-aged lady in an orange jumpsuit whose blond hair was done up in an elaborate beehive, shades of yesteryear. A motherly looking lady who introduced herself as Sal took my order for a brandy and ginger. When she'd served it up I took a long, satisfying swallow, and said, "Ahhhh."

"Sounds like you needed that," said Sal.

"Needed is right," I said. "I've just spent three days in a hospital drinking stale water, ice-cold tomato soup, and once, Hawaiian punch."

"That'd drive anyone to drink," observed Mrs. Beehive. "Speaking of which, Sal." Mrs. Beehive had chubby cheeks, which made her look something like an amiable chipmunk.

Sal obliged with another vodka on the rocks for the lady. A Mrs. Goode. Well, we got to talking, as often happens in bars, and by the time I was making a dent in my third libation, I was Vic to her and she was Katy to me and my back wasn't hurting at all and nor was my front. She asked me what I did. I told her. She said, "Really?"

I said, "Cross my heart." I asked her what she did. She said she ran the mobile home park right down there, see? She pointed out the side window. I looked where she pointed and sure enough, a mobile home park, all prettily lit up, is what I saw. It turned out, what she was angry about was she'd had another robbery over at her place, which made it umpteen million in three months would you possibly believe it, which was why she was so interested in anyone in my line of work.

"Am I to assume the police have not made a lot of progress up until now?" I ventured around a mouthful of microwaved pepperoni pizza Sal had just deposited in front of me.

"They show up right away, in carloads," Katy said. "They're polite, they look around diligently, they say all the right things, they make notes, they spray that powder stuff around, they put it all in some computer, but." She shrugged. "You know."

"How well I do know," I said. "Those guys in robbery, they do their best but they've got huge case loads and for anything under five or ten grands' worth, they just don't have the time."

"How about you, Vic?" Katy said, sucking the end of her swizzle stick. "You got the time to spend if I've got the money to spend?"

"I got till two o'clock tomorrow," I said.

"So come on down," she said. "Senate Mobile Estate. I'm the first home on the left inside the gates, it says 'manager' on it. It's got yellow roses all up one wall. And a doghouse out on the porch."

Given that wealth of detail," I said, "I should probably be able to find it without getting totally lost." She smiled, then touched the top of her hair carefully to see if it was all still there. It was. How I wish I could say the same.

We had a nightcap, me and Katy and Sal and a huge tattooed truck driver called George and his tiny wife Doreen, then I gingerly eased myself off the stool, made my farewells, and wound my way back to the motel and, a few moments later, to dreamland. On my back, Doc, too. Was I glad to get that fool corset off. Was I glad I wasn't a lady living in Victorian times when the wasp waist was *de rigeur*, my dear. I was glad I wasn't a lady living in any times, come to think about it. Imagine having to kiss some jerk good night on your doorstep after he's just taken you for a meal of fish curry. No, thank you. Imagine having to stifle yawns while some Romeo is taking twenty minutes to figure out how to undo your Cross-Your-Heart bra. No, thank you. Imagine having to take some Lusting Lothario's word for it when he swears he had a vasectomy two years ago this Wednesday. Imagine . . . I fell asleep imagining.

CHAPTER NINETEEN

It was nine-thirty the following A.M. when I knocked on the door of Katy's mobile home, using for the purpose a brass knocker shaped like a horse's head. *Knock knock knock.* The door opened; Katy greeted me and bade me enter. She was wearing a floor-length satin-looking house robe and her hair was as immaculately coiffed as it had been the night before.

"I wasn't sure you'd show," she said. "But I made some coffee just in case. Coffee?" She led the way into the living room.

"You bet your boots." I said. Just inside the door, on the wall, was a notice board that had pinned to it among other things, a calendar of the estate's events for the month.

"Sit yourself down," she said. "Back in a jiff."

"Thank you," I said, lowering myself with some trepidation into a wing chair by the front window after removing a bag of knitting from the seat first. Katy came back from the kitchen carrying a tray on which were a Pyrex coffee maker, full to the brim, two mugs, creamless cream, sugarless sugar, and a half a Sarah Lee coffee cake.

"Nice place," I said politely as she poured out the coffee. Actually, it wasn't bad if you like living in a converted DC-10. And on top of nubbed carpets.

"It's your standard single," she said, cutting me a piece of the coffeecake. "Twelve feet wide, 56 long, expandable, naturally. Runs upward of fifteen thou, thirty-five for the double. Your lot rent here about one seven five. This here is an older model, the siding's aluminum, the panels plywood. In the newer ones, and I'll show you one if you like, you've got all wood siding and your Sheetrock insulation, of course."

"Of course," I said.

"Ten percent down is customary," she said. "The rest we can finance for you over twenty years. If you're at all interested, I've got a realtor's license, as a sideline, like, I could give you a really good deal on one.'

"I am a detective, madam," I said. "I did realize what your sideline was when you were three words into your spiel."

She grinned.

"Caught in the act again," she said, without sounding overremorseful.

"The robberies," I said. "I want all the details you have—when, where, how, from who, what was taken, everything and anything."

"Back in a jiff," she said. I know she took longer than a jiff because while she was gone I had time to leaf through a copy of *Sacramento Single Souls* that chanced to be on the cocktail table right beside me. I skipped past "My Most Creative Date," also "Make-over of the Month," but deeply perused the following female ad: "I am the woman your mother warned you about!! My dream is to participate in a mutually beneficial relationship with an exceptionally sexy and intellectually stimulating male. His often exotic behavior and cosmopolitan view of life only helps to support his desire to change and grow." Me—to the very tee!! "He is adult both emotionally and financially and he is particularly attracted to brilliant, positive women who are in touch with their own physicality." Right on again!! "Age?" (Oh-oh) "Old enough to know better, young enough to walk barefoot in the rain." Damn—tripped at the final hurdle.

I was glancing at an ad tor sensual boudoir portraiture (a thrilling memento he will long remember) when Katy returned with a bulky green cardboard folder, which she plunked down on the table beside the tray.

"That's all there is, there ain't no more," she said. I took out my notebook and a pen, opened the file, and began detecting. Katy watched me with undisguised fascination.

Number of thefts—eight, not umpteen million. From eight separate mobile homes, no repeats. I noted the names of the home owners. I inquired of Katy what protective devices, if any, the homes had when they were burgled— they all had something more than a lock on the front door; in a few cases, a lot more. I made a list of what had been sto-len—there were a handful of small items but mainly money, quite a lot of it, considering. Of course the biggest hauls came from the homes that were the best protected; it stands to reason that if you spend a lot of money to protect, you must be protecting something valuable, any crook could work that out. All this money had, also of course, been clev-erly stashed away in unfindable places, so much so that it might have taken the thief as much as say five minutes to unearth it.

When I'd gotten that far, I asked Katy to take me on a tour of the estate, please, and to make sure the tour included all the homes that had been broken into. So off we went, down Election Lane, into Convention Lane, around Representative Circle, and son on—well, it was the Senate Estate and Sacramento was the state capitol—get it? I noticed that everything was clean, the grass was well tended, likewise the flowers, that the swimming pool had no customers, nor did the rec room, and that all of the homes that had been burgled all had back windows that faced the high, wooden, slatted fence that enclosed the estate, not back windows that faced someone else's windows. I left Katy talking with an elderly resident we met on our meanderings, the subject being animal droppings, and made two complete tours of the exterior fencing, one outside and one inside.

Some half an hour later I rejoined her in her home. When we were sitting around the cocktail table again, I said,

"The story so far. We are dealing with a professional, not kids. He's done eight successful break-ins, and according to the police report they sent you, they don't have a clue. He's also a professional because he's not frightened off at all by alarm systems or weight sensors or whatever, *au contraire*, he loves them. And it looks like an inside job to me. There's been some small attempt to make it look like someone climbed over the fence but I'm not convinced; the couple of places where the grass near the fence was disturbed on the inside, on the other side is cement, which doesn't show traces."

"So?" said Katy.

"So, I as a resident here could find plenty of reasons for wandering around inside making all the traces I wanted, walking the dog, picking wildflowers, but who's going to walk around no man's land outside, looking for what, weeds, used tires? And it goes without saying that he's also a pro because wherever you cleverly hide your emergency fund, he's on to it pronto, but you know what is outside that fence?"

"No," said Katy. "What?"

"A service road that leads back up to the highway. So the reason only small stuff was taken wasn't because of the difficulties of moving it, you could hoist a grand piano over that fence as long as someone's waiting to catch it and shove it in the van. Or VCRs, TVs, rugs, you name it, but if it is someone living here, what's he going to do with a grand piano, stick it in his living room? Or ten TVs, stick them in the den? There's no way he could truck them out of here without some kindly neighbor watching. Something else, Watson—in every case the homes that got burgled were empty at the time of the crime. How did he know? Most of them had lights left on, I noticed, and in a couple of cases, radios, too. All right. Next step. I need a list of all residents. Also I need that." I indicated the calendar of events pinned on the notice board. "Ages of residents, too, if you've got them," I said to her as she was heading for the notice board.

"I do," she said, " 'cause I send them all birthday cards." She unpinned the calendar and brought it over to me. "I had a thought. This awful man who's making my life a misery—well, it has to be a man, doesn't it, I can't see any of the old biddies who live here creeping around at dead of night climbing into windows, bless them. Anyway, why doesn't he know a home is empty because he sees the people inside leaving?"

"Excellent, Watson," I said. "However, the eight homes in question are all scattered around the periphery of the estate, there's no central location he could be in that would allow him a line of sight with them all."

What if his home is like where mine is so he can see every car that leaves, 'cause there's only one way out?"

"A fine feat of ratiocination yet again, Watson," I said. "But recall." I showed her one of the lists I'd made. "God knows why the cops didn't pick this up." In all the burglaries the residents were away from home all right, but they weren't off the estate, they hadn't driven into town to catch an X-rated film or gone to a drive-in. They were still on the estate attending one of the regular social events put on in the rec room, which is why I wanted to check out the calendar. So I checked it out. It said things like, "Monday—social club meeting." "Tuesday—sewing group." "Wednesday—executive board meeting." "Thursday— paper pickup—have them out by 8 A.M." "Friday—special meeting." "Saturday—bingo!" "Sunday—breakfast in the park." Also entries like "Wednesday—gamblers, bus to Reno." "Thursday—Talk 'n' slides on South Korea." 'Sat.— dance." "Tuesday—Spanish group." And so on, amigos; starting to get the idea? Deduction by elimination is the idea, for you slo-pokes. Katy, at my request, came up with membership lists for all the various groups, classes and what have you. She also came up with copies of the estate's monthly newsletter, in which were published news 'n' views and new residents and of course the monthly calendar of events and occasionally a tidbit like, "The sewing group is pleased to welcome new member Mildred Baker, blah blah blah . . ." It also helpfully listed the members in attendance at the various meetings, following the old small-time news-paper principle that what a reader wants most to see in a paper is his or her own name.

Elimination—from the list of residents and their ages, I eliminated all males under twenty-five (none) and over, just guessing, seventy. We had already eliminated all females, remember. That left me fourty-four clients. Then I eliminated all those attending social functions on the estate the nights of the robberies, what else. One man from the sewing circle. The Reno bus took care of another eight. Spanish class, two more; obviously if someone was brushing up his Mexican he wasn't likely to say, "Excuse me a momento," slip out and go looting and pillaging. It was possible, OK, but it was later shown the burglary took place when he was gone, then where would he be? Old-time dancing eliminated three more, including me. Still too many names left. I took a wild stab at it and eliminated all married men, because you try hiding something from your wife and see how you get on. That cut it down to four possibles—all right. I asked Katy what she knew about our four potentials—she knew them all personally, of course, she said. All seemed ordinary. No one was a newcomer. The only thing . . .

"Speak to me," I said.

"Mr. Elkins," she said, pointing to one name on the list. "I seem to remember he paid cash for his home, which you don't see often."

"Well, well," I said. "When was that, can you remember?"

"Eight or nine years now," she said. "I could look it up if you want."

"Doesn't matter," I said. "Use your phone? it's to L.A."

"Help yourself."

I called Sneezy. He was out. I sighed, and asked to be transferred to my brother. He was in.

"Lt. Anthony Daniel, Records," he said.

"Tony? It's me," I said. "How's the wife? How're the kids?"

"They're fine," he said guardedly.

"Mom?"

"Not so good last time I was out there," he said. "When was the last time you were out there?"

"Tony, give me a break," I said. "I've been busy, haven't I. I've even been up in Canada, for Christ's sake. I'm still shivering."

There was long pause. Oh-oh. Somehow I didn't get the feeling that Tony was about to give me a break.

"Tony, I need a favor," I said. "I'm up in Sac on a case, can you run three or four names through the computer for me? I wouldn't ask if it wasn't important."

"No," he said, not trying too hard to keep the satisfaction out of his voice. "You know it's against the rules."

Helping your brother isn't, I thought. What I said was, "OK, talk to you later," and hung up. I dialed the same number again and this time asked to be put through to Momma. Momma was in. Momma was delighted to hear from me, she claimed. Sure she'd run a few names for me through the system, no sweat. While she was doing so, I asked her if by any chance D. Gresham the Third had spilled all, thus leading to the recovery of all the stolen antiques, thus leading to a hefty payout from certain insurance companies to a certain highly-skilled investigator.

She laughed.

"Forget it," she said. "All he did was smile like a cherub, then he went back to his chanting again, three times I talked to him. He's already walked, what have we got on him? Possession of one stolen article, value, who knows, five hundred bucks? Seven-fifty? Hang on, it's coming through."

I hung on. I rolled my eyes at Katy. She rolled hers back.

"Dunno why this one's still in the computer." she said after a minute. "Pearlman, Arnold J. He was wanted in Kansas for nonpayment of alimony, but hell, it's ten years out of date. Now, your Elkins, William, no middle initial? Guess what?"

"I guess you are an OK doll, and I guess I owe you an intimate candle-lit supper," I said.

"He's got more aliases than I've got gray hairs," she said. "Real name, Paul Horbovetz, that's H-o-r-b-o-v-e-t-z."

"Horbovetz," I echoed, writing the name down.

"Reading between the lines," Momma said, "and noting the company he used to keep, I'd say he was your specialist B-and-E pro, probably did hundreds of jobs, mostly for one of the New York families, one conviction only, did 18 months of a one-to-three. That do you? You can have the details if you want, there's only about a page of them."

"That'll do me fine, darling," I said. I said I'd call her as soon as I was back in town, blew her a kiss, and hung up.

"Bingo!" I said to Katy. 'Who's the lucky boy today."

"Mr. Elkins?" said Katy, who had been hanging on to my every word, to say nothing of my arm a couple of times. "I can't believe it. He's the sweetest little thing. He doesn't join in much with our group activities, but he's always polite as can be whenever we meet."

"What does someone who breaks and enters for a living look like, Katy me dear? Riddle me that. A sweet little inoffensive citizen or a blood-stained Jack the Ripper with a bundle of swag over one shoulder? If you'll kindly provide me with Mr. Elkins' particulars, I think I might stroll over and have a word with him."

"Well, I'll be damned," Katy said, beginning to get angry. "I think I'll just stroll with you." Her cheeks started to redden.

"You are not strolling anywhere," I said firmly. "You are paying me to stroll down dark alleys and into enemy territory, not vice versa. You are staying here by the phone, which you are picking up and dialing the fuzz with if I'm not back in an hour or haven't called you in that time."

"Oh, shoot," she said. "OK. But be careful."

"I'm always careful, except on the dance floor," I said, getting up. "But I don't think our Mr. Elkins is the violent type or Momma would have mentioned it. It doesn't go with the job, either."

"By the way, who is Momma?" she asked, pointing out for me on a map of the estate where Mr. Elkins' home was.

"A friend, a lady cop, who has access to police files, unlike my brother I spoke to, too, who is not a friend and who has access to police files. Well, toodle-oo."

I toddled. She saw me to the door and watched me amble down Representative Way until I turned the corner. A lady with pink hair who was out walking her pooch said good morning to me. I said good morning to her. An elderly gent in jogging togs, breathing heavily, trotted by me. He said good morning. I said good morning. I passed an orange cat sitting under a tree. I said good morning.

I found Mr. Elkins' home without any difficulty; it looked just like all the others. A well-maintained but elderly Chevy sat in the drive beside it. I knocked on Mr. Elkins; aluminum-sided door. When it opened, I said to the man who opened it, "Good morning."

He said," Good morning."

"Mr. Paul Horbovetz?" I said. "That's H-o-r-b-o-v-e-t-z."

"Never heard of him," he said, eyeing me carefully. As Katy had mentioned, he was an inoffensive-appearing little fellow, although I'm not sure I would have used the work *sweet*. He was maybe five foot seven or eight, bald as a coot, with a pleasant but unremarkable face, in his sixties probably, attired in a white shirt buttoned at both neck and cuffs and a pair of baggy black trousers that seemed to be belted somewhere just below his armpits. The belt was snakeskin, I perceived.

As for me, I merely smiled enigmatically. After a minute he sighed, then said, "Oh, shit, you better come in out of the rain, whoever you are."

I followed him in, over another nubbed carpet, into his rather sparsely furnished front room.

"I'll tell you who I am," I said. I told him. I even presented him with one of my business cards. He gave it a glance, then handed it back.

"That's nice," I said. "In fact, that's gorgeous." I was referring to a wall hanging that was maybe three feet by six, it was a sort of Noah's ark scene full of animals and birds and butterflies and jungle and clouds and sky and a crocodile or two. There was even an ark in it, with three windows—two were blank but the head of a man who looked remarkably like Mr. Paul Horbovetz appeared in the third. I walked over to get a closer look at it.

"Needlepoint, it's called," he said. "I learned to do it up in Attica. I shared a cell for six months with what they call a child molester, Harry, he got me into it. Shit, it passes the time."

"How much time would it take to do something like that?"

"On and off, a year," he said. "You might as well sit down, I can see you're planning on staying awhile." I sat down carefully on the sofa. He sat in a straight chair by the bookcase.

"Well, here we are," I said brightly.

"Ain't we just," he said. "So what put you onto me?"

"Oh, a spot of elimination," I said modestly. "A spot of deductive reasoning. Mostly luck. Then I ran you through the computer, and bulls-eye."

"That I knew, didn't I," he said. "As soon as you came up with my right name, you had to know my form, being a dick and all. Talk about a ghost from the past, shit, I'd almost forgotten what my real name was. Nine years I been here, can you believe it? Nine years of playing canasta and doffing my hat to old ladies with hearing aids. Stir crazy ain't in it."

"I can see how a man of the world like yourself might get a trifle bored here after a decade or so," I said.

"Shit, I was bored after a week," he said. "But what's a guy to do? I'd rather be alive and bored than dead and bored, any day."

"So what happened?" I said. "I hope you didn't suddenly take off with a suitcase of greenbacks that didn't belong to you. Someone else I know just did that very thing, giving me all kinds of problems, including French."

"Nah," he said. "But I might as well of, I just took off, but when you're in my line of work working for the types I was working for, you can forget about retiring and going to live on a chicken farm somewhere on your old-age pension. Something came up, a job, I didn't like anything about it, so it was either disappear or get disappeared, if you get my meaning, friend."

I allowed that I got the general tenor.

"Funny," I said. "That guy I just mentioned, I helped him to disappear, too, but I sure never thought of disappearing into the Senate Mobile Estate."

"I never spent none of the money or nothing." he said. "Shit. I dunno. Maybe I can give it back."

"So how come?" I said. "If you didn't need the money?"

"How come?" he said, getting up and walking around the room. "How come is I can't go to the track. How come is I can't go the Reno, or Tahoe or Atlantic City. How come is I'm afraid to go bowling or to the stock car races or even to some nothing demolition derby. Those guys don't forget—I show my face anywhere I'm long gone. And this joint—you see me taking up Scottish square dancing or learning modern Greek or something? And they're all straights out there, I wouldn't know what to say to them even if i wanted to. You want a beer or something?"

"I'll take a glass of milk, if you've got one," I said. He headed for the kitchen; I followed him just in case he was up to something like spiking my milk with instant oblivion capsules, although I didn't really think he would.

He opened the fridge; there was nothing in it but a couple of six-packs, olives, and a half carton of milk.

"Don't you eat?"

He opened the freezer compartment; it was jammed with TV dinners. "Who can cook?" he said. 'My mom did the cooking, then my wife, all I can make is coffee and that's shit the way I make it. You know how long it's been since I saw a basketball game or a decent fight?" He opened a can of Bud for himself and poured me out a small glass of milk.

"If I get the picture," I said, 'What you are suggesting to me is you began to crave a little action. Any action. And, finally, what is sneaking into someone else's home in the middle of the night but action, and a lot of it, I would guess."

"You guess rightly, friend," he said. "I'm here to tell you it is a charge and a half."

"Well, friend," I said, "I'm here to tell you, you better start getting your charges some other way, because you sure got yourself in the shits this time and I don't know if I can get you out."

"Why would you want to?" he said. "C'mon, let's go back inside." We went back into the front room. "What's in it for you?"

"Maybe your sad story has gotten to me," I said. "Or maybe it's the difference between you and another old fart I ran into recently. He was on the lam, too, but he came out shooting everyone in sight, including my best pal. Come to think about it, everyone I've met recently has been on the lam, there must be something going around. Let me think a minute."

"Take two, they're cheap." He sat in the straight chair again and picked up a smaller piece of needlepoint he was working on. He expertly threaded a length of red wool into a huge needle and began pointing or needling or whatever.

It was a good ten minutes later by the time I had thought it all through. "Try this on for size," I said to him. "You still got all the money?" He nodded. "Do you know how much of it came from where?"

He nodded. "Kept a list."

"Hope you kept it somewhere safe," I said. He grinned. "The other stuff, the trinkets, likewise?" He nodded again.

"The money, the knickknacks, you give to me. I mail them back, registered mail, to their rightful owners, from L.A. I say I had an attack of conscience or my old lady got at me or I got religion. OK. Next—in the forthcoming edition of whatever it's called—the *Senate Estate Mobile Home News?*—after Katy the manager's bit about how delighted she was that all the money and stolen goods were recovered, thanks to the tireless efforts of Yours Truly, she puts in a bit about you. What it says is, to try and avoid such-like problems in the future, one of our distinguished residents, you, now retired but who at one time had extensive contacts with various law enforcement agencies, to put it mildly. . ."

Here he grinned again.

" . . . has kindly volunteered to help. He will visit any resident who so desires on a one-to-one basis and advise them on home protection systems, completely free, of course, merely as a service to his neighbors. Meantime, to ensure you get a little something out of it above and beyond that warming glow that comes from being a good citizen, you go into town. You make a connection with a local locksmith or security outfit or a hardware, even to work for them strictly on commission. They saw yes, because what have they got to lose. Then every time you legitimately suggest someone replaces the lock on his front door, you stand a chance of getting a piece of the action. *Capisce?*"

"I *capisce*," he said, biting off the end of the wool.

" 'Course I have to sell all this to Katy," I said, "but I think I can, giving that everything's been returned and that She's a nice lady, also that the alternatives could be highly unpleasant as well as costly, the cops called in, your real name getting out, your old employers seeing your name in the headlines, plummeting mobile home values due to the bad publicity, need I go on? Next."

"I can't wait." He picked up a skein of yellow yarn and looked at it critically.

"As for all those so-called straights out there," I said, finishing up the milk, "when I ran a check on you, I also ran one on every male resident in the estate. I can't name any names but I came up with one nonpayment of alimony, two with juvenile records, one car theft, one assault and battery conviction, and one guy banned from all racetracks in the United States and Canada for life." What the hell, dress it up a bit.

"No kidding?" said Elkins, his face brightening. "Wonder which one he is?"

"So there it is," I said, getting slowly to my feet. "Thanks for the milk." I checked my watch. "I'm going to give Katy a call so she doesn't send in the marines while you dig up the loot from wherever it's hidden. Wherever it is, I bet I could find it in five minutes."

"Bet you couldn't," he said. He trotted off toward the bedroom. I called Katy and told her all was well and I'd see her anon. Elkins came back with a well-stuffed money belt and a shoe box.

"List is in the belt," he said as I was strapping it on under my shirt but over the corset. His eyebrows lifted when he spied my unusual undergarment but he didn't say anything. We shook hands at the door.

"Thanks, friend," he said.

"What the hell," I said.

"In the shoe box," he said. "There's something for you. If you don't like it, chuck it out."

"Those other two windows in the ark," I said. "Who goes into them?"

"My two girls," he said. "But I haven't seen them for so long who knows what they look like now."

"So do them as they looked then," I said. "See ya."

"Anytime, and I mean that," he said.

I walked back to Katy's. I didn't see anyone to say good morning to, so I said it to a bench. Katy, kindly lady that she was, agreed completely with my plan, I didn't even have to start listing the unpleasant alternatives. When I mentioned the state of Mr. Elkins' icebox, she snapped her fingers and said, "Now it's my turn to have an idea. Mrs. Galanti and Mrs. Swaine."

"Elucidate," I said.

"They're both great cooks," she said, her dimples bigger than ever. "I'll get them to give Mr. Elkins cooking lessons."

"He'll love that!" I enthused. "Oh, and by the way, tell the ladies, anytime they're short a fourth for canasta, he's their man."

CHAPTER TWENTY

Not a bad morning's work, I thought to myself on the way back to the motel, checking the money belt every few seconds to see if it was still there and clutching the shoe box to my manly chest. Mr. Elkins was out of the shit, and out of that fuselage he lived in, going around being an expert on home security devises—and if not him, who—also enjoying tasty, dimly, lit *intime* supper parties with Mrs. Galanti and Mrs. Swaine. Eight upset citizens would soon be mighty relieved to have their lucre back, Katy was mighty relieved to have everything resolved without any fuss, and also relieved of five hundred smackers she pressed on me as I was taking my leave and bending over to kiss her curvaceous cheek.

Back at the motel, I packed up what little I had, paid my bill, dropped by the Bunkhouse for a microwaved hot dog, then had Sal call me a cab. When it appeared, I said goodbye and catch you next time to her, and eased myself into it rear end first, Doc, then took in the passing scenery, what there was of it, as the cabby drove me sedately to the airport.

As the Sacramento city fathers had wisely located their airport in a reclaimed swamp, fog commonly descended or rolled in or formed or materialized or whatever it is fog does, most afternoons; I believe my flight was the last one out that day. *Adiós*, Sacramento and all whom there do dwell. *Buenas tardes*, Burbank, likewise, and hour or so later.

I cabbed it to my apartment, waved a hello to my landlady, Feeb, who had the apartment below mine and who
was watching afternoon TV game shows as usual, receiving
a spirited wave in return. I then let myself in, went up stairs,
myself in, opened a window or two to air out the place, took
off the money belt, then made myself comfortable on the
sofa with the telephone and my address book both near at
hand.

I called up Mom. The receptionist said she was napping
and better I didn't disturb her. I said please tell her I'd drop
by tomorrow, late afternoon, all being well. She said it would
be a pleasure. I called up Precious, who I estimated should
be just home from school, and she was. She answered me
from her garden, on her portable phone she was so proud
of, where she was thinning her parsley, she informed me. I
told her that I was tiptop and that Benny was progressing
better than could be expected, according to the doctor.

"How's his wife?" she said, giggling. "Bet you were surprised when Sara walked in."

"Nothing that birdbrain does has the slightest effect
on me anymore," I said. "You are the one who surprised
me, quite frankly. Thanks for forewarning me. Thanks for
telling me you two flew up together, in adjoining seats no
doubt, giggling away, just like you're doing now, knocking
back Shirley Temples and having a right old time."

When her merriment had subsided somewhat, we made
a date for that eve. I made her promise no serious messing
about as I wasn't sure my back was up to it. She said she was
having second thoughts about our date already. Then I dug
out the yellow pages and began calling airline charter firms.
On my third attempt I found one that had a flying ambulance service—they used a Cherokee 100 that had been
converted to hold four stretchers, pilot, copilot, attendant,

and one other passenger. I made a tentative booking early the following week. Then I obtained the number of Sara's motel from information and tried her, I figured it was safe enough.

"Yeah?" she said when we were connected.

"Yeah yourself," I said. "So how's it going, Mrs. Clam? How's the patient?"

"He's doing OK," she said. "It's me who's freaking out. You should see this dump I'm in. I'm thinking of moving, like maybe to the Sheraton."

"No, no!" I said. "Stay right where you are, I need you there. Anyway, you should be out of there soon." I told her about the plane I'd booked.

"I didn't know they had planes like that," she said.

"I did," I said. "Any more visits from Kalagan and his straight man?"

"One," she said. "Just for a minute. He says as far as his department is concerned, they've closed the case."

"Sure, sure," I said. "Remain alert is my warning to you two, even if he says he's been transferred to a desk job in Death Valley."

"That old guy," she said. "They buried him today, you want me to send you the bit from the paper?"

"Forget it," I said. I told her to write down the name of the charter airline so she wouldn't forget it. I told her if the lieutenant did come back, your story was, having your hubby in L.A. would be a lot more convenient as you had a place to stay there and the use of a car so you wouldn't have to keep paying out for the motel and cabs twice a day to and from the hospital, and restaurant food all the time.

She said she got it, she got it, she wasn't totally thick. Then she asked me in a heavily casual fashion if Marlon had just happened to call, looking for her.

"No, he hasn't, sugarplum," I said. "If he should chance to, what do you want me to tell him?"

"Aw, forget it," she said. "He's not going to anyway. Even if he does, don't tell him where I am, promise?"

I said I promised. There was a pause.

"Were you ever in love, Vic?" she asked then.

"Twice," I said, "not counting juvenile follies."

"Oh yeah? Who with?"

"Well, before Evonne, there was Benny's Aunt Jessica."

"What happened with her?"

"She went back east."

"That ain't no answer."

"It's all you're going to get, nosy, I'm no kiss and tell. Talk to you soon. Give us a call if there's problems."

She said, "OK, adiós, V.D.," and rang off. I did likewise.

There followed a brief conversation with Mrs. Leduc in Canada, and an almost equally brief one with Will; all seemed to be progressing smoothly up there in the land of the Northern Lights. Big John D., too, had put my plan into operation, he informed me, with no mishaps so far, but he was finding it hard to bowl strikes with his fingers crossed. There were other things as well he was finding it difficult to do with crossed fingers, he said. Do not be crude over the phone, I said.

Then, without enormous expectations, I tried the Lew Lewellens again. To my surprise, I got Mrs. Lew. After greeting her politely, I inquired if I could have a word with her husband, if he was back from wherever it was he hadn't been. As soon as he was on the line, I said, "I just called to tell you I'm never going to one of your movies again."

"Oh come on, my main man," he said. "What would you do if someday someone said to you, 'Your country needs you, so put up or shut up?' "

"I'd probably put up," I said, "but I'm still never going to one of your rotten films ever again. Do you know what you got me into?"

"Yes, I do," he said. "And I'm sorry, Vic, especially about your good buddy."

"Me too," I said. "But how did you find out about it all."

"Had a phone call."

"Gee, wonder who it was from. Well, let me be telling you this, Mr. Patriot. I've booked an ambulance airplane for Benny this weekend to bring him down here if the doc is saying it's OK, you are in for half. You are also in for daily deliveries from the delicatessen of his choice when he does get her."

"Anything else?" he inquired mildly.

"I'll let you know," I said. "That blabbermouth who phoned you with all the latest news, I don't suppose you know where I can phone her."

"No idea," he said.

"Good," I said. "I never want to see her or talk to her again. Oh, by the way, Lew, if you've got Michelle Pfeiffer in your rotten film, I'll think about it. Farewell forever. Love to your wife." I hung up forcibly. Well, you have to forceful with movie producers, otherwise they'll steamroller all over you. Then I bestirred myself all the way to Mom's closet, where she stored all her useful some-rainy-day you-never-know items. Such as used paper bags in assorted sizes, old wrapping paper, Scotch tape rolls with only a couple of inches left (and you could only get at those if you broke a fingernail), an assortment of empty boxes of various sizes, used Christmas cards, ditto Easter, ditto Mother's Day, a one-glove set of gloves, a string of plastic beads without the string, need I go on? Ah, women! Would that we could fall into their arms without falling into their hands, or something like that.

I do not mean to suggest that we men do not have a shelf in our own bedroom closets where we store our rainy-day bits and pieces, our flotsams and jetsams from other tides and times. However, ours do tend to be either of obvious value or undoubted practicality, such as my rubber band collection, my old Gil Hodges first baseman's mitt, an almost intact five-thousand-piece "Fisherman Unloading Their Catch" jigsaw puzzle, and several Scandinavian publications of an uplifting nature, to name but a few at random.

Anyway, Mom's one-glove set of gloves gave me an idea: gloves. So before I went any further, I squeezed my digits into a pair of leftover washing-up ones. Then I extricated the Scotch tape, the string and some brown wrapping paper from the jumble, then exchanged the brown wrapping paper for Christmas wrapping paper as it seemed more fitting. I emptied the money belt of its contents, which turned out to be one list and $7,545.00. I emptied the shoe box of its contents, which turned out to be one snuff box, I guessed, silver; one set Eisenhower commemorative dollars, mint; one cameo brooch; one unrecognizable pointed thing, mayhap a jeweled hatpin and mayhap not; and one pearl-handled ladies; two-shot .22-caliber Derringer. Plus my surprise gift from Mr. Elkins. It was a small—say, a foot by a foot and a half—needlepoint portraying an airport at night, much as a child might see it—there were rays of light done in yellow wool beaming out from the windows of the control tower, and old-fashioned biplane taking off, the pilot waving, and in one corner an owl with orange eyes on a post and in the other a bunny rabbit sleeping under a bush. If you want to see it, drop by the office, it's hung where that outdated calendar of Armenian lovelies Mr. Amoyan had given me used to hang.

I wrapped up the right amounts with the correct artifacts, then tied them and sticky-taped them. Then addressed them clearly, using the street addresses provided by Mr. Elkins. He hadn't provided any names, and I couldn't remember them all, nor had I remembered to bring a list of the names with me, so I packed them all into the shoe box, where they just fitted snugly, and addressed that to Katy, whose last name I did remember—Goode—and wrapped that most securely. Then I unwrapped it, went downstairs to Feeb's.

When she came to her door, I said, "Feeb, you look lovelier than ever. Do you know how to write?" I gave her crimson rinse a pat.

"Now what are you up to?" she said. "Come on in. Want some date and nut loaf?"

"Always," I said. After I'd taken care of the inner man, I dictated and she wrote in a large, plain notebook: "Sorry for what I did. I was just trying to get even. You should put a couple of feet of bobbed wire on top of that fence, electrified. I feel better now."

"What do I sign it?" was the only question she asked.

" 'Remorseful, San Diego,' " I said. "Thanks, honey, I'll tell you all about it someday."

"Sure you will," she said. "Like you told me all about it that time I pretended to be your grandmother on the phone."

"I'm going out to see Mom tomorrow," I said hastily. "Want to come?"

"Sure," she said. "Just give me five minutes to get ready."

Back upstairs, I regloved, then rewrapped the shoe box, this time with the unhandled-by-me note inside. Why take even a one-in-a-hundred chance and write it myself? And leave my prints all over everything? To purloin a phrase much used by a certain tedious saphead I happen to know, No way, José. As I believe I have mentioned before, kids, do cover your stern, especially when all it costs is a modicum of time and a minimum of effort.

Then I changed my shirt, gave my endearing cowlick a hasty brush, tucked the package under one arm, and ambled down to a post office I didn't normally patronize. Wherein I nudged, with one knuckle, said package across the counter toward the clerk, and off it went on its registered way. Unbelievably, I had to fork out fourteen dollars and forty-five cents just to do someone else a good turn. Maybe someone would do me one some fine day for a change. Sure, and maybe Hawaiian shirts would be all the rage someday. Well, my joke of a car made it, didn't it?

That evening Evonne and I ate Japanese, which she liked to do once in a while although the green horseradish was the only part I really liked. Then we sat in her garden on her swinging sofa and billed and cooed. I am probably better at billing than she is but she had few if any equals when it comes to cooing.

The following day, it being a Saturday and thus not one of my regular working days, I didn't open up the office; we drove out to Manhattan Beach instead, where I did some gingerly paddling, which was supposed to be good for me, while she did some serious swimming. In the early evening she and I and Feeb drove out to the Pasadena Hills to Hilldale, where resided *mater*. We found her in high spirits in the pool room, kibitzing loudly a game that was in progress between her usual opponent, Erwin, a miniscule but most dapper geezer dressed today in a skin-tight aubergine suit with yellow high-heeled shoes and a taller, older man I didn't recognize. Erwin was beating the high-cuffed pants off him.

Mom led the way into the cafeteria, but not before calling out to Erwin, "You lucky little stiff. You get to live for another day." Mom was small, attractive, and when in form, full of energy, with curly hair and great legs, both of which she was vain about. I mentioned she suffered from Alzheimer's disease; the prognosis was a gradual and irreversible decline into increasingly aberrant behavior, with a good chance of pneumonia thrown in. But when she was like she was that day, like she had been up until a few years ago, you couldn't believe it, you didn't want to believe it. But when her control slipped or she didn't recognize you, then you believed it.

I got us all drinks and told Mom about Canada and watching Les Habitants and eating moose soup and she told us about the latest scandal at Hilldale—two of the residents, both over eighty, one male, one female, had been caught swimming in the nude in the pool at two o'clock in the morning, and with all the lights out, too. Also in the pool at the time were two empty wine bottles. Then Evonne and I took a little stroll through the grounds while Mom and Feeb got caught up to date. On the way we bumped into Dr. Donald Fishbein, the guy in charge of the joint, out for a little stroll himself, only he never strolled, he ran. Doctor Don was half energy, half beard, and half brains. He must have had a little common sense as well, to say nothing of the odd male hormone, because when he caught sight of Evonne's legs in those minishorts she loved to wear, he skidded to a stop and almost fell over her.

"So you are human after all, eh, Doc," I said. "I always wondered. Yes, it's me, Victor, Mrs. Daniel's eldest. Any more problems since last I was here?" He'd had series of petty pilfering one time that I'd helped him with.

"One," he said, when he finally finished shaking Evonne's hand. "Someone's been lifting Mr. James's copies of *Penthouse* from his mailbox before he's had a chance to read them."

"Hum," I said. "A tricky one. I'd look for a man who's got a faraway look in his eyes. A sort of bemused expression."

"Also extremely listless," said Precious, to my surprise. Doctor Don's teeth gleamed through his bushy black beard.

"How's Mom?" I said.

"No miracles yet," the doc said.

"Ah, shit," I said.

"Right on," he said. We made our good-byes and off he ran. Evonne and I sat for a moment on a bench under a magnolia tree which we shared with a ruddy-cheeked elderly lady with a walker, dressed, in a T-shirt that said, LIE NO. 371—LIFE BEGINS AT 40, shorts, and sneakers with no socks. She was industriously working away at something in an embroidery hoop.

"Ah, I see we're busy at our needlepoint," I remarked.

"I'm tatting," she said. "Which isn't the same thing at all, as anybody but an ignoramus would know. Now go away. Your emanations are muddy."

We went away. As soon as we were out of earshot, I said to Evonne, "What was that all about?"

"I don't know, sweetheart," she said, taking hold of my arm. "But they are muddy."

"Yours would hardly be crystal clear, whatever they are," I said, striding along, "if you'd been through what I've been through this week. Some fucking old Nazi is dead and so is Solomon, who I never even met and I'm alive and Benny's in the hospital getting reinflated. And Fats is doing God knows what, and who knows or cares what the twerp's up to and her heart throb is having it off in the snow with Tits McGurk and I don't know what else."

"And your mother's dying," Evonne said, tugging me to a halt.

"Well, there is that too, Evonne Louise Shirley." I enfolded her in my arms in the middle of the path. An old man in pajamas and slippers, using two canes, passed us by.

"Sure could use a little more of that around her," he said.

"Around anywhere," I said. After a minute she raised her face toward mine.

"That's new," I said.

"What's new?"

"That freckle on the side of your nose." I touched a finger to it and it came off. I showed it to her. "See? It was just a mote after all."

"Maybe a spore," she said.

"I like that idea better," I said. We walked back, arm in arm, to the reception area, found Feeb, and went home. Young Doctor, I am being sorry about the relapse that followed. It was all my fault. See, I didn't sleep on my back that night. I slept on my right side, as close as I could possibly get to Evonne Louise Shirley without inhabiting the same epidermis.

Chapter the Last

Well, it started with her, whoever she was and still is, I hope, so it is only fitting that it end with her, if only for neatness' sake.

Salmon was the color of her blouse, pitchblende the color of her hair, forest green her skirt, short jacket, and shoes. Her earrings were a still-darker shade of green jade, her lipstick and hair clip, scarlet, me' Open your paintboxes, kids, and color me any color you want to.

I was sitting in my office trimming my cuticles and waiting for a client who was late for her appointment when she walked in. It was on a Monday, almost two weeks to the moment from her first materialization into the life of that well-known Studio City boulevardier, V. (for Victor) Daniel.

"Miss Braukis, as I live and breathe." I stood politely to greet her. She proffered a hand. I pretended I didn't see it.

"Mr. Daniel," she said in her throaty voice.

"Please be seated," I said. "Anywhere you like." She sat demurely in the only other chair in the office aside from mine. "I am awaiting a client," I said, sitting down myself, "at any minute, one of Burbank's leading society matrons, so please be brief."

She let me have one look from those unfair eyes; one was enough.

"I would have come sooner, she said, 'but I've been sitting shivah."

I used to dog-sit myself," I said. "A beautiful Labrador puppy she was. She's in doggy heaven now."

"To sit shivah is how the Jews honor their dead," she said.

"I apologize," I said, blushing to the roots. "I didn't know. What does it consist of?"

"Seven days of mourning," she said. "Shivah means seven. Officially it is only performed by the immediate family—brothers, sisters, father and mother, sons and daughters—and the deceased must have been buried within three days of his death. You could perhaps think of it as a Jewish wake"

"What do you do?"

"Traditionally, you sit on wooden boxes, although now stools are often used, without shoes. To combat vanity, all mirrors are covered. Food is served, of course, and there's no lack of conversation, it's not entirely a sad occasion."

"Were you related to Solomon?"

"No," she said, "he had no relations at all as far as I knew, they were all killed in the Second World War, except one cousin he mentioned once, he was one of the few tank commanders we lost in the Six-Day War. But I wanted to do something so myself and a few friends, we did the best we could."

"God damn it anyway," I said, or something equally impolite and meaningless.

"How's your friend?" she asked then.

"He's doing terrific," I said. "We flew him down here the day before yesterday, he could be out in the world and up to his old tricks again in what, ten days, two weeks?"

"I knew you moved him," she said. She opened up her purse (also forest green, I neglected to mention) and put an envelope on the desk in front of me. When she leaned forward, her blouse parted slightly; I averted my eyes. Inside the envelope were travelers checks totaling two thousand dollars. "Half for the plane," she said. "The rest for you if you'll take it."

"I hope they're kosher," I said.

"They are," she said.

"The half for the plane," I said. "Is that my half or Lew's half?"

"Yours," she said.

"Oh," I said. "Jolly decent of you." I put the money away in a drawer. "If I decide it's too contaminated, I'll buy you a couple of trees. Who was that old guy, anyway? I hope he was worth it all."

She rummaged again in her handbag, then slid a sheet of paper across to me. This time I failed to avert my eyes in time and couldn't help noticing her undergarment was black and lacy, unlike mine, which was sweatstained, fraying around the edges, and getting to be a bigger nuisance than Mickey Rooney at a beach party. Luckily I only had to wear it another couple of days.

The name at the top of the sheet I didn't recognize although no doubt Nathan Lubinski would have. There followed his date of birth,—some small town in Austria— school records, and so on. The came the date of his joining the Nazi party, then the SS with his SS number. Passed some course. Transferred to Essen. Got his commission. When the war started, served with a Waffen-SS group blitzkrieging French, Belgians, and anyone else who had the temerity to resist the mighty Third Reich. He got promoted. Sent as second in command of new extermination camp at Riga. One year later promoted to commandant. Estimated one million (1,000,000) slain 1941–1944. Assumed he escaped late 1944 by boat from Riga or Ventspils, then via Portugal to South America.

"That little guy?" I said. "It's unbelievable."

"Want to see a picture of him as he was then?" she asked me.

"No, thank you," I said.

"Would you like to know what his particular specialty was?"

"No, thank you," I said.

"So you tell me," she said. "Was it worth it?"

"It's not a question of worth it," I said.

"What is it a question of, then?"

"How should I know?" I said. "Ask the rabbi, maybe he knows. What I do know is you set me up, lady, and good."

"I'm sorry about that," she said.

"You're sorry," I said. "I've had some time to think about it, and here's what I think, correct me if I'm wrong. The purpose of the whole number wasn't for Uncle Theo to recognize Cookie, it was for Cookie to recognize Uncle Theo, and did he ever. I don't know if they knew each other from a camp or before or after, but as soon as Cookie got one look at him he knew what was involved."

"After," said my ex–dream girl. "Theo tracked him from Argentina to Chile to Mexico. He had him, then he lost him."

"Theo should stick to picking grapes," I said. " Anyway. After a while, our favorite nightmare pops up again, this time in the U.S. You're going to have a hell of a time extraditing him from here after all this time and you probably don't want to go through another one of those show trials that break everyone's heart, no, no, what you need is some stumble-bum to do the job for you, some gun-toting hick who's as dispensable as a used throwaway diaper. So Lew puts you on to me, the perfect goat. Thanks again, Lew."

"To be fair," she said, "he said you were not only quick on the uptake, but perfectly able to take care of yourself if you had to."

"Lucky for me," I said bitterly. "You make it all mysterious enough and potentially dangerous enough with your hints and lies and following people around to ensure I do pack a gun. Cookie sees Theo. Cookie comes looking for Theo. Brilliantly, I've even suggested Theo and I change rooms. If I hadn't suggested it, I'll bet he would have. *Bang bang*—me and Cookie in a shootout. Hopefully, I nail Cookie—if he nails me too, ah well, *c'est la guerre*. And there's Solomon, armed to the teeth, prowling around to make sure at least Cookie's had it, if not, ideally, the stooge too. God knows what Uncle Theo was packing, just in case. I never thought to look. He went through the airport detector with no trouble, so it was probably some new-fangled all-plastic capsule shooting gizmo you've come up with."

"What an imagination," Miss Ruth Humbug Braukis murmured. "And by the way, the handgun to which you refer is called a Glock. And it is not all plastic, either, although it is partly made of polymer two. Or so I've read."

"Oh really? And what would you have done if I hadn't sneaked a gun up there?"

"Provided you with one. Believe me, no one wanted to see you killed, Mr. Daniel."

"I'd love to believe you," I said. "Sure would make a change. How did you know I already had my own weapon, anyway?"

"Theo searched your room. Twice."

"I might have guessed. Luckily I guessed right about most of the rest of it."

"I'll tell you something else you were lucky about," she said, crossing her legs in a vain attempt to distract me. "Or rather your friend was. That Cookie, as you call him, had to use a gun with a silencer."

"What's so lucky about that? You mean he could have used a bazooka?"

"Silencers only work efficiently on small-caliber handguns, about up to a twenty-two," she said. "I hate to think what might have happened if your friend had been shot with anything larger at so close a range."

"You seem remarkably well informed," I said. "Have we been reading the gossip columns again? Or were we lurking in the underbrush waiting to drive the getaway vehicle? That Uncle Theo. He even remembered to collect his teeth. And as for all that stuff about silencers, these days you can silence weapons of any caliber up to and including thirty-aught-six rifles. Or so I've read."

A movement outside my reinforced picture window caught my eye. It was just what I needed right then—the twerp herself, snub nose pressed against the glass. "Pardon me the nonce," I said, rising. I went to the door, opened it an inch, hissed, "Beat it!" closed the door again, locked it, then regained my seat.

"The Burbank society matron?" suggested Miss Ruth Braukis, who of course had turned to watch.

"Hardly," I said, giving her a withering glance. In return she gave me a slow, sweet smile that, if I wasn't imagining things, had a touch of sadness at one corner. She looked down at the elegant timepiece circling her tanned, slim wrist.

"Going somewhere?"

She nodded.

"Somewhere nice?"

"Home." She arose. So did I.

"Give my love to the grapefruits," I said. She came around to my side of the desk,

"Bend over," she said. I bent over. Naturally, the twerp was watching all. She pressed her cool lips to my hot cheek. "*Leshana habaa beyerushalayim*," she whispered.

"Thank you," I whispered back. "That's one of the nicest things anyone's ever said to me."

The most beautiful woman in the world swayed to the door. Just as she opened it, I asked her, "What does it mean?"

"Next year in Jerusalem," she said.

"Wasps gather," I said, but by then she had gone.

A moment passed.

Then enter the twerp, eyes goggling.

"Holy shit!" she said. "Who was that?"

"An ex-client," I said. "Her name is Ruth. Or perhaps Barbara. It might be Agnes for all I know."

"What did she want?"

I smiled in a nonchalant fashion. "What do all beautiful women want with me? She wants to meet me again sometime, that's all."

Sara whistled.

"No shit?"

"No shit."

"You gonna do it?"

I patted the nerd's head fondly. "Are you jesting, child? I am strictly a one-woman man, as well you know, unlike some I could name. I've never even thought of another woman since I met Evonne Louise Shirley, the very idea revolts and upsets me. Yeech. I'm surprised at you, Sara, I really am. I know you've been through a troublesome phase, but that is no reason to suppose all men are fly-by-night cads and rotters. Oh, seeing as you're closest, do us a favor, hand me down that cheap atlas you gave me, will you, there's a place I want to look up."

APPENDIX

Answers

I forget how he did the pyramid and the alternate heads and tails. Write to him care of the Round-Up Saloon, Lafayette, Ca.

The lightweight bag. Weigh any three against any other three bags. If they are equal, the remaining trio must contain the light bag. Weight any one bag from it against any other. If they are equal, the leftover bag is the light one. If they are not, the light bag is the light one. Similarly, in your first weighing, if one trio is lighter than the other, proceed as before, weighing any one bag from it against another.

The traveling salesmen. One traveled east around the world, one west, thus one kept gaining days, the other losing them.

The Rileys are not twins because they are what is left of triplets.

The five matches: IIIII. The answer is not given here due to a wish to avoid vulgarity whenever possible.

To pour a whole pint of beer into a half-pint mug, supposedly you fill the half-pint mug with sawdust.

Those lipstick traces. The lucky winner reasoned like this. Time has passed. Both other guys are still in the room. If either one of them saw two pink kisses, they'd know they had a red one. So if either of the two others have a pink one, the winner couldn't have, otherwise there would be two pinks in view, and one of his rivals would claim victory. If there are no pinks in view, the winner reasons that he can't be pink either because if either of his opponents spotted his pink kiss, from the reasoning above they could deduce they couldn't have a pink kiss as well. So the winner knows he has a red one. Clear? I figured it out, or at least I think I did, on the drive the following day.

That's all folks.

Printed in Great Britain
by Amazon

42811553R00169